Copyright          Alastair Walker

Published 2016      ISBN 978 152 39 72579

Other books by Alastair Walker

Scooterama – Carlton Books 1999. Reprinted 2001.

The Café Racer Phenomenon – Veloce Books 2009

Kawasaki Triples Bible – Veloce Books 2010

Circles In The Sand, Inside the Paris-Dakar – Amazon Kindle/Creatspace 2014/15

Jacks, Knaves and Kings of Speed – Amazon Kindle 2014

Notes From The Margins – Amazon Kindle 2014

Due Autumn 2016

Grievance – Amazon Createspace

# THE LIVES AND LOVERS OF THE PINK PEPPERMINT LOUNGE

# CHAPTER ONE: *"NOW YOU'VE GOT THE BEST OF ME, COME ON AND TAKE THE REST OF ME, OH BABY"*

Somewhere off the M60 motorway, there is a mythical palace of faded disco shirts, glued-on eyelashes, blinged up heels, Sainsbury's Basics sausage rolls and a car park CCTV that's seen more porn than a 14 year old boy with his Dad's wi-fi password.

Come with me now, be an angel on my shoulder, as we walk through the double doors of dating Hell. It's Wednesday, £5 Singles Nite, and the walls are gently perspiring a cocktail of Christmas gift aftershaves and £1 market stall body sprays, while a gaggle of middle-aged singletons tap out a morose code with their fingertips, as they nurse the first drinks of the night.

Look, there are the three `pot of tea' ladies; Vera, Angela and Trish, sitting like *Strictly* judges, at the table with the `Reserved' sign on its faded Rioja-spattered tablecloth. This *X Factor* trio start their evening with a simple cup of tea and a chat each Wednesday. But whatever dirt is being dished during their early doors gossip, however juicy the details may be, all three of them keep their eyes peeled for new guys in town, married people meeting for illicit affairs, or worse still, an appearance by their ex-boyfriends, now chaperoning a *new* woman into the Peppermint's arthritic arms. Sometimes, even a cuppa with two sugars has a bitter aftertaste.

Once, this fraying red carpet of lost dreams was a real nightclub, where people queued patiently behind a red rope and the car park heaved with Merc S Classes, BMW 5 series, Jags, Rollers and even the odd Ferrari. Admittedly it was generally the 80s Ferrari that Magnum PI used to drive, but still, the Pink Peppermint had once been a byword for flash clothes, big hair, spray-tanned legs and self-made men with money to burn. It was even rumoured that Peter Stringfellow came along one sultry Friday night, and got into a fracas with Owen Oyston, as they argued over who was giving Lynsey de Paul a lift home. You could taste the glamour.

But those days are long gone now. The Peppermint's carpet has yellow safety tape holding it down near the French windows, in case someone trips and sues the management. The car park features so many pot-holes that Audi should be testing 4X4 prototypes in winter. There's a handwritten sign saying `Taxi's Only' outside the main entrance, so that semi-literates feel immediately at home and some joker has abandoned a green Rover 45 in the far corner, with a sign stating `Doctor On Call' nestled in the corner of the windscreen.

Dave the DJ works for free beer all night and a token £25 travel expenses, but as he's officially `on the sick' this is a sweet deal for him. Dave actually spends the first hour of the evening simply playing his own disco compilation from an USB stick. Well, it saves on buying records. He's under strict instructions to only use half the available multi-coloured spotlights set on a gantry above the dance floor until 11pm, so that the Peppermint's electricity bill is cut by a fraction. You can ask Dave for song requests and eventually, he will get round to playing them, so long as you want to hear J-Lo's `On The Floor' every fortnight.

****

I can still recall that warm night in June when I first set my pointy, purple suede Chelsea boots inside the Peppermint.

I'd finished with internet dating, after a traumatic series of meet ups, which included being savagely bitten on the ear by a business studies lecturer from the Midlands, just as I kissed her goodbye, a stalker who brought lamb chops and a slow cooker along to a third date, plus a woman who had been born a man offering me a blow job at a Premier Inn near Swansea. Despite being sent some reasonably convincing topless photos by email, I felt it wasn't worth the petrol money...yes, I'm still fairly sure about that.

So I searched Google for somewhere that a recently divorced, poor man's Colin Firth, with a nice line in paisley shirts and Cuban heeled boots, could have a midweek boogie for a budget of £15, including soft drinks. It took a while, but eventually I found a scrappy, almost 1990s website, with cheesy photo galleries and the magic dress code; `No jeans or trainers.' Cool. I fired up the VW Golf and put some Calvin Harris on i-Tunes to get in the mood.

The moment I paid my fee, bagged my free buffet ticket and walked into the main lounge, I knew that this was my spiritual home, a kind of Happy Valley of lost souls. Here, in this pink and green neon purgatory, all our sins would stay a shared secret; what goes on `Mint, stays on the `Mint...

This illuminated dance floor, with its corral of white-shrouded, wedding reception tables, was irresistible to my eyes, a magnet for my footloose boots, and the last chance love train for a middle-aged man who had run out of options.

Instinctively, one glance around the tables, which were set alarmingly close to the dance floor, told me all I needed to know. Here, a guy could meet man-hungry divorcees, have your heart frozen by sugar-frosted career women, or meet bored, sex-toy testing housewives, sick of spending weekdays folding ironed clothes, shopping and wondering why their husbands sat slumped like burst beanbags in front of the telly every night. There were tiddly, flirty ladies out for a 40th birthday bash, thin girls looking aloof, fat girls oozing voluptuous lust, betrayed wives with mad staring eyes, or cheery oompah-loompah tiny women, who danced in circles to deter bullying. I smiled and wandered slowly around the room, listening to Rihanna and Roxy Music, Motown mixes segueing into a bit of Rizzle Kicks. You could just take it for what it was; fun, music, a good laugh, or you could throw yourselves to the she- wolves of the night. Your choice.

****

I knew one thing for sure within ten minutes of meeting Vera, Angie and Trish; this disco was full of real women, who – despite succumbing to magic pants made of industrial lycra - were still holding out for the real thing: True love. Bless their hearts. But failing that, they would settle for a wild weekend in Lytham St Annes, a riding crop from Ann Summers and sharing all the hot, filthy gossip over a pot of tea every Wednesday.

That was the unspoken understanding, the shared, knowing glances, the very essence of the Peppermint Lounge; everyone secretly hoped they might still find someone and fall in love, in spite of everything that life had thrown at them. Like the 12 inch version of Soft Cell's *Tainted Love*, you had to stick with it to the end, even though you'd forgotten exactly why you liked the track in the first place.

"So you're single, just turned fifty, and fed up with crazy internet dates then Cal?" asked Vera, once we'd made small talk about jobs and failed marriages.

"Yes, thought I'd just get out and have a dance."

"Good for you. Well you can sit at our table and we'll tell you which women to avoid in here, because some of them will eat you *alive* sunshine – never mind biting your ear lobes."

"Ah thanks Vera." I smiled, pulling a chair closer to the three sixty-something ladies.

"You're welcome pet. By the way, you don't mind having sex with older women for money do you?"

There was a second's pause and then all three of them burst into laughter as a look of total, paralysed fear crossed my face. We all laughed, and Vera patted my arm, as if giving a Papal blessing. They were good fun and I knew at once that every Wednesday would be a bit brighter with them and their circle of friends in my life. Vera, Angie and Trish were adopting me in a way, because just like them, I'd found a place where I could dance away the past.

This is the story of the ladies from the Pink Peppermint; the men in their lives, plus all the heartaches, hard-ons and hot flushes along the way. These are our moments, the snapshots that made us laugh, the dances where romance bloomed, the secrets uncovered, the truths that hit home when the music stopped. After divorce, you can hide away from the world, or go out and shake it; dance like nobody is looking at your less-than-perfect body, and stick two joyful fingers up at the idea of ever growing old gracefully.

****

## TRISH'S RATHER FISHY THIRD DATE

It had started with an invitation for a drink and smile that cracked the corners of his eyes. Trish had seen Brian a few times in the Peppermint but never done more than lock eyes and smile. Now here he was, arriving at her door in his BMW X5 diesel, dressed in a pale grey shirt and dark blue trousers, his face crinkled with a little outdoor work tan.

Third date. Been for a drink. Been for a meal...Thai as it goes and very nice too. Things were looking up for Trish.

"Had a busy week then Brian?" she asked, settling into the passenger seat and running the seat belt carefully across her cleavage. Trish didn't want the belt to press the front of her dress down too much and reveal the red M&S bra cupping her more than impressive breasts. Better to let him discover that a bit later on, if things went well...

"Yeah, had a job on over in Wigan, rotten old shops being turned into flats, should be all sorted in a week or two. You're looking sunny side up Trish, very nice."

He leaned across before belting himself in and kissed her on the lips, not pressing too hard, not smudging her lipstick with a little swirl of passion, but just enough to let her know he was keen.

"Nice dress." he said, starting the engine and skipping a couple of tracks on the *Top Gear Sub Zero Driving Anthems* CD on the Beemer's functionally black music system. Amy Winehouse's *Valerie* kicked in as they pulled away from Trish's place and six cylinders of German engineering meshed beautifully together, with a silky growl.

"Thank you Brian, you look very nice too – new shirt?"

"Well, yeah. Gotta make an effort for the Peppermint, haven't ya?"

"Oh definitely, said Trish, smoothing down her floral pattern, crisp cotton dress, so it kissed the top of her knees. "the Peppermint's the highlight of my week...tragic really isn't it?"

Brian shot her a knowing smile, glanced in the mirror then gunned the BMW past a couple of fuel-sipping hatchbacks as they joined the dual carriageway.

"Let me know if you need the air con on Trish...I cater for everyone, think it's even got a hot flush setting on the climate control."

"You cheeky thing!" blurted Trish in mock outrage, letting a little laugh escape and break the ice between them. "Anyway, I'm on HRT, it's all under control."

"Well, we'll see how y'get on after three or four dances. I kinda like it when there's a bit of colour in your cheeks, gives me the horn."

She gave him a playful dig in the ribs,

"Stop it, you're making me blush."

Brian let his hand fall from the mock leather gear knob onto her freshly shaved, and moisturised, leg,

"Now ya talking Trish...keep it going love."

She gently removed his hand, letting him squeeze her thigh just long enough for her to feel the rough edges and callouses on his skin, the spread and strength of his fingers. She wanted to feel his hands on her skin, cupping her breasts, pulling her waist close to him. She loved that feeling of being taken sometimes. She missed it.

Divorce was a bitter business, and she was glad that pain had passed, but the lonely, silent space afterwards was like a desert in the night. Being on her own every night was rubbish really, bloody lonely – though she'd never admit it.

****

The Peppermint was filling up nicely as Trish and Brian breezed in, signed their names in the `book of shame,' as she liked to call it, paid their £5 and headed around the corner to the main bar.

The usual suspects were already sat at their regular tables: Trish's close friends Vera and her volatile younger sister Angie were at `the top table' directly opposite the bar, enjoying the last of their pot of tea.

Trevor and Penny were just settling down next to the sisters. Trevor had a new shirt on, well new to him, but obviously from a charity shop. He had the look of a down-at-heel geography teacher, binned off in the local authority's brutal budget cuts of 2010. Penny looked careworn, exhausted by working all the hours she could get, just to keep their family ship afloat, but each time she glanced at Trevor –

her little Trev – there was a candle of affection in the window of her soul.

Two tables away, a trio of social services care assistants, Jen, Sadie and Karen were already ripping into their first bottle of red wine like jackals in an abattoir. The stress of dealing with two dozen mildly delinquent teenagers at the special needs unit was etched into their forty-something faces, like a roadmap to Hell, disguised beneath a layer of Superdrug cosmetics.

Sadie, who was a mere 4 foot 11 inches tall, but liked to draw a crowd on the dancefloor, had a bright white dress on, that clung to each curve of her Zumba-toned body. Her foot tapped inside her white sparkly heels as DJ Dave's usual MP3 `mood music' filled the room.

Sadie leaned over to Jen, who was busy fluffing up her hair and drawing it back, to show off her earrings.

"Y'know it must be the moon or something, I'm just dyin' to get laid tonight."

"Well Sadie pet," noted Jen, "there's plenty of volunteers in this place who'll give you a good seeing to. Some of `em will do ya in the car park, then get y'back in here for last orders."

Sadie's boobs jiggled as she laughed.

"Awww, fookin' hell Jen. Class guys eh? How lucky are we?"

****

The music got louder around 9.30, as the buffet was served: A selection of greasy sausage rolls, loosely packed with grey meat product and gelatine, plus a reasonable imitation of mini pork pies and a few token samosas for the vegetarians in the room. The retro feast was dispensed from the hatch style window which joined the kitchen to the disco area. Some tucked in, others picked suspiciously at the food and sensible people who were driving – and therefore not drinking – skipped on the buffet completely.

Sadie and Jen started the dancing, soon joined by northern soul legend Colin, spinning his spats and tipping his fedora as he warmed up. Then a gaggle of ladies on a 45th birthday party began to shimmy on the far side of the dance floor. Soon, the pink fluorescent lights, and blinking disco spots, were beating in time to *Red Light Spells Danger, Young Hearts Run Free* and a dozen other disco era classics.

Brian and Trish waited until it was busy on the floor, and then joined her circle of friends. Vera placed her handbag in the middle of the group, like she always did, because she didn't want to leave it at her table, not after the great purse nicking incident of 1998. Deep down, she'd never got over it, despite years of therapy which involved her quizzing almost everyone who was in the room that fateful night.

There was a Motown section, electro 80s hits, a taste of R&B and even a birthday request or two as the night rippled by, in a sea of hookey aftershave, sweat and over-flowery perfume. Sadie did a salsa with tall Dave and when he dropped to his knees, to bump up the comedy value, she generously rubbed her boobs in his face for a second. Vera and Angie had words over some half-forgotten family disagreement and Angie skulked away into the back bar, where Kevin the car dealer chatted her up and bought her a double vodka and Coke.

Brian and Trish went outside around midnight to get some air, sitting at one of the smoker's tables that lined the front terrace. They chatted and kissed, letting their arms fold around each other for a few minutes, but aware that others were watching their courtship.

"Let's get you home Princess." said Brian.

\*\*\*\*

"Mind if stop for a little cuddle, just here like?"

Brian didn't wait for an answer, he braked sharply and pulled into a side lane off the main road. Trish said nothing as he parked up in the car park of a pub that had been closed by the brewery last year.

"Well, you're getting keen." she observed, unclicking her seat belt.

He undid his belt and sidled across the leather seats towards her. They were both still warm from dancing and Trish was quite tipsy on the two glasses – large glasses – of Pinot Grigio she'd had. Brian kissed her, moving his tongue inside her mouth and letting his hand settle beneath her mighty bosoms.

"I do like this dress." He whispered, reaching inside and stroking her breast, drawing a tiny circle of pleasure.

They kissed for a while longer, and then Trish broke away from his lips.

"Brian, please don't think I'm being funny, but it sort of smells a bit...well, fishy in here. Can you smell fish?"

"Er, yeah. That's because there's a couple of fresh trout in the boot probably."

Trish pulled herself up in her seat and moved back an inch or two from Brian's face, which was burrowing, like a hungry gopher, down her cleavage.

"But why have you got trout in the boot?"

Brian gave a sigh and sat up straight, easing himself back to the driver's side of the car and letting one arm fall over his bulging trousers.

"It's because I tell the wife I go night fishing with my mates on Wednesday nights, so I always get two trout or summat from Asda before they close at eight."

"Oh for god's sake – you're married?"

"Yes, I'm married...but so what? Let's just have some fun, and then I can get us home eh?"

Trish adjusted her clothing, popping her boob back inside her dress like a wayward, half-melted jelly, and felt a wave of anger and embarrassment fill her.

"Brian, I'm not doing it in a car at my age. I'd be absolutely mortified if a Police car turned up! I've got grandchildren and my daughter's an accountant! You're an absolute swine you are. Can't believe you were going to do me in the car. I thought you were different, but you're just like the rest of them in the Peppermint!

Brian sighed and started the engine, then gave Trish one last chance;

"If you want some comfort, we can get a room at the Premier Inn down the road?"

She glared at him, and then said, "Just take me home."

And so that was the end of Trish and Brian's third date. It's a true story...even though there was a fish involved.

\*\*\*\*

## CHAPTER TWO: `LOVE IS THE DRUG'

A weighty wedge of junk mail ker-plunked through the white front door on Angie's three-bedroomed, Redrow detached house and she stood the steam iron up on its fancy little stand as she marched through the hallway to check it.

"Crap...more crap. Charity crap. Oh look, another bill. The joy never ends."

Mrs Angela Steel. That's what it said on the front of the broadband bill and the echo of her marriage whispered around the kitchen as she ironed. Sometimes, she still cooked her husband, Keith, a meal, but otherwise, apart from a family event, their paths rarely crossed.

It was their `arrangement' and it suited them both, most of the time. He had his woman, a dreadful cow called Sylvia who lived on the Wirral and had hair like badly dyed candy floss, and Angie had Rahim.

Well, correction, she used to have Rahim. But he was feeling guilty about their affair now, and had slunk off back home to be with his wife and children. Doing the right thing. This sudden end to their relationship was much to Angie's annoyance, as she liked the constant, flirty attention; all the sexting, the secret meetings and the no-holds-barred bonking that Rahim used to deliver on a regular basis. Younger men were great, especially when they were keen in bed, and equally as keen to vanish back down the M6 once the spanking action had finished.

Angie's white diamante encased iPhone chimed as a Whatsapp message came in.

**Hey hun, you at the Peppermint tonite?** asked her friend Sue.

**Yep. Not got a clue wat 2 wear, how bout u?**

**I'm thinking glam. Probs a black dress, feel I need a big Wednesday nite out. Been a rubbish week x**

Angie smiled as she batted messages back and forth like a game of tennis, sitting with her legs crossed on the faux leather dining chairs, her foot tapping to some half-forgotten beat. The pile of ironing stayed untouched in the basket. The iron gently hissed a quiet disapproval.

When she had finished texting, Angie switched the iron off and emptied the water out. Ironing more clothes could wait for a bit. She switched on the kitchen television and saw Phil and Holly giggling over some food that looked like a willy. The day was lapsing into a kind of coma.

Angie heard a distinctive chime and checked her Whatsapp again. She had a new message from Rahim.

**Still miss you baby, how's things? Wen u comin 2 see me, fancy a trip to Bham wiv me, got a show to work in a few months time?**

"That's nice. Keep quiet for ages, then try and book me in for a dirty weekend when you're away with work. You sly bastard." hissed Angie to herself, flicking through TV channels whilst she pondered her reply options.

She could feel herself getting worked up, heart beating quicker, the adrenaline rising. She took a deep breath, flicking the switch on the kettle. It was time for a brew, then a big think about things. For all his cheek, and his calculating suggestion that she let herself simply be used for a night out, she was tempted.

The ironing pile stared back at her across the kitchen as she sipped her tea. Apart from that, all she had to do was some supermarket shopping later today. Then her dull, sulky husband, Keith, would return home for another evening meal punctuated with fractured conversation before he burrowed himself away in his garden shed, or headed off to Sylvia's place for a few days. The joy of life seemed to be vanishing into the past. She was dreading the day that Keith retired from work and then it was just the two of them in the house. All day, every day.

Fact was, Angie missed being thrown over the edge of the bed by Rahim, being taken from behind, filled up with her hardness of him. It reminded her that she was still a woman, still alive and sexy, not quite dead or ready for a nursing home.

She needed that feeling, those moments of pleasure. So she texted him back.

**Hi sexy man. Missed u too and u r hot body pressed against mine. Yeah, Bham nite sounds good, can't wait 2 buy some new knickers for u to rip off me. Kisses babe xxxx**

\*\*\*\*

## WOKE UP THIS AFTERNOON

Trevor wiped the sleep from the corners of his eyes and sat up. His bones clicked noisily as he leaned over to glance at the clock radio. He sighed as he picked up his phone from the top of the bedside drawers.

"Ahh, what's the time...bloody hell, lunchtime – how did that happen?" he said to himself, scratching at his chest hair and catching the scent of Penny as he shifted beneath the duvet. She had long gone to work of course, but even though she had been busy, Penny had found time to poke at Trev as he slumbered.

There were three terse messages:

**R u up yet? x**

**Get that wallpaper stripped mate, come on x**

And finally,

**Oh FFS. You're hopeless, get uppp!!** That message had been sent at precisely 11.01 am.

Once again, Trevor was busted. Staying up late browsing eBay for old collectable comics, silver cigar cases and spare parts for his classic Alfa Romeo GTV sports car had been a bad idea. He could see that now. Trev scratched his leg as he texted how he was busy attacking the back bedroom with a steamer gadget, had worked on sci-fi novel and tidied up the conservatory too. All lies of course. He then added a little romantic touch;

**Can't wait to lick the sweat off your gorgeous boobs hun, love ya x**

That should do it, thought Trev, as he pressed the send button.

Strangely, there was no reply. Penny must be very busy at work deduced Trev. He switched on the TV and settled back into the pillow to watch a little bit of the BBC lunchtime news. Best not to rush things.

****

### THE BEAUTIFUL BENDY WENDY

Wednesdays meant two things to Bendy Wendy. One was Hot Yoga class at the local health club, to fine tune her already impressively flexible body, and the other was an evening of gold-digging at the Peppermint Lounge.

So far, the years had been kind to Wendy, who at 62, was wearing surprisingly well apart from some hair loss. She had a selection of good quality wigs, and it was interesting to see how different men reacted to the guises of blonde, redhead or brunette that she applied at various singles nights across the North West.

For example Ronnie in Stockport liked her in the blonde wig, plus sporting his cowboy hat, as she bounced up and down on his barrel sized belly. Ronnie liked country and western music, but otherwise was a kind-hearted soul and their holiday in the USA had been wonderful.

On the other hand, tall Paul from Warrington preferred Wendy in her shoulder length brunette wig, wearing a clinging velvet purple dress. He said she reminded him of a `skinny Nigella, and believe me that's a good look' as he gave her a good seeing to, bent over the writing desk in a Best Western Superior Room near Wigan. Like Ronnie, tall Paul was a generous kind of guy as well, and had treated Wendy to a new kitchen, complete with black-painted appliances and a double-door fridge. These men were married, of course, but everyone was getting what they wanted, everyone knew the score.

Wendy breezed into the Hot Yoga class, nodded to some of the regular ladies waiting for the class and placed two bottles of water on the floor. Her friends Lisa and Jo, came in and found their usual spots, laying their towels down carefully. Caitlin, the yoga teacher bounced in, chatting to a couple of new ladies, who looked nervous as they stripped to their swimming costumes, letting soft, doughy lumps of flesh poke out from unlikely places.

"Hiya Wendy, y'alright?" asked Jo.

"Yes thanks, still creaking on."

"Give over, I can't get into the positions you can, you're amazing. I bet they love it when you're on the dancefloor at that…Pink Panther place is it?"

Wendy gave a little laugh and corrected her over the name of the greatest disco in the North of England. Then Lisa joined in.

"I heard that some of them chuck their car keys in the middle of the tables about midnight, and then go off with anyone. Is it really a swingers place or what?"

"No," said Wendy, leaning back as she sat on the floor and began to stretch her legs, "it's just a fun night out really. I've met some nice guys there to be fair. And a few players…one even took me on a date and had two salmon in the boot of his car – he told his wife he went night fishing."

Lisa and Jo threw their heads back and laughed.

"Oh Wendy, you should write a book…you've seen it all love!"

Caitlin came over with one of the new ladies and introduced her to the trio, just to make the class more sociable and make sure the new girl would turn up again and pay her £10. It was always that bit easier to drop out of classes if you didn't really know anyone.

"And this is my star pupil; Bendy Wendy I call her – she is amazing! Sorry Wendy, I hope you don't mind me calling you that?"

"No problem Caitlin. I've been called much worse." she said with a straight face.

The thing was, Wendy had been called many things; cold-hearted user, slag, cheat, money-grabber and plenty of other things. None of it touched her. She drove home from the hotels in her Audi A3 Sportback diesel, had a shower, deleted the willy pictures from her phone and then planned her next cruise, or conservatory upgrade. People could say what they liked, because in the end, she had an independent life, free from any man dipping into her bank account, or arguing over gas bills and hair appointment costs.

Wendy had her detached house in Cheadle, (thank you second husband!) her beautiful red car and could still do the splits in her 60s, a feat which several men like to admire in five star hotel rooms from Manchester to Marrakech. Wendy wasn't interested in growing old gracefully, doing the gardening each Sunday, or gazing, dopey-eyed, at the telly, alongside with some grumpy bloke who wanted cups of tea and his toenails clipping. Sod that.

Bendy Wendy was determined to go out with a bang, not an 8-pack of Aldi bangers.

\*\*\*\*

## GET LUCKY

I stepped out of the shower, shook some water from my hair and wrapped a towel around my waist. From the living room I could hear Daft Punk's *Get Lucky* thrumming its addictive beat from the speaker dock. I sang along with the chorus as I sprayed on deodorant, and then grabbed my shaver.

My iPhone pinged. It was a text from my current stalker, a middle aged lady called Annemarie from Swinton. We met at Big Reg's disco nite, held in the basement of the Lord Devonshire Hotel. If you can imagine a museum of waxworks, which has been trashed by drunken football supporters, then hastily redecorated using cast off furniture from Scope, you've got the lie of the land.

I liked Annemarie, don't get me wrong. She had a real sense of adventure about her, owned a string of rental properties in Worsley, an apartment in Turkey and did that ace thing when she danced, where she put her arms above her head, and shook her impressive boobs from side-to-side.

Trouble was, on our second date, which was an evening at the theatre, she brought along her brother, plus his two grown-up children, her daughter and someone's cousin. The date was like being interviewed by half the audience from *University Challenge*;

"So Annie says you've been married but divorced...why do you suppose it failed?"

"You're Annemarie's new bloke then, where did you meet, not through the internet I hope?"

"Do you mind me asking, how old are you exactly and what do you do for a living?"

Kinda intimidating. So when I clocked Annemarie's Whatsapp message, which consisted of a photo of herself, wearing a bright turquoise bikini, with a message that read; `just in my brother's swimming pool, it was lovely today, wish you were with me here. x' I knew what to do.

Nothing.

The thing about female stalkers, in my limited experience of about five of them, is that any response feeds their need. Texting back is like methadone for their man-hungry wet pants. Just don't do it.

I dried myself off properly, and then chose some bright blue underwear for the Peppermint. Not that I planned on getting lucky, all I ever wanted was the music, the lights, the feel of my boot heels skimming that floor. Friends around me.

Santana's *Smooth* came on the iTunes and I swayed a little bit as I shaved, and then sprayed a little dab of Dolce & Gabbana onto my chest and neck. As I headed back to the bedroom, I sang along to that ace bit in the track,

`Gimme your heart, make it real, or else forget about it!'

It was all or nothing for me at the Peppermint. Either I'd be hit by the lightning bolt one night, meet someone really special, or I would stay single forever. In truth, the only thing left to do was smile, dance and flirt. Like half the crowd in the Peppermint, I'd kissed goodbye to real love a million years ago. It was better to just stop hurting people, and getting hurt.

I ran the steam iron across a Hawkes & Curtis shirt, which was a rich purple paisley, with square buttons and a high collar. Then I tucked the shirt's crisp, soft cotton into my Armani black jeans, fastening a heavy black leather belt, with a chrome buckle, around my skinny waist.

Tonight, I felt like wearing my fake snakeskin Paolo Vandini boots, winklepicker style, with a faded lilac pattern on them that went well with my shirt. I changed my belt for a red one, but it didn't quite work, so went back to my original choice. The Peppermint was the tragi-comic highlight of my week, I had to look sharp.

I wiggled my hips in the mirror as I grooved to the faint sound of Amelia Lily's thumping *You Bring Me Joy* oozing from down the hallway. I flicked some gel into my darker strands of hair and left the grey sides alone.

"Still got it." I said to myself, grabbing my car keys, watch and wallet.

That was true, but the thing was…nobody wanted it, except mad stalker women, bitey internet daters, lamb chop stew boilers, chubby gay men and arthritic grandmas gone wild on HRT. The only thing to do was to dance and forget all about bad romance.

## CHAPTER THREE: "WE FOUND LOVE IN A HOPELESS PLACE"

It was just another steady Wednesday at the Peppermint. Vera, Angie and Trish installed themselves like man-tracking software at their table facing the bar. This gave them a perfect view of the empty area in front of the bar where single men gathered, or `Meerkat Manor' as Vera called it.

It was still only 8.35 but within an hour or so a steady stream of head-darting, loose change-fondling men would gradually populate the bar area.

They lurked together for safety more than anything else, too scared to sit at a table and actually speak to women. Staying near the bar also kept them well away from the dance floor, which was a forbidden zone, until most of them had consumed enough booze to float a corner off-licence. Bathed in a motley cloud of supermarket aftershave, `Meerkat Manor' was a Greek chorus of chat-up artists repeating the same lines every Wednesday to any women who looked new to the Peppermint.

Some guys slowly supped beer, watching the women dancing with blank, staring and envious eyes. Their gaze suggested they were in a state mid-way between internet stalker and marriage-induced coma. Others swapped sexist jokes with their mates, having downloaded the very best filth from Facebook earlier in the day. Staccato bursts of manly chat about football, cars or gambling was also another good way to fill in time until a foxy woman walked by – or even stopped to say hello.

Each time a group of women came into the club, moving like panthers, with sensuous feline grace and power, the men looked them over. The genuinely single men craned their necks as the ladies sashayed their hips towards the tables, eyes drinking in all the beautiful curves, the glistening smoothness of skin and readiness of their smiles, which was always a good indicator of how receptive the women might be to a chat, or a dance.

But the married men simply homed in, like laser-guided RAF missiles, at the ladies' boobs and bums. After a witty remark or two about `plastic tits' or `an arse you could ride from here to Southport beach,' they generally went back to chatting about football.

****

"Shall I order the tea?" asked Trish, as Vera sent a text to her new fella, Derek, and then placed her pink coloured phone inside her shiny gold handbag.

"Ooh yes love, let's get a brew in first before we watch tonight's action."

Trish trotted off to the bar and ordered a refreshing pot of tea for three. It was good to start the evening with a good old fashioned bit of man gossip, general family news and an update on any medical ailments.

"Action?" asked Angie, raising one of her perfectly plucked and shaped eyebrows in mock disdain, "I'll bloody join a convent before I get any action in this place. The men in here are like useless yard dogs. You know that bloke I was talking to last week..?"

"The tall one, him with the red car?" asked Vera half-heartedly.

"What? No. That was the other week, this was Graham. He had a grey suit on, bit podgy, and going thin on top, but still didn't look as ugly as Phil Mitchell."

Trish arrived back at the table. A group of friends celebrating a 40th birthday came into the room and made a beeline for one of the bigger tables at the far end of the room.

"Oh how did you get on with that bloke Angie? Did he text you?" asked Trish as she sat down again, catching the last fragment of conversation.

Angie leaned forward and smoothed a stray hair away from her lip gloss-coated mouth.

"Yes, he certainly did. First, there were a couple of nice texts...y'know, `great to meet you properly...lovely dancing with ya babe....' that type of thing. Then he sends a photo of his *cock* with the words `can you find a hiding place for this?' I mean, for fuck's sake."

"Oh dear." said Trish, smiling broadly nevertheless.

Vera shrugged and then asked,

"Well, go on then sis, can we have a look then, or what?"

"Wouldn't bother," noted Angie, with a look that mixed decades of marital experience with a lifetime of disappointment, "I've seen thicker bingo markers, talk about pencil dick. And it was hard too!"

Trish squealed with laughter and threw her head back as the young waiter; Gorgeous Gary With The Blonde Hair brought their tray of tea things over. Vera cackled and shook her cleavage in delight.

"Evening ladies, here's your tea. Anything else I can get you?" said Gary, smiling from the tempting 24 year old corners of his kissable mouth.

"Don't tease me Gary." quipped Angie, powering up her phone and sifting through her photo archive with a slick dab of her manicured fingers.

"No Gary, Angie needs a man who can deliver, do you deliver son?" quizzed Vera, pouring the tea and shooting a knowing look at the lad, who blushed deeply and smiled in embarrassment. This was like being harassed by your Nan's pissed up mate at a wedding...which had actually happened to Gary.

"Oh leave him alone, he's lovely. We love you Gorgeous Gary...in a good way." said Trish, breaking the awkward spell between the barman and giddy trio. Then Angie found the photo of Graham's appendage and showed it to Vera and Trish.

Trish and Vera both rummaged in their handbags and, in unison, put on their spectacles to check out Graham's tackle with some degree of clarity.

"OMG. Too much info there ladies - I'll leave you to it then. Have a good night." muttered Gary, already turning on his Shoe Zone heels and beating a retreat as he spoke.

The three women passed the phone around, tapping patiently on the screen to make the image larger, and then chuckling as they compared star ratings. The overall judgement was a disappointing six out of ten.

"Very poor of him isn't it? He seemed nice." observed Trish

"Men are all the same Trish, animals, every one of 'em." stated Vera, with a look of bitter experience in her eyes.

"I just don't get why you'd send a photo if you knew that you were distinctly average in that department." added

Angie thoughtfully, "it's like he doesn't realise that he actually has the Tom Cruise of cocks in his trousers. I mean, he's basically saying `prepare to be disappointed love, but let's have a ding-dong anyway.'

"Maybe he's like them little Kia cars?" noted Trish, "bit boring, no real go, but comes with a seven year warranty? There's something to be said for being a steady loyal type – he did have a nice suit, I'll give him that."

"Trish, I don't care if his suit is Hugo Boss, I prefer a bloke who's dressed like a tramp but is more Huge-o Boss."

Vera and Trish threw their heads back and laughed. It was going to be a fun night all round.

****

DJ Dave finally dragged himself to the console and switched on his microphone. He muted the free disco mix that he'd downloaded from the file sharing site a month ago, and made the announcement that was always a crowd pleaser:

"Good evening ladies and gents, just to let you know, that the buffet is now being served. The buffet is now on. Thank you. Please don't forget to show your ticket – no ticket, no buffet."

A straggle of hungry punters made their way to the serving hatch immediately. Others carried on chatting as the room filled up. Sadie, Jen and Karen were sitting at their usual table, which was right next to the buffet queue. Karen was partial to sausages and made Jenny get two, even though she hated them.

"I'll always have an extra sausage." said Karen as Jenny and Sadie joined the line. Sadie winked and bantered with Karen;

"Yeah, that's what it says on the walls in the Ladies loo – ha!"

"Oh you cheeky bitch," said Karen, before firing back, "I heard that there's a guest book in the Gents about you."

\*\*\*\*

It was nearly ten, so by now most of the regulars had arrived. The two tall skinny ladies, who danced like wonky flamingos, were working their usual corner. No men were biting at their waterhole though. Dancing Derek, a 60-something, rakish guy, with a love for Northern Soul, had warmed up his two-tone shoes on the dance floor to Rihanna's *SOS/Tainted Love* remix.

Derek's green suit jacket flew open, as he spun around next to the big, beefy couple, who were having a secret affair. Everyone in the Peppermint knew about the affair, in fact the only two people yet to hear the news were the respective partners of the two smooching chubsters. The pair of them arrived separately, danced for an hour, mauled each other's behinds for ten minutes and then vanished.

In the centre of the dance floor Monkey Man was dancing with a trio of bemused women, who all tried their best to avoid his outstretched, and frequently wandering, massive hands. He didn't really dance as such, just stamped vigorously from side to side on his flat feet, smiling broadly and taking every opportunity to place his hands onto a female arm, waist, or bum cheek.

Sometimes women complained about this 70s style harassment to Tall Paul, the Peppermint manager, or Marco, the feisty Maltese owner of the club. But as Monkey Man was a former Detective Inspector who had taken early retirement, the management let most of his dancefloor crimes slide past with a nod and a cautionary wink. Now and then, like all night club owners, Marco needed a friend, who still had friends in the Police. That was how the world worked; always had, and always will.

At Vera's table, all the seats were full now. Trevor and Penny were finishing off their buffet and chatting to Sue and Kevin, who were fellow Motown fans. Once DJ Dave played his usual set of Northern Soul classics, the four of them would be up on the floor, Trev chucking talcum powder onto the floor and Sue shimmying sideways with that classic crossover step.

As Angie and Vera got up to dance, Sue sat next to Trish for a chat.

"Hiya Trish, y'alright, how did things go with Brian on your date?"

"Oh well, probably best we don't mention it…let's move on."

Sue smiled and made a little `Gladiator' thumbs down sign, then flicked her long blonde hair back and got closer to Trish's ear.

"Well, never mind Trish, but listen, we've been chatting with Trev and Penny we were all thinking of going on the disco boat at Chester. You know the one where you get a buffet then you dance on the rear deck of it. Do you fancy coming along?"

"Ooh yeah, that sounds nice. Who else is going on it?"

"We've asked Trev and Penny, Vera and Angie are definites…and you might like this, we asked Cal, the original Aldi Travolta himself and he said yes!"

"Callum's going? Ooh, I wonder what shirt he'll wear – I love his crazy shirts."

"He's still single Trish…god knows how with those hips, but he is! Get in there girl."

Just then Rihanna's *We Found Love* came on and Sue jumped up,

"Ahhh, I like this one, let's have a dance Kev – Trish come on, shake ya booty girl!"

They eased their way past the pillar with its peeling stick-on glitter and joined the milling press on the dance floor.

Jen and Sadie wiggled their asses against each other, teasing the men around them with some comedy lesbian actions. The overweight couple continued their secret affair by letting their hands roam across each other's ample buttock cleavage, like Bear Grylls looking for shelter in dense, steaming undergrowth.

On Meerkat Manor, Brian the fisherman was casting his net far and wide, searching for a bit on the side who perhaps fancied kippers for breakfast sometime.

Sue, Kev and Trish wriggled their way to a space near Angie, Vera, Trev and Penny, forming a little circle. Sue sang along with the lyrics and shimmied herself close to Kev, grabbing one of the lapels on his suit.

"We found love in a hopeless place." Then she drew Kev a bit closer by his suit lapels and added, "So what the hell are we still doing here?"

Kev smiled at her,

"Dancing hun, just dancing and watching all the crazy people."

\*\*\*\*

### THE CITROEN PICASSO – SURPRISINGLY ROOMY

Little Davey danced next to Sharon, the two of them grinding away to the beat of Barry White, Olly Murs and Robin Thicke's *Blurred Lines*.

"Can't believe I've just met you tonight!" shouted Davey, taking in every second of Sharon's mighty bosoms making their break for freedom from her little black dress. "I mean, I've seen you around a few times, but was always scared to chat you up...I didn't think you liked me."

Sharon wiggled herself closer to Davey and ran her fingers down his sweaty chest hair, and then pulled him really close, smiled sexily, before planting a deep smooch kinda kiss on his surprised lips. Sharon was on heat tonight, feeling inexplicably horny, plus her ex-boyfriend was in the Peppermint, watching her every move from Meerkat Manor. She was determined to give her ex a show that was worth a standing ovation, the annoying prick. He could watch now, while she nailed this comical little guy...unless he had the guts to do something about it.

As the music pumped its seductive throb around the room, Sharon and Davey danced in slowly decreasing circles, arms interlocking, him spinning her out, salsa style, than reeling her in again. As they drew close, he was crushing her breasts close to his face, letting his hand drift lower down her back and cup the rippling curves of her sexy, swaying arse. He could feel things stirring in his pants.

"Listen, I have to ask you one thing Sharon..."

"Anything."

"Does it bother you that I'm a bit...short? At all?"

Sharon threw her arms around his shoulders, kissed him again and pressed her hips against him. At the bar, her ex turned away, placed his pint glass – still half full – on the top of the brass drainer and then left the Peppermint. He'd seen enough and was off home to join Match.com at precisely 1.12am that night. He would subsequently meet a nurse from Timperley who had rediscovered sex after a hysterectomy and live happily with her for four years, but that's another story...

Five minutes after her ex left the building, Sharon more or less dragged Davey outside to the smoking area in front of the Peppermint's French windows and proceeded to snog his face, with the power, suction and ball action of a rogue Dyson.

"I think you're dead cute Davey. Is your car parked in a dark bit of the car park?" She placed a hand on his tackle area, just to reinforce the point that she was getting at, so Davey knew, absolutely hundred percent understood, that she was up for it. You had to spell things out to blokes sometimes, in a kind of `join-the-dots' book of seduction.

Davey gleefully escorted her across the car park, walking like a frisky terrier that has just learned there's a new butcher's shop in town, and shoehorned Sharon into the passenger seat of his Citroen Picasso. She moved the seat back, pulled her dress up halfway along her mighty thighs, and then popped her boobs over the lacy rim of her black bra.

"Go on lover, have a play with these puppies."

Davey dived in as if he was a penguin in a paddling pool full of sardines. When he came up for air, he offered a bit of sexy chat to help get Sharon in the mood.

"Ahhhh babe, you're so sexy. I want to make you wet."

She took his hand and guided it across the sensitive skin that she needed to have touched, caressed.

"Don't keep talking Davey, just do it."

Sharon kept kissing Davey, and then deftly reached beside the seat for the seat-back lever, ramming the seat down with a thump so loud that horses three fields away were startled. She then lifted herself upwards, slid her knickers past her knees and threw them into the footwell, next to a half-eaten packet of mints and a scrunched up Ginsters pasty wrapper.

Davey fumbled with his trousers and shoes, struggling to get half stripped off as the steering wheel and gear lever proved tricky to navigate in the dark. He also accidentally beeped the horn as he dragged his right leg over the steering wheel.

"Oops," he gasped, trying to make light of it, "me so horny, ha ha!"

It didn't help that his arse cheeks then brushed the CD player as he wriggled loose from his sweaty disco trousers, accidentally hitting the on/off button. The Best of Robbie Williams suddenly chimed into life, blaringly loud.

`Jump on board...take a ride!'* sang Robbie and Kylie, before Davey groped in the dark, pushing various buttons, eventually lowering the volume.

"Bugger it, stupid CD player. Sorry."

On the upside, Sharon felt his hardness in her hands. He was still keen.

"Bloody hell, you're not short in that department. That whole shoe size thing is complete bollocks, this is a right good tool!" she noted with genuine surprise, and a distinct note of satisfaction.

"Yeah, they used to call me tripod at school." winked Davey, as Robbie sang *No Regrets*. The music reached a crescendo, as the Picasso rocked on its knackered shocks in the far corner of the Peppermint's car park. People leaving the club crept past, like unlucky witnesses at the scene of a brutal road accident, trying with every fibre of their being not to look at the raw, damaged meat on display, but copping a sneaky glance anyway.

Inside the club, big Steve the bouncer and Marco the boss watched the CCTV in horrified fascination, flicking the camera to infrared night vision to get a better view of the two bodies coupling like diesel locomotives in Crewe goods yard.

"My God," observed Marco, "that little guy should be a bloody porn star, look at him go. Are you taping this?"

"Yeah." agreed Steve, "He's got the moves boss, proper Duracell bunny. Wonder if he's on Viagra?"

"Yeah, probably," agreed Marco, then adding pointedly, "wonder if he's buying it from you?"

Marco selected normal vision again on the CCTV and zoomed in on Sharon's face, which was turned to one side, eyes closed, unsmiling. Davey continued to go at her, eyes closed in rampant pleasure. Sharon lay in the uncomfortable seat, letting him finish. The camera couldn't see it, but if you looked closely enough you would have seen a teardrop slip quietly from the corner of her eyelid.

Revenge isn't always sweet, sometimes it's just love, in a hopeless place.

\*\*\*\*

## CHAPTER FOUR: `WHILE HE IS BUSY LOVING EVERY WOMAN THAT HE CAN'

The tension was thicker than a budget Christmas cake from Lidl.

Angie poured out some tea for both her and Keith, and then sat down opposite him at the kitchen island. The toaster began to emit that pungent, insidious scent that told you the bread was too thick, it was about to burn.

She ignored it. Scanned her copy of OK magazine instead.

"Kate Middleton's gone too thin, she looks like a kidnap victim." observed Angie. Her husband made a vague `Huhhmm?' noise and continued studying the sport pages in the Daily Mail.

"I did two shirts for you last night," she said in a softer tone, "which one are wearing for the races?"

He looked up from the paper, then noticed the toast begin to smoulder and leapt over towards the work surface to rescue it.

"Erm...the pink one most likely, looks well with that grey suit I got in the Greenwoods sale."

"Yeah. Weather seems alright for it anyway." ventured Angie.

"Yep. Should be a good day out."

Keith selected his favourite knife from the kitchen drawer and smeared Lurpak with utmost precision, right to the corners of the toast. When it came to spreading butter onto bread, he had an engineer's eye for accuracy. He liked things neat and tidy, like their `arrangement.' Keith didn't ask about Angie's weekend plans in any great detail, and in return, she was expected not to probe too deeply into his exact location. Things were easier that way.

He sat down again and bit into the toast, eating it as quickly as possible. He wanted to be on the road to York in about 20 minutes if possible, taking a detour to the outskirts of Ellesmere Port, in order to pick up his mistress, a no-nonsense doctor's receptionist called Sylvia. She was happily divorced, went to the gym once a week, liked to be plied with Prosecco at York racecourse, and then fucked senseless at a Marriott hotel afterwards. She didn't want a man living with her full-time and she certainly wasn't going to get married and hand over half her house, which she'd won the hard way on life's divorce lottery.

It was another neat, tidy arrangement. Everyone got what they wanted, nobody was hurt.

Angie and Keith's children and grand-children were none the wiser about the lovers who existed only in compartments of the couple's shadowy, secret lives. Things were easier that way and although family get-togethers were always a strained affair, Angie and Keith could usually keep a simmering lid on their feelings until dessert was served, a christened child was photo-bombed, or the bar closed.

Meanwhile houses, pensions, secret bank accounts full of emergency cash and the odd classic car, were all preserved intact. Inviolate as their separate souls.

Angie went back to her magazine as Keith chewed gamely away, making that annoying lip-smacking noise that some blokes do when they eat too quickly. Her phone buzzed and she checked her Whatsapp. It was Rahim.

**Hey gorgeous, I'm coming to Manchester today on business. Let's meet up hun, I wanna see you bad, miss ya babe xxx**

She switched her phone off and flicked the pages of her magazine, catching sight briefly of Jodie Marsh and making a mental note to get some gravy from the supermarket later. She was still debating with her own head about seeing Rahim again. She hated being in love with him, despised herself for being used, but still…he was keen, almost twenty years younger than Angie too. Tough decision.

She texted Rahim; **Hi babe, dunno if I can make it to Birmingham, got a girls day out planned that day, will let u know xx**

Keep him guessing, make him work for it, she thought to herself. There was always a Wednesday night at the Pink Peppermint, plenty of fish in the sea. Angie's toast wasn't quite cremated, not just yet.

**Come on babe, I miss you. Come see me this Friday, wear something lacy and black, I wanna pull your clothes off with my teeth.**

Angie smiled as she read his text. She glanced at Keith, but he was oblivious, studying form at York.

****

### CAL'S RIVERBOAT SONG

The night on the disco boat was one of my favourite Peppermint-On-Tour excursions. Partly because the whole idea of about 70 people trying to get on a dance floor about 12 foot square was like a giant game of stand-up Twister, but that night also had a kind of genuine magic. It was memorable because something happened; I met someone.

I parked at the posh rowing club, figuring nobody would question someone wearing chameleon patterned Jeffrey West boots, and a blue silk shirt that Jonathan Ross might have deemed `a bit gaudy.' I didn't want to park the 2.3 V5 Golf on the street until one in the morning, just in case someone fancied nicking it, or vandalising it – it's a guy thing, we love our classic cars.

As I walked along the tree-lined Groves, catching the chilly wind pulling at my hair, the sound of Take That's *Relight My Fire* rippled across the river, as the last heat of September ebbed away into the sky. *The Lady Diana* disco boat gently chugged its engine as the crew stood on the jetty, smoking and chatting before the party people arrived.

I nodded at Vera and Trish and kissed them on the cheek as I joined their table.

"So, no Angie then?" I asked.

Vera shook her head in exasperation at her sister's no-show and said nothing, but Trish made the peace.

"Well, she's not feeling so good, she texted us before, but never mind eh? You're here and Sue and Kevin, plus Trev and Penny are coming along too."

"It will a great night," I underlined, "the crew told me before they've got two hen parties and a 40th birthday party booked on – full house."

"Oh Lordy." observed Vera, knocking back the last of the white wine and lemonade she had on the go. I offered to get some drinks in and as I stood up Trev and Penny arrived, with Penny looking flustered.

"Sorry we're slightly late," explained Trev, "we struggled to find free parking, and Chester's a nightmare. Never mind."

I checked out Penny's shoes, being something of a connoisseur of footwear. She was wearing silver, strappy heels, touch of glitter on the heel and across the toes. Nice to dance in, not so hot for trekking from a back street somewhere beyond Grosvenor Park I imagined.

"Shall we go inside now?" asked Vera, gathering her wrap thingy around her shoulders, "I'm freezing my Lancashire arse off out here."

**** 

## THE IRRESISTIBLE RAHIM

Angie wriggled her shoulder as Rahim leaned across and ran his hand down her the bare skin of her arm. She pulled away a bit from him, but still smiled into his dark eyes.

"Babe, I've missed you...missed touching you."

Angie pursed her lips in annoyance and took another sip of her cranberry juice. She was determined to stay sober.

"Yeah well, you chose to go back home and play happy families, remember?"

Rahim leaned back from her, opened his arms expansively and as he did so she could glimpse his chest hair poking up from his unbuttoned shirt collar. The little triangle of tanned skin grew bigger for a moment and Angie recalled pushing her fingernails across that caramel soft flesh almost a year ago.

"Come on Angie, I was never the type of guy who would walk out on his kids...you knew that right from the start."

"Yeah well, you didn't have a take a job in friggin' Leeds and relocate as well did you?"

"Babe, we went through all that…it was another 12K a year, and an Audi A5, only a knob was gonna turn that down. But listen right, this new role they got for me means I travel more…shows, shop visits, client pitches…all that shit. We can be together, we can see each other again. Like this…yeah?"

He touched her hand gently, less intrusively than before. She didn't pull away, but looked him straight in the eyes.

"I dunno. Too much time has gone by…and you hurt me Rahim. You just stopped replying to my text messages. I'm worth a text OK? If I'm worth a night in a hotel and some fancy knickers from Boux Avenue, then I'm worth a few texts and a phone call. Fuck's sakes."

Rahim sighed and looked furtively around the hotel bar, in case anyone was listening to her raised voice. For a second he looked as if he was about to get up and leave. Then he reached across and gently hugged her, whispering in her ear,

"You're like a drug Angie. There hasn't been a week without thinking about you, wishing I could take back the crap things I said to you. Times I ignored you. Come on babe, give us another chance. We had a good thing goin' yeah?"

She patted his back and shoulders, but gave a lukewarm response, then went back to nursing her cranberry juice.

"You can't just switch things on again, it isn't that easy Rahim. All the promises you made, all the things you said to me...it all turned out to be a load of crap really. And I still feel like crap inside, I feel used. Don't you get that?"

Raw emotion filled her eyes. Her head fell lower and she reached for her handbag, rummaging for tissues. Like most men, Rahim sat immobile next to her, because he just couldn't cope with a crying woman. Especially when it was his fault.

"Come on, it's OK." he soothed, holding her hand. "It will be OK babe."

Across the bar a couple paused as they demolished their Hunter's Chicken and Lamb Shank, the woman tapping her husband with her foot under the table, then whispering,

"See, told ya. They're having an affair, and he's finishing with her - written all over her. Poor woman."

"Yeah. Poor show if all she's getting is a seeing to in a Premier Inn on a Friday night." Agreed her husband, chewing thoughtfully on a pleasantly burnt strip of lamb, and then adding;

"Mind you, she looks quite a bit older than him, so she's punching above her weight just to get a bit of action there frankly. Talking of affairs, I wouldn't a good seeing to later in the garden shed, never mind a cheap hotel. B&B in Skegness, anywhere really. How are ya fixed later?"

"Dream on. How's the lamb shank?"

"Not enough gravy, there's never enough gravy at these places."

He went back to flicking through Facebook updates on his mobile, between chewing mouthfuls of meat. His wife had a quick glance at Angie and Rahim, who walked out of the bar together.

Friday night out for married couples; work related conversations, family squabbles, gossip about the neighbours. Smartphones set on the restaurant table, like blunt, glowing daggers pointing at each other. Conversation stoppers, distractions from the all-too-familiar flesh and bones parked just opposite. Date night passion killers.

\*\*\*\*

## MEETING NEW PEOPLE

"Shall we make a move, the disco boat sails in 15 minutes?" Trev asked, finishing off the last of his lager.

The rest of us glanced at each other and nodded in agreement. As we walked out of the Old Orleans pub Sue and Kevin came marching along the pathway next to the city walls.

"Oh sorry we're late," explained Sue, "we had to see to the horses." Kev just smiled and stood next to her, his grey suit fading into the background next to Sue's stunning white party dress. She had a blue CZ and mystic topaz bracelet on, plus her white gold watch, and sky blue high heels, with little white hearts on the toe. Sue may have been nearly sixty years old, but she still oozed glamour when she wanted to.

"See to the horses eh?" observed Vera as we strolled over to the Lady Diana's gang plank, "that's a new euphemism for me!"

Trish, Penny and myself chuckled as Vera gave a saucy, *Carry On* style wink. Vera was a game old bird. Kev blushed faintly as Sue replied,

"Can be struggle getting the bridle off sometimes...off Kev I mean!"

****

The lower deck was filling up now and I was glad that Trev had shooed us along earlier, as we had good seats close to the bar at the front of the boat. The first hen party were settling themselves in just across the way from us.

I let my eyes wander over the group of ten or a dozen women opposite. The long bench seats were a soft parade of caramel skin, glittery heels, raven dark rivers of hair and flickersoft blonde bobs.

Handbags staked claims on tables, some bulging with the unmistakeable outline of miniatures full of vodka or Baileys, some were slimmer with just a smartphone, some lippy and a mini Tampax in there. Youth, hope and the joy of life bubbled and fizzed from their conversations as they greeted each other and admired the bride's Pink Princess style outfit, complete with tiara, Ann Summers accessories and ridiculously high platform heels.

At the far corner of the deck, near the perilously steep steps, which led to the disco dance floor at the rear of the boat, there were a group of four mums, hunkering down in sensible cardigans, lower heels and dresses from M&S, BHS or Next. This quartet of 50-something ladies wore lines of care on their faces beneath the Superdrug make-up and knowing smiles. But still, they were ready for a big night out.

The mums sported bulky, more utilitarian handbags than the younger generation. These were stuffed with tissues, Polo mints, Tesco mobile phones, spare panty pads in case a belly laugh caused a bit of wee to leak out, unpaid electricity bills, nail clippers, eye liner, dark red lipsticks, headache tablets, a morning after pill, spare tights and enough small change to fire a volley of grapeshot from HMS Victory.

I liked the look of one older woman. She had an indefinable warmth about her, from the way she leaned close into conversations, to the expansive hugs that adorned her as she greeted her daughter's friends. She made a point of applying a dab of make-up to her daughter's face, wagging her finger at her and telling her to `go steady on the drink.'

The captain made a few announcements regarding safety. Laughable really, I mean how are 50-odd drunk people going to get off a sinking boat calmly? He then asked if I was wearing my jazzy disco shirt for a bet.

For a second I was tempted to make some smartarse reply concerning the amount of ballast he was carrying under his jumper, but then I considered that the Captain might know how to deploy the lifejackets and rafts in an emergency. I just shrugged and smiled.

"Aww, leave him alone," said Vera, "he's single and hasn't figured out what a colour catcher is yet."

"Smoothly done, now every woman on the boat knows Cal's single. It'll be mayhem." said Trish, with just a little hint of annoyance in her voice.

**\*\*\*\***

After an hour's slow chugging along the river, passing the millionaires' gin palaces on the banks of the Dee, the two hen parties were both coming to the boil nicely. Team A, who had come in matching blue and white sailor suits, with short skirts and tiny little hats had staked a claim to the dance floor early doors. Vodka fuelled alcopops in hand, they bumped, grinded and twerked like extras from a freshers week condom advert.

Team B meanwhile had gone for a `Where's Wally' theme, surrounding the pink themed bride like a motley collection of stripey burglars. In fact one or two of them looked as though they might break open your back doors with a rampant rabbit. As my old Gran used to say, `these women with tattoos on their legs are often a bit rum.'

Somewhere in the middle of this volatile cocktail of mating hormones, celebrity-endorsed perfumes, spiky heels and sex toys, I danced to The Killers, Calvin Harris and Lady Ga Ga. Occasionally I was bashed by a stray handbag, at other points a random hand darted out and slapped my bum cheek. It was all going so well.

Then the boat had to perform an awkward three-point turn, before heading back and this resulted in a fog of rancid diesel fumes drifting across the arse end of the deck. Two things happened in the space of three minutes; first, a completely hammered girl called Ellie fell to her knees and then projectile-vomited over my trousers and shoes.

"Oh my God..." slurred Ellie, "I've got to go home...I'm in work tomorrow." She added, before summoning up another portion of blue-tinted puke and dribbling that onto the back of her hand and on my left boot, simultaneously. Great aim.

And then the older woman that I'd seen before hurried over with some wet wipes from her handbag and began dabbing at my clothes.

"Sorry about my daughter's friend, just stay there and I'll get some water." she soothed, without a trace of awkwardness. I stood up and moved to the edge of the dance floor as people began help Ellie and empathise with me.

"Aww no, not your lovely shiny new boots." said Trish as she noticed the fracas and the music stopped whilst the crew started a bit of a clean-up.

"Ah, they're not really expensive." I lied, and then added "It's OK." To placate Ellie, who had got emotional and started crying with a mix of shame and alcopop depression.

"It's a shame when people can't handle a drink, but you're so good about it Cal. Oh look at your trousers too, it's all over your left leg there. Nasty." said Trish, firing a quick look of disgust towards Ellie and her Wally-fied friends. Then the nice lady came back with a bottle of water and some kitchen towels.

"I do apologise," she said, nodding slightly at Trish, "here get some water on those boots as quick as you can. Maybe we can save them."

Trish stood awkwardly to the side of us as I dabbed at myself and made small talk with the older, petite, blonde haired lady, who smiled at me.

"Listen if they're ruined, let me know and I will pay for them. I feel really bad about it all. My name is Lisa."

I told her it was OK, don't worry. Told her my name too.

"Is this your wife?" asked Lisa, smiling at Trish, who was taken aback.

"No, we're just friends on a night out. This is Trish." I explained.

"Well, you wanna get this guy down the aisle Trish, he's a bit of a mover on the dancefloor." smiled Lisa. Trish smiled back weakly, as if she was swallowing laxative chocolate. Then Lisa rummaged in her big handbag and found a business card.

"Well listen Cal, if you change your mind just phone, or email me and I'll make sure Ellie coughs up for some new boots, as I know her Mum pretty well and she'll make her pay. Those are probably ruined now. It is a real shame, they look fantastic."

"Wow, that's so kind of you. You don't have to, but thanks."

Trish looked like she was trying to swallow an ostrich egg as Lisa passed me her phone number.

For a second there was a strange, heavy silence between the three of us. I stood with vomit-coated tissue in my hand and wearing stinking clothing, wanting to kiss her on the cheek and say it was lovely to meet her. But instead I just smiled gormlessly and reeked of alcopop puke.

Lisa broke the spell.

"Well, I should help Ellie, instead of leaving it all to my daughter. I would say nice to meet you Cal, but let's be honest...it could have been nicer. One of those things. Bye bye."

And then she was gone, back to the far end of the boat deck. But I watched her walk all the way there. I liked her. There was something about her that hooked me. The chemistry crystallised in the air between us, we both felt it.

\*\*\*\*

## CHAPTER FIVE: `HEART OF GLASS'

It started with a throwaway line.

Wendy had woken up early, showered and then put on some clean knickers. Ronnie was still flat out, snoring after his exertions from the night before. Forty-five minutes of high octane sex action basically did for him, bless, thought Wendy as she looked at his flesh pouring out from under the quilt like a badly bleached walrus.

She plugged in her iPhone headphones and flicked through her music until she found the *Best of Chicane*, then she started some gentle warm-ups and stretches on the floor of room 282 in the Holiday Inn, Harrogate. The vertebrae in her arched back stood out, like wisdom teeth pushing through, as she folded her knees beneath herself and let her head and arms tip forwards. Then she slowly lay down and stretched herself all the way out, bones clicking, muscles working gently.

The music took her mind away from her surroundings, as she raised herself into a crab position, thrusting her hips up and feeling her breasts slip up her chest towards her neck. She lowered herself a few times, and then pushed up again, each time a little higher, feeling the strain in the back of her tanned, lithe thigh muscles.

"Bloody `ell, you should be charging for a show like that Wendy." Said Ronnie, who suddenly woken up. As had his penis.

"Get yourself over here girl." instructed Ronnie, a wicked smile creasing his flabby face in delight, "I want you to do that Boston crab thing on my cock – how much?"

\*\*\*\*

That chance remark got Wendy thinking. The holidays in Morocco, Crete and Cuba were great. Weekends in Harrogate and the Lake District were fine too. But she could feel the clock ticking within her clicking, creaking bones. Sometimes she caught a glimpse of herself in a mirror and saw the ripples of skin, folded like parchment near her elbows. Time would catch her, one day.

Maybe a little work here and there, a few lines redrawn, some fuller lips and smoother eyelids wouldn't be a bad idea. But all that cost money, big money, because it had to be done right.

But Ronnie's request had a grain of truth in its jokey heart. In essence, he was paying for her favours with the hotels, the spa treatments, the dinners washed down with Marlborough Estates Sauvignon Blanc. What difference would another £200 or so make to Ronnie's company accounts anyway – almost all of these trips were down as `business shows, sales meetings' or `client entertainment.'

Wendy had an idea. She would build a room of her own. A room of pain, dreams, whips, chains and all the *50 Shades* fetish gear that older men seemed to relish like HP sauce on a full English breakfast. The dirty old dogs.

Well, strictly speaking *she* wouldn't build it.

No, in fact her good friend Joe the Builder would. He was really good with his hands. Very good indeed and if he was a really good boy he might get to road test some of the equipment first as well. Wendy had a plan. It was like a pension plan, but a hell of a lot more fun and much better paid than anything you might get from Aviva.

****

## MATHS LESSONS

Gorgeous Gary with the Blonde Hair felt a set of well-manicured fingernails teasing his tackle into life. He shifted uneasily in the strange bed, feeling the buzz of alcohol still clouding his head and slowly sifting the fragments of last night into a jigsaw picture that made sense.

The room smelled of sex. A thin cotton sheet covered him from the waist down. Strands of blonde hair tickled his chest as a woman's mouth laid a daisy chain of kisses across his firm 20-something flesh.

"Mmmm, morning Gary."

For one awful second, Gary thought it was his Mum in bed with him, as he caught a trace of Chloe perfume in his nostrils and felt the softness of hair and skin enveloping him, warming his shoulder.

Angie let her fingers fold expertly around Gary's balls and began stroking them, moving upwards, pausing to cup them for a few seconds, then starting again. As if by magic, things started to happen.

"Ooooh, hello there big boy!"

Gary smiled and properly opened his eyes.

"Morning. God it's early...what time is it Angie?"

"Ummm," she pondered wiggling his willy in fascination this way and that, "about six-ish. Do you know, I am so glad I dodged out of that disco boat trip last night. You were soooo good."

Gary rolled his eyes and tried to turn away, burying his head in the pillow. Three hours sleep after two hours of bum-spanking, up-against-the-wall, no holds barred sex, on top of some late night drinks, had taken its toll on him.

Besides which, he wasn't quite so sure about loving Milf action now. Thing is, he'd seen Angie without her make-up on and her unrestrained boobs lolling about like two balloons, half full of chip shop batter. But still, her hand gradually, inevitably, worked its charm upon his now rock-solid willy. Boys will be boys after all.

"Do you watch *Countdown* Gary?"

"Er yeah, sometimes...why?"

"Well," explained Angie, propping herself up on her right elbow as her left hand kept on doing the Harlem Shuffle in Gary's groin area, "I'm fifty-seven, and you are..?"

"Twenty Five." He replied sheepishly. Blushing even.

"Yes, twenty-five. Good age by the way. Enjoy it son."

"Please don't call me son. It's kinda freaky."

"Really? OK, sorry Gary. Right so, I'm fifty-seven and you're twenty-five, so like the skinny bird does on Countdown, I want you to double 25, which is 50 yeah, then add three bonks from last night, then subtract one `BJ', which you received last week, after doing all that gardening work for me. Cheers for that by the way, nice trimming on my shrubbery."

"Riiight," ventured Gary, smiling as he folded one arm behind his head and leaned back into the pillow, "that leaves five, I think..?"

"Give the lad a gold star! Correct."

Gary chuckled to himself as Angie grinned like a Cheshire Cat at him.

"I can't do it five times Ange, honestly!"

"Tell ya what, I will accept one bonk, but in five different positions, you super-stud." Then Angie added the sugar on top by performing the Countdown theme tune; "Do-do, do-do, do-do-do-doodley-do - doo!"

"Oh Angie. You are pure filth. I fuckin' lova ya." said Gary, pulling her on top of him and playing with her swaying boobs.

"You don't have to love me big boy. Just give me a good seeing to, keep your mouth shut at the Peppermint and then nobody gets hurt. Now then, let's see what this little fella wants for breakfast, eh?"

The faux leather headboard began to thud, to a steadily quickening beat. It got noisy within a few seconds, too noisy for Angie to hear the ping, as a text from Rahim echoed plaintively from her iPhone.

\*\*\*\*

## TIME WAITS FOR NO ONE

Vera turned the Yale key in the lock and cautiously pushed the green painted door open. The smell hit her immediately; an acrid, stale, perishing stink of piss. It hung in the gloomy hallway of the flat, like an echo from Vera's council house childhood all those decades ago. She half expected to see the coat hooks on the wall, one of Dad's caps there next to his `best' Mackintosh. But the hooks had long gone, removed some two years after her Dad had died and all his clothes had gone to the *Heart Foundation* charity shop.

Now there was just Mum. Wonderful Mum, Joan, who had slaved in shops and offices until 9pm cleaning other people's messy desks, emptied half-eaten food from waste paper bins, hoovered rich folk's houses and scrubbed pub floors after closing time on weekday afternoons.

Joan had washed so many bags of laundry that her hands had that luminous, raw pinkness that a wartime generation sported like medals of austerity and want. The veins stood out bluey-purple on the back of her hands, like a map of some long forgotten battle scribbled onto damp, peeling wallpaper.

There she was in the living room, propped up on pillows, the TV remote next to her on the single bed that had replaced the sofa about four months ago.

Her eyes lifted from the TV screen and she looked at Vera's beaming smile.

"Oh hello love."

"Hiya, shall I put the kettle on and have a little tidy up for you then?" asked Vera, putting her handbag down on the high back chair and taking her coat off.

"Well, I suppose so. But would I have to vote for you then?"

"Vote for me?"

"Well yes. You're the lady from the Conservatives aren't you? Betty something isn't it?"

Vera sat down on the edge of the bed and took her Mum's hand and looked at her. Grey hair flew away in wisps, straying from her worn-out eyes and crumpled forehead. The ache of a life slipping inexorably into dust, cell by cell, grinding joints seizing slowly up, was written a thousand times over upon her milk-soft skin.

you." "It's me Mum, it's me, Vera. I'm here to look after you."

Joan looked at her for a full few seconds and then a wave of recognition, like bittersweet déjà vu, swept across her face. The blueness of her eyes glittered a little, as she summoned up the last remains of the fight, stitching together the threads of life still left inside her soul.

"Oh good. You're a good girl Vera. I always told your Dad that you were my favourite."

"Aw, that's nice Mum. Thank you. Listen you just carry on watching *Emmerdale* and I'll make us a brew, then get some stuff from the bathroom and give you a little wash eh? Just to make you feel a bit nicer."

Vera held her mother's hand tightly for a fraction of a second, and then let go. She passed the TV remote to her mother's limp, slightly swollen fingers, then got up and headed into the kitchen. Vera's brother, Jim, had been round in the afternoon, and made lunch, but not washed the pots. Typical bloke.

Vera ran the hot tap and looked out of the kitchen window at the garden. Once neat and symmetrical, when Dad spent hours looking after it, the patch of land was now half jungle, half local recycling centre, with an abandoned barbecue, plant pots, gro-bags and a broken brush lumped together in a corner. She filled the kettle just enough for two mugs of tea and clicked it on.

Then she gathered up a tea towel, some Carex, Johnson's baby wipes and ran some warm water into a plastic basin. She knew deep down that Jim had probably smelled the wee on Mum some four of five hours ago, but as a man, he felt he couldn't clean her up. That, ultimately, was a daughter's job.

You could cry some days, you really could, thought Vera. But what was the point? That was life and you had to get on with it. She finished off the tea, grabbed a few biscuits from the cupboard and took them through to the living room. Joan looked at her like a guilty puppy.

"Vera, I've messed meself love. I'm so sorry." There were little blobs of tears forming at the edges of Joan's eyes. Her face reddened with the shame of her admission.

"It's OK, we'll get you cleaned up love. Just have this brew first, and then I'll set to. Don't fret."

She patted her mum reassuringly on the arm and made ready with the wipes. Vera's mum blew a few wheezing breaths onto her tea and then took a sip of it. She closed her eyelids for a moment, opened them and stared rheumy and vacant at the wallpaper and ceiling.

"You're a good `un. You're the best carer I've had, where is this place dearie?" smiled Joan, as Vera set her own mug of tea down on the bedside table, almost spilling it as she shook with suppressed sobbing. She was losing her mum, day by day, watching her soul sail away to god knows where.

"It's your house mum, this is your room."

"Oh. Who are you then?"

"I'm Vera, they call me Vera."

\*\*\*\*

## IT STARTED WITH A TEXT

The chameleon boots sat forlorn, on top of a Sainsbury's carrier bag, still emanating the faint aroma of sickiness. Despite two soapy wash-downs and a spray of Febreze, there was a faint whiff of something nasty ingrained into the leather. No doubt about it, they were write-offs.

I dropped the boots inside the carrier bag, and then quietly slung them in one of my neighbour's recycling bins on my way to the supermarket. Whilst I drove through the fractured shoal of traffic, I pondered on the idea of texting Lisa. I always tried to make it a rule not to text someone on the first night we met. It just looked too keen and I'd made myself too vulnerable, far too easily, in the past.

But I liked her. The picture of her sashaying down the deck, her beautiful hips moving with an easy grace, the way she carried herself. Her shoes. They were silvery glittery things, possibly from Schuh, maybe Next, but she was definitely a size 5. I could tell that in an instant.

I trollied around the aisles for a bit, then stopped by the low calorie microwave meals section and composed a text.

**Hi Lisa, it's Cal. Boots received much love from baking soda and are drying out. Sure they'll be fine. Hope you enjoyed rest of nite, it was lovely to meet you. x**

With a little deeper intake of breath than usual, I pressed send. Yes, I'd lied about the boots, but I didn't want her to feel bad.

My trolley slowly filled up, people in their jim-jams wandered past me, chucking BOGOF pizzas, sugar-laced breakfast cereals and offal pasties in their baskets like there was no tomorrow. Twenty minutes later, just by the checkout, Lisa replied.

**Hello lovely Cal. Nice to hear from you and good to know the boots survived! I have three very hungover young ladies in my house this morning. Ellie sends apologies. How did you like the disco boat? xx**

**Good fun. Nice to be there with a good bunch of friends too. Is the wedding day soon? Have you got a hat sorted? x**

**Yes. Hat, bag, shoes, the works. Cost a fortune but my best friend's daughter Catherine is a bridesmaid so have to look my best. It's a competitive thing being invited to a wedding. Happens in 2 weeks time. Everyone starting to panic now. ;-) xx**

I loaded my shopping into the car, and then settled down with the radio on to text a little bit more.

Sorry it took a while 2 reply, just out shopping. How exciting for you! Hope it's a nice day for the photos. My brother got married again last year and they had sunshine, makes big difference. Xx

It only took a second or two before she pinged me back;

Ah how nice, how romantic to go for a second marriage, not sure I would :-/ xx do you mind me asking if you've been married? X

No u can ask anything u like. I would've talked more last night, but well...there was the vomit n everything ;-) Was married for a long time and it didn't end well, but a wonderful woman and just because it didn't work out I would never say never again. You have to believe in love. Xx

There was a pause, as she had a little ponder on the message, then replied;

It's nice you are a man who talks about feelings Cal. I like that. Most blokes don't like to talk about relationships. And some men I know say nasty things about their exes, but you don't. I like that. xx

Well that's lovely of you to say Lisa. X I leave the judging to Simon Cowell and just try to be happy. You can't be a prisoner of your past xx

Listen Cal, I really want us to text a bit more. You're an interesting man, so would like to chat more if that's OK with you? Gotta go for now, stuff to do, but text me later this evening won't you? Xx

That would be wonderful. I'd really like that. You're a lovely person to chat to Lisa. Xx

That's how it started with Lisa. Lovely Lisa.

\*\*\*\*

## CHAPTER SIX: "AND I KNOW THAT IT'S TRUE, I CAN TELL BY THE LOOK IN YOUR EYES."

The Peppermint was busy.

It was just a few weeks until Halloween, which was a fancy dress themed night, with tickets already on sale. The room was filling up nicely and it wasn't quite 9.30. Vera, Angie and Trish were enthroned at their usual table, with Jen, Sadie and Karen just across the way at the next one.

"What was that *Plenty of Fish* night in Wigan like then Sadie?" asked Jen, as she sipped at a red wine and offered a dabble of Walker's Cheese `n' Onion crisps to the girls.

Sadie waved the crisps away and scrunched her lips up in disappointment.

"Same old faces really. Big Nigel was there trying to get into my pants again and I had a drink and a chat with Ginger Graham."

"Oh yes? He's quite nice really Ginger Graham, isn't he?" observed Jen, between munching her crisps and spilling fragments down her impressive cleavage.

"Well yeah, he's alright. It's just the thought isn't it?" asked Sadie, looking at both her friends in rapid succession, who replied as one chorus.

"Ginger pubes!"

Jen pulled a face and put her crisps down, she'd gone right off them.

****

"Evening ladies, got some drinks here for you."

"Oh Gary, that's good of you bringing them over, I can't carry the jugs at my age y'know." said Vera, as Gary gently lowered a tray, heavy with a jug of fruity cocktail, three glasses, plus a bottle of water, onto their table.

"No problem Vera, you're welcome."

"Service with a smile, can't beat it." said Angie, giving Gary a big smile back and a cheeky wink.

"Ooh Gary, you'll make a lovely husband one day." noted Trish as she poured some cocktail out into the glasses.

"I know, he's good isn't he?" agreed Vera, "How do you feel about older women Gary, is the age gap a problem for you?" said Vera. Gary looked at Angie, who maintained a mask of innocence across her face. Gary started to blush, and then shrugged at them.

"Actually girls, you're all a bit young for me."

"Oh you smooth talking bastard," replied Vera, tipping her head as she laughed, "get your coat sunshine, you've pulled."

****

Sue and Kevin breezed in just after ten, bought their tickets for the Halloween bash and then Sue said hello to Vera, Angie, Trish and greeted me at the table with a peck on the cheek.

"Cal, how are you luv, have you heard anything from that lady?"

"Yeah, we texted a little bit. She's really nice to talk to."

Kev joined us with the drinks and we chatted away as the Peppermint filled up and the dancing got going. Sadie shook her ass with a touch of burlesque flair, Jenny shook the last remnants of crisps from her Primark top as she boogied to *Blurred Lines*. Little Davey was in too, floating across the floor like an eager puppy, the glove box of his Citroen Picasso filled with flavoured condoms. Tonight he felt lucky, on fire even.

Sue and Kev told me they were coming to the Halloween as Gomez and Morticia from *The Addams Family*, Vera said that she would `wear less make-up than usual and just scare everyone that way,' whilst Trish quite fancied a bit of *Twilight* action. It was just so great to talk with friends and plan a great party night. I felt lucky.

"Aw I love this song, *Lady,* let's have a dance, come on." I urged, getting hold of Vera by the arm and lifting her up.

The others followed suit and Trev and Penny walked in just as we formed a circle on the dance floor. Trev threw some self-raising flour on the wooden block floor, pulling a few northern soul style spins and super-fast shoe shuffles. Trev liked to bust a few soul moves before he started really hammering the beer.

Dave the DJ switched on all the disco lights and cranked the volume up a bit too. It all came together and suddenly the Peppermint felt like a real discotheque, like it had always meant to feel; a gaudy bubble of pure dancing joy, sexual fantasy, escapism, friendship, one drink too many and spinning heels.

Man, I love this place, I whispered to myself, shaking my hips in time to the beat, lifting one arm above my head, Travolta style, and taking a turn in the middle of the circle. We all tried a few seconds worth of crazy dance moves, partly to entertain each other, and also to prove we were still alive.

We lip-synced to the song lyrics, smiling at how great it felt to be middle aged and dancing around like giddy teenagers. True, we were creaking a bit at the knees, and bruised by relationships gone bad, or impoverished by divorces. Yet still, you could shrug and feel philosophical as you counted the years that had flickered by. We were all still here, in this sacred place, skimming the surface of the Earth, in a glorious last stand against the dying of the light.

\*\*\*\*

## THE WENDY HOUSE

"What are you planning down here Wendy, some kind of disco?"

Joe stood back for a moment and put his hands on his hips as he surveyed his handiwork. Half of the basement was a mass of spring-loaded scaffolding poles, wires dangling from the ceiling and bits of rubble. The rest was an even bigger mess. But the space, the sheer space gained by opening out the cellar into one long room – that had potential.

Wendy set a proper builders brew of strong tea down on the workmate bench near Joe and smiled as her vision began to take shape.

"Well, there will be music Joe. It's going to be a place where I can do a bit of Zumba sometimes, maybe get on the pole, just for the exercise." She soothed. Joe gave her a knowing look, as he guessed the pole dancing area in the corner might well have a few other uses beyond toning up tummy muscles.

"Bloody hell, you could fit half the Peppermint crowd down here and still find room for a DJ's console. D'you want me to add a few flashing lights maybe?"

"Joe, we are creating a VIP club down here, something rather exclusive. You will be invited to the basement lounge warming do, I promise you that hun."

Joe took a sip of his tea and looked her up and down. Wendy was a fine looking piece of kit, whether she was in a party dress, or – as she was now – just some tight black leggings and a pale pink jumper. Their eyes met across the tops of their tea mugs and Wendy sent a little flick of her eyelashes towards him.

"This place will host the mother of all parties Joe. It's going to be great."

Joe set his tea down and picked up his plasterer's board and began folding and chopping the plaster, getting it nice and jelly-like before applying it.

"Oh there'll be some mothers down here I reckon."

Wendy laughed and watched him work. She liked to see a man get a bit of a sweat on.

\*\*\*\*

## DEREK'S LAST DANCE

It must have been about midnight and I was all danced out. Trev and Penny were going and as they said their goodbyes I just caught a fragment of conversation between Penny and Trish.

"Hold on, did you say that Derek has died?" I asked above the din of the music. Trish nodded. Trev shrugged his shoulders and opened his arms out in a gesture that was half-frustration, half-regret.

"An absolute legend. I can't believe it." said Trev, who looked wiped out by the news.

I chatted at the door for a few minutes before heading for my car. Trevor said he'd seen Derek in action at a soul weekender at Prestatyn just last spring, twirling and spinning like it was still the glory days of Wigan Casino; parallel trousers, short-sleeved Ben Sherman shirt and black loafers. Derek was maybe 65, 67 years old and old school soul, through and through. He was the kind of guy who brought a spare suit, shirt and a towel to the Peppermint lounge, so he could freshen up after 90 minutes solid dancing.

"That is bad news, the Peppermint has lost one of its soul stars." I said, "does anyone know what happened?"

Trish looked upset as she put her coat on, making ready to leave. The news had kind of frozen the night for the group, especially as they had all known Derek for years, whereas I'd only really spoken to him a few times on the edge of the dance floor in the last six months.

"Well, not really," explained Trish, "all I know is that Sam's heard about it. Apparently Derek's been unwell for a few weeks and he's died in hospital."

"God, 66...it's not that old really is it?" noted Trev, who had celebrated his 60th birthday just a few months ago.

"Old enough." added Vera sadly, but smiling, as she hugged me and Trevor, then said her goodbyes, "Listen you lot, take care and I'll see you all next week eh? Keep dancing!"

There was an odd deflation of everyone's spirits, although Sue and Kevin were still inside, dancing closely to *Young Hearts Run Free* and still oblivious to the news. I waved at them and then walked across the pot-holed car park, feeling my suede boots wobble occasionally. It wasn't the usual night at the Peppermint and although I didn't really know Derek that well, I felt like texting Lisa.

**Know it's late but just wanted to say that I had a nice night with friends, though I heard that a guy who used to go to Peppermint has sadly passed away, aged 66. So little time really, it makes you think. So glad I met you and think we will be good friends, nite x**

I got inside my car, hooked up the iTunes and scrolled through to Saint Saviour's version of *Love Will Tear Us Apart*. Once I was out of the car park and stopped at the traffic lights, my phone pinged a little message alert.

**Hi lovely Cal, sad to hear that. Strange feeling for you all I'm sure. Glad you texted me with that news, cos that shows we are good friends. Ring me if you like, I'm not asleep yet, or just text me when you're home. Nite xx**

I phoned later and we spoke for over an hour. As we got to know each other, and words tumbled out naturally, I began to like her very much. Lisa was a wittier, sharper, more incisive woman than I recalled from our meeting on the disco boat, yet still full of kindness, of love for animals, and people...probably animals first, then people. As we spoke I felt like she was someone I had met years ago, when we were both younger and more impulsive and we just hadn't clicked. She was so intelligent, so perceptive, I listened to her talk about all kinds of things and we laughed at fragments from each other's past lives. That, to me, was a good sign.

I drifted off to sleep, wanting to dream about her.

\*\*\*\*

Trevor took a sip of his tea and tapped away at the screen of the Galaxy tablet. Penny shuffled herself over towards the edge of the bed and ducked her head under the duvet.

"Trev, I've gotta be up in 5 hours, can we not just sleep?"

"Yeah, you're right love. It's sleepytime." said Trev switching off the bluey-white light of the tablet screen and placing it carefully on the bedside chest of drawers, next to his charity shop copy of Dan Brown's *Angels and Demons*. Trevor eased himself carefully out of his pyjama top and snuggled down next to Penny, folding his body close against hers. He felt lucky, really lucky.

"Can't believe it was just two months ago we saw Derek, spinning around to Tainted Love like there was no tomorrow. Don't think he's on Facebook either and I've lost his mobile number. One minute we're here, dancing, and then we're gone."

Trev sighed and gently kissed the back of Penny's long blonde hair.

"Night hun."

"Night night."

****

## ANGIE'S CONFERENCE CALL

It was an early start for Angie. She stepped, eyes still heavy-lidded and sleepy-glued into the shower and felt the shock of the water power against her skin. She gave it a few seconds, then squidged out some shower gel onto her arms and legs, lifted her impressive boobs up and soaped beneath them.

Draped in a pale blue towel she padded softly into her room and began to carefully search through her knickers and bras drawers. Eventually she found the Boux Avenue set, satin soft, with a pink rose design trailing across both the chemise and the hot pants style knickers.

Before she put the knickers on she took out her Lady Shave, and carefully trimmed the top edge of the tiny tuft of hair, that lay in a strip just below her belly button. She wanted every detail to be perfect, just right.

She sprayed a little Daisy Dream scent between her breasts, and then wriggled into a crisp, plain white top, with its scalloped neck, that showed plenty of cleavage, but also had the clever lycra panels at the side that pushed her boobs together. Angie gingerly unpacked a pair of stay-ups, 20 denier, caramel brown coloured, with darker brown lacy tops, and rolled them up to the top of her thighs.

"Hmmm, shoes?" she muttered to herself, opening the wardrobe doors and checking various boxes, stacked neatly like the foundations of a Wimpey home, beneath her rows of tops, dresses, trousers and skirts.

She pulled out the navy skirt and jacket that wanted to wear today and checked various shoes against the material, finally settling on a medium heel pair of black, high shine shoes from Kurt Geiger.

"Yeah, these are definitely `fuck me' shoes."

She took her time gathering her blonde hair up, choosing a simple, light brown clasp to hold it in place. Then she began with foundation, added eyeliner, some shadow, lipstick and gloss. She applied her make-up ultra carefully, listening to Smooth FM as she made herself ready.

"Me and Mrs Jones...we gotta thing goin' on..." she sang to herself as she applied a bit of neon pink varnish to her nails. Angie couldn't resist a dab of glamour, even she was going to the hotel dressed as a `businesswoman.'

She was finished. Gazing back at her eyes in the mirror was a professional looking lady, but with her bosom pushing hard beneath her suit jacket, and her tights – or stockings – hinting at something interesting going on between those womanly, curvy legs. She picked up her phone, took a `selfie' in the wardrobe mirror and texted him.

**U are so gonna get it this afternoon. Brace yourself xx**

Then she gathered her bag, car keys and brolly from downstairs and got into her red Audi. As she plugged her phone in a text message chimed back.

**Very sexy. Cant wait for u to get on top of me, nail me. Totally nail me Angie baby. Have you got suspenders on? xx**

She smiled and licked the edge of her lip gloss.

**U will have to wait to find out, dirty boy xxx**

Angie set up her Sat Nav, keyed in the Hilton's postcode and slowly reversed down the driveway. As she flicked the A3 into Drive, she took a last glance at the house just to check she hadn't left any windows open upstairs. She found the radio and turned up the volume.

"Rahim, I'm coming to get ya." she smiled to herself.

\*\*\*\*

# CHAPTER SEVEN: "CALL ME MAYBE"

Rahim walked into the Hilton's lobby, dragging his trolley style overnight case behind him, its wheels making an irritating humming noise as they tracked across the floor. The Latvian girl on reception smiled at him broadly as he approached.

"Hello sir, welcome to the Hilton Metropole, checking in today?"

"Yes, just one night. I have a room booked in the name of Ahmadi."

"OK, let me check...yes, here it is. You are all booked in sir, to ahhh...oh yes, an executive suite. Do you have a card that I can swipe please, it's just for any extras on the room?"

Rahim scratched at his ear briefly, and would have blushed, but his skin was dark enough to hide the heat in his face.

"Erm, no it's OK, I'll pay cash at the bar or for any room service. It's OK thanks."

Rahim had learned a long time ago to pay cash for everything else above the cost of the room. The less paper trail, the better. No awkward questions about restaurant receipts, or odd looking transactions on credit card statements opened `accidentally' by his wife. No thank you very much.

He took the lift and checked into the room. It wasn't as big as the photos, but still, it was nice, with a little lounge area too, including a sofa. Very nice. With a practised efficiency Rahim unpacked his case and put his shaver, toothbrush and some aftershave in the bathroom. The bath was unusually large in this suite, it looked big enough for two, which was interesting, full of possibilities.

Rahim fished his Durex out of the secret compartment he had inside his suitcase and placed them carefully inside the bedside cabinet drawer. He liked everything in its place, every detail had to be just right. His phone vibrated and he saw a text message from Angie.

**Hello lover boy. I'm here for my business meeting, waiting for you in the bar area. Angie baby xxx**

Rahim smiled to himself and felt his willy stir inside his suit trousers. He absolutely loved bored middle aged housewives. They knew what they wanted and mostly, that was tanned, slim, younger men like him, with a pocketful of Viagra gel sachets, a weekend on expenses and no strings.

He texted back; **Hey sexy, will be down in 2 minutes. Xx**

As he walked to the door, his phone rang. It was his wife. He muttered a curse in Farsi but decided to take the call.

Better to speak now than in a crowded bar later, especially as Angie didn't know that he was actually married.

"What's wrong, why are you calling me again?"

"Rahim, it's Amir. He's very hot, I think he should see a doctor."

"OK then, take him to a doctor. You have a car, so drive him there now."

There was a second's pause, as Rahim's wife, Maryam, marshalled her thoughts.

"Yes but he isn't just hot, like a bad case of the flu, it's different. I don't want to put him in the car with the baby and I might have to wait at the doctor's, or go to the hospital. So it would be better if you come home. This jewellery thing is just a trade show, I mean it's not really important is it?"

"Oh, so earning money, so that you can spend it on trips to the fucking White Rose shopping centre every week is not important now, is that it? I have a business to run, the shows are where I do the deals that make us the money. You don't need me to come running home every time our children have a temperature. Who has been filling your head with this crap Maryam – your mother, yes?"

"What crap? Your son is ill, he needs you Rahim."

"Really? OK then, put Amir on the phone.

Rahim began to pace up and down in front of the TV screen, his blood was up.

"Come on, that's stupid. The boy is ill and he's just four years old – what is he supposed to do, diagnose his own illness over the phone to you? You're an idiot. Come home tonight. Stop this nonsense."

"I want to speak to him, now." snapped Rahim, playing with his car keys as he stood by the window of the room."

But Maryam wasn't having any of it. They squabbled for a little bit longer and finally, under duress, she agreed to phone her mother and get her to mind their baby girl, whilst Maryam took Amir to the GP surgery.

Whilst they were arguing Angie texted from the bar; **Where R U? x**

Rahim hung up and took a moment to think about things. His son had been unusually quiet this morning, a bit tired maybe. But Maryam could cope and in any case, looking after children and all their ailments was a woman's job, not a man's.

He sprayed on some aftershave and texted back to Angie;

**Sorry babe, work called me. Just changing my shirt and b with u xx**

Then he texted Maryam;

**Sure Amir will be alright and glad u let me know. Putting my phone on charge n going for drink with the watch reps. Txt u later xx**

Well, maybe he would text later. Maybe not.

****

**THE FIRST DATE**

I'd chatted to Lisa twice in the last three days and wanted to see her again, so in the modern way, I texted her, like you do.

**Hi Lovely Lisa, we get on so great chatting, would you like to go out for a meal this weekend, or watch a film maybe? I just really love listening to you and want to be in your company, get to know you more. x**

She left it for an hour or so before replying, which could have been work related, or maybe she was mulling things over. It didn't matter in the end.

**Hi lovely Cal, I would like a meal with you. I thought about you today when someone said something at work, and I wondered what Cal would think about that. You're an interesting man, and I need that in my life I think. xx**

**Ahh thanks, I will book a table at a nice place for Friday or Saturday, which is best for you?**

**Friday. Can't wait! I shall wear a dress for a change. xx**

**Lovely xxx**

It was exciting having a proper date, for the first time in over a year. Once I'd finished off some work and it was lunchtime I spent 10 minutes online looking at some new shoes and boots. Dropped lucky and found some pointy toed black numbers, with red embossed soles in the Jeffrey West Sale section. Then I tracked down an Italian place online, which seemed like a safe choice. I phoned and booked a table for about nine, which let us have time for a drink first.

I arrived at the restaurant early and waited outside. She arrived in a taxi and slid her luscious legs out of the door, her feet encased in red, velvety soft, suede heels. Her damask dress had a shimmery edge to it and she wore a small cardigan over her bare shoulders. Her bobbed blonde hair swayed as she walked a few steps towards me.

We kissed, in that offbeat way first daters do, arms almost encircling but not quite, lips closed, but brushing slowly, promising more. She looked beautiful and I told her so. She smiled a little, in that way women do when they've heard the compliment so many times. But as we drank a little Sicilian red, we warmed to each other and lowered our guard gradually.

When I tackled my calamari starter I dropped my knife, which left a comedy stain on the leg of my trousers, and I glowed red with embarrassment. But she just told me to use my fingers, she was from the north, she didn't mind. I laughed at her jokes, and was impressed by her job, working as a radiographer in the NHS.

At times, the date felt like a job interview, but I forgave her shop talk. Her mouth was a pleasure to watch and her voice put a spell on me. She held my hand in the taxi on the way home and kissed me goodbye with an easy swirl of her lips against mine. There was heat in her face. Partly, the flush of wine for sure, but something else too and it got beneath my skin. I wanted her.

On the taxi ride home, she texted me;

**Lovely time with you, great company, good food and wonderful kisses too. Let's do this again soon, love and hugs. Sweet dreams xx**

\*\*\*\*

## HER SMILE UNFOLDS THE DAY

"Morning Mum, only me!" said Vera, rattling the key in the front door lock as she entered the house, smelling the urine and something else, the second she stepped into the hallway.

In the lounge, Vera and Jim had set up a kind of bedsit, with a single bed parked where the sofa had once been. There was a wall mounted TV – so Mum couldn't get at it and press the buttons – plus a high-backed chair, footstool and zimmer-on-wheels. But the zimmer was knocked over and poor Joan lay on the carpet, her nightclothes stained with faeces and urine, a terrible mix of fear and embarrassment written across the pale parchment of her face.

"I'm sorry, so sorry." she mumbled.

Vera put down her shopping bags in the doorway and bent down to help Joan up, propping her on cushions for now, using a tissue to wipe away tears from her face.

"It's OK Mum, I'm her, I will look after you."

She set to with a will of iron. Finding clean clothes and disposing of the soiled ones. Then she began gently cleaning Mum up with baby wipes and a warm facecloth. Vera ran more hot water, dropping bleach into the bucket and then getting busy with a scrubbing brush on the carpet. It took an hour to settle her down and clean the place, let the smell evaporate through the open windows. It took almost 20 minutes to stop Joan from crying and apologising, but the TV distracted her in the end and she settled down, eventually falling asleep as clean, warm clothes brought a kind of womb-like relief to her.

Vera finished cleaning up, stroked Mum's hair, then went into the kitchen and had a quiet, racking, stifled sort of cry. There was nothing more she could do now except move in. Or call social services and have Mum put away in a home somewhere. Vera stood at a grim, hard-edged crossroads, standing on the worn kitchen tiles, looking into the future.

Vera picked up her mobile and began to dial Jim's number. Then she stopped. She went back into the living room and sat down on the high backed chair, smiled at Mum.

"Mum I'm stopping over for tea tonight, what shall we have – fish, chips and mushy peas?"

Joan pondered on the menu for a while, racking her memory to try and place what on earth mushy peas might be. Then it clicked.

"Aye go on then, just a small fish though. And crispy batter."

It would be alright, thought Vera, everything would be alright in the end.

\*\*\*\*

## STUFF HAPPENS, THEN YOU DIE

The room phone rang with an incessant tone, jarring as a game show host reading a eulogy. Rahim grunted and nudged Angie.

"I'm not answering it, the room's booked in your name." said Angie, shoving her naked bum cheek at him in disgust. He slapped her arse playfully and took the call.

"Yes, what is it?"

"Hi Mr Ahmadi it's reception here, could you come down to the lobby as soon as possible please?"

"What, why? Hang on…it's 6.30am, what's the problem?"

"Your wife is here sir. She seems upset and we thought it best if you came down."

Rahim was about to answer and then Maryam snatched the phone from the receptionist's hand and yelled;

"Get that bitch down here as well, because I want her to see the family she's wrecking, the piece of white trash!"

"There's no one here Maryam, I'm alone OK?"

"OK, see you in 2 minutes then, I'll join you in your room."

There was a bit of general shouting of `give me the phone' and `get security now' before the line went dead. Rahim shot out of bed and began dressing rapidly.

"Don't just lie there, get up, get dressed!" he shouted at Angie.

Angie propped herself up on her elbow and yawned.

"Why? The hotel staff won't let her run riot up here…anyway, I could take her, skinny little bint, talking like she's hard."

Rahim suddenly lunged across at her, slapping her face hard and then grabbing her by the neck.

"Listen you stupid whore, this is my family, my life. So pack up your stuff and get the fuck out of this room in 90 seconds or I'll throw you from the fucking window."

Angie tried to fight back, tears and adrenaline rising inside her, but he pinned her down and raised his hand again. She turned her face away and sobbed `No, don't...please' as he drew back his fist, then thought better of it and jumped off her, gathering her clothes together and stuffing them into her overnight bag. He cleared her make-up, toothbrush and hair stuff from the bathroom in one swoop, dumping it all in the bag in a jumble of mess and noise. She was scared of his anger, which filled the room with menace.

"Are you driving home naked, or putting some clothes on?" he barked at her. She lay there, stinging face reddening up and blobs of tears running down her face.

"You bastard, you fucker."

"Get dressed and fuck off back home to your husband. It's over Angie, do you need me to spell it out? Just go and don't contact me again."

She struggled into her underwear, pulled jeans and a top on, then found her shoes under the desk. Rahim passed her car keys to her, and then flipped the pillows over, brushing her blonde hairs onto the floor. He was as cold and efficient as a scenes-of-crime officer at a murder, checking and double-checking the room for evidence of a female presence.

"She'll smell our come on the sheets Rahim, so she will *know*. So fuck you."

He stood glowering at her, his mobile ringing, then going to voicemail, then a text pinging in. Angie picked up her bag, coat and scarf and then walked out of the door. Rahim carried on vainly trying to clean the room up. She walked down the corridor, still groggy from the harsh slap he'd given her, and the lack of sleep from the night before. The lift bell dinged and out stepped Maryam, seething with the same quiet rage as her husband.

Angie dropped her bag on the floor and made ready with her bunch of keys to settle things with Maryam. Angie had grown up in a place called Walkden near Manchester, where bitch fights had only one rule when it came to a set-to; there are no rules. But Maryam had a moment of clarity and thought about her children, her family's shame if the truth emerged…and ultimately, whether Rahim would come back to her. She sneered at the older woman, bereft of dignity and make-up, face reddening where a slap had been delivered.

"I can't believe he'd screw an old tramp like you. Look at the state of you, pathetic fat cow."

"He seemed happy enough to give me seconds last night love, more than you're getting lately I reckon."

"Fuck off you cocksucking white slag."

"Make me, you towel-headed, baby machine."

The two women would have settled their argument right there, but Trevor, the hotel security guard came huffing and puffing out of the second lift, having been given the slip by the more agile Maryam down in reception. He placed his chunky body between them as they traded more insults, then Rahim came out to join the action and pulled his wife past a screaming Angie into his room.

"No Maryam, no...come on, let's talk about it, I'm sorry."

"How could you, with...that...old woman? How could you Rahim?" Maryam began to wail, as if in deep mourning. The anguish, the betrayal, overwhelmed her. Rahim had promised her faithfully that all this business was over and done with last year. Here he was again. It hurt deeply, ate away at her like a kind of cancer. Angie was ushered away by Tomas, who had a sly look at Angie's pendulous boobs as they swayed bra-less, inside her loosely buttoned top.

"We'll get you to your car now Miss, it'll be OK."

"It's not Miss, it's Mrs."

"Oh right." said Tomas sheepishly. There was an uncomfortable moment in the lift as it gradually headed down to reception.

"Shit happens eh?" said Angie, as she grabbed her bag and walked over towards the main entrance, shrugging her shoulders at the receptionists who had both come to the desk to view her walk of shame.

She'd had better days.

**\*\*\*\***

## A TOAST TO DANCIN' DEREK

It had taken Trev a week or so of texting and phoning around to organise, but this Wednesday would be a little bit different, as the gang saluted Derek, the oldest soul boy on the scene. There was a cake, with a mod-suited figure iced onto the top, which Penny had made with her own fair hands and a single candle to place upon it, next to the inscription; `Derek — Keep The Faith.'

That was Trev's own idea, a nice touch he thought, as he and Degsy had spent many a soul weekender together back in the day, before he'd met Penny and Derek had lost his job and gone through all kinds of problems before returning to the Peppermint just a few years ago. Trev would miss his mate.

I got there early doors and the group were in a slightly subdued mood as they arrived. Vera wore a black dress, with a bit of sequin action peppering the cleavage area, just to add some glamour to the night. Trish was in a green dress, vivid as a Wimbledon lawn just before the tournament started, as a kind of homage to Derek's legendary lime green suit, which he used to wear with an orange shirt and hat.

Sue and Kev were in quite early, Bendy Wendy, Little Davey, even Jen and Sadie came over from the next table, just to join in the candle ceremony. We raised our glasses and

Trev said a few words. Most of us couldn't hear exactly what he said, because the disco music was already fairly loud at 9.30-ish, plus half of us had suffered hearing loss over the years. But we nodded and smiled, drank a little bit and then chatted about everyday stuff to each other, so we didn't dwell too long on Derek's passing.

The room filled up quickly after that and everyone drifted away. I got dancing with Sadie and Jen, Sue and Kev stood chatting to another couple at the bar and Vera, Trish and Angie danced as a trio. Angie seemed upset and had arrived late, plastered in make-up.

It must have been about quarter to eleven when Vera suddenly pulled my sleeve as I danced to *I'm Sexy and I Know It,* wiggling my arse seductively as the DJ activated the smoke machine.

"Am I seeing things?"

"What?"

"That's Derek, standing over there by the pillar, Jesus Christ! Get me a stiff drink someone."

"No, it can't be." I said, squinting hard as I tried to focus on the figure just 20 feet away through the haze. But Vera was right. There was a pale, washed out, almost bleached bone white, version of Derek standing in the corner. Jen and Sadie stopped dancing for a moment, with Jen putting her hand to her mouth in disbelief.

"Oh frig! The cake's still on the table." She blurted, hustling her burly frame over to where Trev and Penny sat, engrossed in a discussion about Alfa Romeo suspension problems. Well, Trev was engrossed anyway…

"The cake, the cake!"

"Oh, would you like some more Jen?" asked Trev.

"No, hide it quick, he's here." Jen threw her cardy over the cake.

"Who's here?"

"Derek's here you pillock! He's not dead."

"Oh shittin' hell." said Penny, grabbing the cake and glancing towards Derek, who was already striding across the floor towards them, waving cheerily. Derek just wanted to say hello, and thanks for all the lovely text messages, which his new phone had finally downloaded now the tech guy at Carphone Warehouse had helped him out.

Sadie tried to distract Derek by dancing in front of him and grabbing his arms, but just as she did so, Trev lunged at the cake, knocked over a bottle white wine in his haste and then skidded sideways as he tried to save both wine and cake. He failed in spectacular style, and with a crushing inevitability, Sadie walked backwards into the mess, falling arse-first into the mess. The remnants of the iced words, *Keep The Faith'* were embossed onto her black skirt and a pool of wine rapidly penetrated her underwear.

"Fooookin' hell, my arse is covered in it!" Sadie exclaimed, moving gingerly up from the mayhem on the floor.

"Oh bugger." noted Trev, as he reached down to help Sadie up, Jen and Penny also assisted. Sadie looked over her shoulder and dabbed at the back of her skirt.

"Fuck's sakes Trev, my arse is covered in cream."

"Not for the first time." said Jen, and then adding, "Sorry mate, someone had to say it."

Penny and Jen began wiping lumps of squidged cake from Sadie's hindquarters.

"Derek, you're…OK! Great to see you mate." said Trev, looking temporarily stunned and then offering a cake spattered handshake to Degsy, who stared baffled at our shell-shocked group, just for a second, before the penny dropped.

"Oh God, you all thought I'd croaked it."

"Well, we didn't hear anything, rumours kind of spread…sorry mate."

"Oh well, at least there was cake, and a drink. My phone got swiped in hospital - I was in with some odd viral thing, all better now. Hey, nice that you bothered actually, it makes me feel pretty good. Thanks, yeah thanks everyone." smiled Derek, feeling much improved after his initial shock.

"We should all have a dance, great to see you looking well Derek." said Vera, smiling broadly and making the peace, as she so often did.

"I want some cake first." laughed Derek, looking at Sadie's rear end, as it was being wiped down. He reached out and scooped a bit of icing and sponge off her and then stuck it in his mouth. Sue took a series of phone photos as we put cake down Sadie's cleavage, placed a candle between her bum cheeks, got Derek to blow the candle out once we had lit it etc. Later on, Sue uploaded them all to Facebook, with an album caption that read;

Derek's not dead everyone! He's back at The Peppermint and just had a Bake-Off with Sadie – reckons her soggy bottom is well tasty. Happy times ;-)

\*\*\*\*

## CHAPTER EIGHT: `I'M IN LOVE WITH THE GERMAN FILM STAR'

Lisa's house was a solid, bay-window, three-bedroomed end terrace, with a little bit of paint peeling here and there on the window ledges, plus tall hedges betraying a few years where the gardening jobs had lost the battle with work emails, nights out and just dealing with people. She answered the door in skinny white jeans and a wonderful loose jumper that had some sparkly bits trailing down on one shoulder. Her blonde hair was immaculate and her make-up looked kissable and not overdone. She smiled warmly as she opened the door.

I hugged her hello and gave her a rose, plus the two veggie starters I'd picked up at Waitrose. We went into the kitchen and she poured me a drink of diet coke as we talked about her house, the renovations, leaks, this and that.

Her dog sidled up to see me, a Jack Russell cross, looking careworn with age but still territorial.

"Oh this is Jess, my best friend in the world, she's come to check you out Cal."

I made a clicking noise with my mouth and bent down to stroke her gently, saying `hello Jessie' as I did so the dog nuzzled me and licked my nose briefly.

"Ahh, my dog likes you…it's a good sign hun, you've passed the important test." she said, and smiled the broadest smile ever back at me. There was a brightness; a glow, that animated her whole face as I made friends with her beloved pet.

"Come on, let's sit down and chat, the food won't be long."

\*\*\*\*

We chatted about films and TV shows and then moved onto the people we both knew a little bit about at the Pink Peppermint. I told her the supermarket fisherman story and a few other risqué tales, and Lisa shared a few secrets from her past too. She told a good story; artlessly mixing wry observations on human nature, with the dirty details that made you laugh out loud. She was a clever woman. I liked the company of a good conversation, the closeness of it.

After the dessert she asked me to pick some songs on her iTunes speaker dock. I flicked through all kinds of albums; classical, Led Zeppelin, Roxy Music, Florence and The Machine, Adele…then I found an 80s electro compilation.

"Oh 80s Electro, how great – what a brilliant time."

"It was, we were all so young and glammed up back then...with big daft hair!" agreed Lisa. I scrolled through the tracks and chose a couple of faves. The opening chords of a slightly obscure song by The Passions kicked into life. She recognised the track immediately.

"This is one of my favourite songs from then, I can't believe you picked it from all of them." She smiled, looking straight into my eyes.

"Shall we dance?" I asked, thinking `she can only laugh and say no.'

"Yes, let's dance."

As the music swayed, its synthesizer beat slowly tapping out an echo of the New Romantic 1980s, we danced on the carpet together. After a few seconds I took her hands and then held her a bit closer in an embrace, slow-dancing and placing my head against hers, kissing her beautiful neck. We parted after a few seconds and then kissed. Her lips brushed tiny swirls on my mouth, I felt the heat of her skin, tasted her softness, and breathed her inside me. I put my hand on her cheek and caressed her, kissing her gently, as if she might break beneath my touch.

"I think I might fall in love with you Cal. Would you mind?"

"No, I would love that."

We danced. The food burned.

\*\*\*\*

Later, we watched TV and lay together on the sofa, but the TV viewing didn't last very long. We held hands at first, but then she arranged the cushions so that we could stretch out alongside each other, me folded up close behind her, feeling the warmth of her body, her slender curves, through her jumper. She drew my arm around her waist, folding my hand beneath her breasts.

"This is like being young again, snogging on the sofa. I love it." she said, kissing my hand, and then settling it back down around the belt of her jeans. I placed my lips onto the nape of her neck, leaving a trail of kisses on her soft skin, letting my left arm support her head. We talked about love, staying friends, children and how marriages crumble to dust over time.

Life.

I felt so close to her, so embraced by her. There was no awkwardness between us now, just love, care and warm conversation. Jess slept on her bed at our feet. The TV blathered away in the background. We were lost in each other; the scent of our skin blending together, the poetry of kisses exploring each other's lips, cheeks and necks. The need to be touched, and held tight, grew steadily inside me. Just feeling this close to her was magical, peaceful and electric. I wanted her.

****

Then her daughter Sarah, plus boyfriend in tow, rattled the key in the front door and came bounding in like curious puppies. We were already sitting up straight on the sofa and looking half decent, although Lisa's wayward hair betrayed the severity of our snogging session. Sarah raised her eyebrows as she took in the scene, it's never easy seeing your mum getting hot and bothered with some guy she met on a disco cruise.

We chatted a little and then it was obviously time for me to go. Sarah and her fella decamped to the kitchen, while I whispered my goodbyes to Lisa in the hallway.

"It was so nice to be with you, talk to you, cuddle up on the sofa. It's been years since I did that with anyone." I said, hugging her close and kissing her forehead. We broke away and looked at each other for a second, and then we kissed intensely, silently, folding our arms around each other.

"I should go, it's late."

"I know, work tomorrow…early meeting with my team. Thanks Cal for the loveliest evening, I just feel so relaxed with you, talking with you. When will we meet again do you think?"

"Soon. Maybe a cup of tea this Sunday, or a walk somewhere, what do you think?"

"I'd like to meet you tomorrow, for a bit more of this, but it makes me sound a bit crazy. Let's keep talking on the phone for now and meet up on Sunday. Then my daughter won't be scandalised. Text me when you're home safe hun."

"I will."

I drove away from her house, watching her wave from the porch and felt that my life had changed irrevocably. Somehow, by a fluke, I'd met someone wonderful and I couldn't really put the complex attraction into words. She just fascinated me, moved me. I could smell the scent of her on my shirt as I trickled the Golf through empty late night streets, with the sound of The Passions grooving from the door speakers.

It really moved me.

**** 

## HOUSEWARMING AT BENDY WENDY'S – BRING A FRIEND

Some things in life are a given thing, mused Bendy Wendy, as she ran her manicured fingernails along the specialist outfits in her wardrobe. For example, most men aged 50 plus will always want to see you bent over a chair, dressed in some St Trinians costume, as they paddle your arse with a variety of implements; slippers, rulers, canes, or even a wet haddock – it doesn't really matter. Another good choice is the traditional French maid, or perhaps the zip-up Catwoman suit. You can't go wrong at a swingers party with any of these outfits.

"Ah, here you are; my absolute Mary Berry style favourite." sighed Wendy, as she took the pristine red, gold and blue costume from its wrapper. She was already wearing her black stockings, red stiletto heels, satin purple and black lace bra and pants set, so all she needed was this perfect outer layer for the debut evening, the basement premiere. Gingerly, she slipped each sleeve of the topcoat over her arms, pulling the gold braid cuffs into the right position, buttoning the jacket lapels across her breasts carefully, letting a bit of bra cleavage show, but not too much. Then she took the whip and the top hat down from the top shelf of the wardrobe.

She surveyed herself in the full length mirror, her long legs vanishing into the cherry red folds of the circus ringmaster's coat, the V of her knickers peeping through, just so.

"Eat your fucking heart out Billy Smart." smiled Wendy, flexing the whip as she pictured the delights that lay ahead for her paying guests.

Wendy checked her make-up still looked minty fresh and then click-clacked her way downstairs as fast as she dared. There was still a fair bit of preparation to do in the house generally, and especially in the basement, before people arrived. She felt her tummy tingle with anticipation.

Joe the builder was in the kitchen, drinking a can of 1664 with his mate Big Nev sorting out a variety of nibbles.

"Oh my giddy aunt!" exclaimed Joe, splurting his lager down his chin, "What time are the tigers on?"

"Fuck's sakes...that is horny Wendy. Top work love." added Nev.

"No real names tonight Nev, discretion always discretion – remember to keep it anonymous."

"Oh shit yeah, what's my name again? Derek Digbeth?"

Wendy sighed in disbelief. Why does a small amount of lager befuddle mens brains so rapidly?

"No, it's Dirk Diggler, like in the movie *Boogie Nights*, remember?"

"Oh yeah. Cos I've got a big knob innit?"

"Yes Dirk, it is. So please don't get pissed, as my guests want to see it in full working order."

Joe and Nev, sorry Juan and Dirk, exchanged a slightly worried look between them. In truth, they were out of their depth with this swinging lark and only agreed to it when they were pissed three weeks ago.

"Ne-I mean Dirk, did you bring that Viagra gel stuff mate?"

"Oh yes. Good stuff this."

"Right give us a sachet now, let's not fanny about here, we need all the help we can get."

"That's the spirit boys," said Wendy, swooshing her whip hard across Joe's behind to warm him up a bit, "now chuck the rest of that beer away and follow me to the basement – there's lots to do."

****

People arrived furtively, in ones and twos, many already wearing their eye masks to protect their faces, especially the women. The internet and word of mouth had worked wonders and almost all had paid in advance, £85 for the full package; food, drinks, gels, condoms...it was all inclusive. Wendy had opened a mini resort in her basement, a South Manchester Sandals, and this private party for the liberal minded co-incidentally had about the same membership as the Lib Dems.

Goldfrapp's *Black Cherry* album warmed up the crowd of about twenty or so, as they mingled and checked each other – and the new venue – out. They were impressed and who wouldn't be, as Joe's craftsmanship and Wendy's design touch had created something glamorous, dark and inviting in the basement.

In one corner, there was a vintage dentist's chair, with chrome handles already fitted with screw-down bolts, handcuffs and silver chains. Over in the opposite corner was a gleaming pole, with iridescent blue, red and purple neon lighting flickering in the glass surround at its base. As a dancer moved, the colours changed automatically - it looked fantastic. An L-shaped seating area had been built into the wall around the pole, covered in slippy vinyl and featuring two pull-out drawers, stuffed with condoms, lube and a selection of sex toys.

Next to this small dance floor area, there was a corner bar, with just enough room for one person to get behind it and serve drinks, operate the iTunes docking station etc. The final corner of the room had half of a yurt-like tent in it, which was stuffed with bolster cushions and just big enough for four people to get inside...or two very energetic people and a close friend who liked to watch...

Wendy had tried to think of everything, because there was a great deal of money riding on the success of her `50 shades club' as she liked to call it. This was a pension plan that stock market dealers couldn't squander on the Greek bond market, it was her passion, the culmination of a lifetime's knowledge about men, and women, and all the secret desires that welled up inside them now and then.

For an hour or so, people simply chatted and warily gauged each other, making sure nobody was doing anything stupid like taking selfies for Facebook, or using real names. Then a blonde lady, wearing a sparkly eye mask, a busty corset and stay-up stockings sat in the dentist's chair and began stroking her male partner's tackle as he leaned the chair backwards, ever so slowly. A small group of people gathered round to watch the show unfold and Wendy held the tip of her whip beneath the blonde lady's chin.

Game on.

\*\*\*\*

**ONLY THE LONELY**

Angie sat on the sofa, flicking through a copy of *Closer* magazine and glancing at the TV now and then. Keith was over on the Wirral, taking Sylvia to a nice restaurant most likely, before they had very boring sex for eight minutes and he then commenced his attempt on the world snoring record.

She checked her phone again. No reply from Rahim to her Whatsapp message earlier today and one tick showed that he hadn't even read it. On the upside, she wasn't blocked now, which she had been for two weeks following the hotel barney.

**Rahim, why don't u just talk 2 me? xx**

Still nothing. She changed channels and found a show about benefits people thieving to get their beer n dope money. One woman had the word `Babe' tattooed on the back of her neck...or it could have been `Beer.' It was hard to tell, as ripples of fat compressed the word a bit when she spoke. Nice work by the cameraman spotting that feature, thought Angie.

**Come on Rahim, you should talk to me xx**

The minutes ticked by, pregnant with tension. She still wanted him, he was like an itch she couldn't quite reach, an addiction, a benefit payment that she needed every two weeks or so. The bastard. But there was only silence. Cold and solid as old lovers now made marble, frozen in their last warm kiss.

Frustrated, Angie texted Gorgeous Gary instead;

**Hey Mellors, fancy doing some work in my garden this weekend? Lady C xx**

It was just a few minutes before Gary replied.

**Yeah OK, cool. Who is Mellors anyway? Was this meant for me Angie? X**

Oh well, shrugged Angie to herself, Gary might not be the sharpest tool in the box, but at least his tool was very hard and very satisfying. Needs must.

\*\*\*\*

## CHAPTER NINE: `THE MOVEMENT YOU NEED IS ON YOUR SHOULDER'

"Sarah is round at Luke's for the night, so it's you, me and Jessie." said Lisa, setting a mug of tea onto the coffee table. "We could watch a film if you like Cal?"

"Maybe...I don't mind, just listen to music and chat."

"OK then, music it is."

She flicked through her CD collection and picked out *Escape* by Enrique, turning the volume down low so we could talk.

"Ahh, Enri-cake. Good choice."

"Enri-cake?" queried Lisa.

"Yes that was my crazy marketing idea years ago; singing celebration cakes made in the shape of Enrique and singing `Hero' when you press a button on the packaging. Just imagine it, `Would you ice, if I asked you to ice...would you run, like a warm lemon bun..?" I sang, in a pub singer pastiche of the Spanish crooner.

Lisa laughed and then pulled me close to her, folding a slim leg over mine,

"Go on, talk in Spanish to me Cal...or Italian, I don't mind which to be honest."

We both gradually fell together, onto that beautifully soft sofa, melting into its depths.

"Ahh, this is so nice." I said, cuddling her close.

"It is, you make me smile Cal, with your daft stories. You make me happy."

We kissed again, letting it last for ages, tasting as much of each other as we could, feeling each other's body heat rise through our clothing. I caressed her neck as we broke away from each other's lips.

"Ditto. I love being this close to you, getting all cosy on this magic sofa."

"True. It is lovely. Be nicer in bed though eh? More room perhaps."

I didn't really know what to say, it's always surprising when a woman brings the possibility of sex onto her lips for the first time. You're never quite sure if she's drunk, slightly bonkers, or there's a recording being made for a potential court case in the future.

"Are we ready yet, it's only our fourth date?"

"I'm so ready Cal I could tie you to the bed with my bra. I haven't had sex for two years and I think I love you, so I can't get any readier really. Do you want to stay tonight and make love to me? I won't ask again."

The way she put it was business-like, yet extremely arousing.

"Yes, a hundred yesses, I want you Lisa." within seconds, I was ready, and aching for her.

****

We went upstairs, feeling awkward as we partly undressed, and quickly diving beneath the quilt. Then we snuggled down in our underwear, kissing and caressing each other, slowly getting warmer. I put my hand between her legs and felt the wetness of her, the beautiful heat soaking through her knickers. She pulled down my pants and let her fingers fold around the tip of my penis, teasing it out from the material, helping it swell with a lovely, swirling touch. I wriggled a bit and let her pull off my pants, then she caressed my balls perfectly; gently cupping and stroking, all the while kissing me tenderly, breathing into my mouth, letting me feel the heat beneath her skin.

"I want to take you Lisa, press your body down and fill you up with me…every bit of me."

"Go on then, I'm yours…come inside me."

I unclipped her bra, eased the cups away from her breasts and let my lips and tongue draw slow, spinning circles against her rising nipples. I sucked and gently pulled at one nipple, filling up my mouth with the taste of her, the sweetness of her sighs, her longing. Then I let my lips swirl down her belly and between her legs, painting delicate brush strokes around her lovely button of flesh, held in that warm, beautiful fold of sensitive skin.

I parted her legs with my hands and worked my fingers and tongue inside her, starting a steady rhythm against her pubic bone, building speed and pressure gradually, drawing a pattern around, and top of her soft, open lips. I could feel her body tense as I pressed my tongue down hard, then let it skim along each side once more, loving every tiny curve and indentation of her, adorning her with soft, pliant kisses. She raised her hips from the bed, bringing her sex up to meet my mouth, pushing it right into my mouth. Just wanting more, giving herself.

She came beautifully, legs spread wide for me, her voice aching with a pleasure that came from a barely touchable place, deep inside her belly. I let her sigh backwards and catch her breath. We smiled at each other and the pure pleasure, the exhalation of the moment she'd given to me. And then I took her, filling her up slowly, so gently, pressing in with my hardness and lifting her left leg high, so that I could push the thickness of me, the base of me, as deep as possible inside her. I wanted to open her belly somehow, touch the edge of her womb with the very tip of me.

I wanted her, like fire needs air.

"Yes…give it to me." she breathed.

I pressed the weight of my body down on top of her, tensing my buttocks as I pushed harder inside, and stirred my penis in slow, tiny circles, letting my wet balls slide against her thigh. I nuzzled her neck, face and hair, telling her I was going to come inside her, feeling it build inside me, forcing the blood, the need and the heat to build up. Possess me. She made little cries of pleasure and more warmth began to flow from her. She grabbed my hair and pulled me closer, watched me close my eyes as I came, letting life pulse into her. I could feel the milky wetness make her suddenly that bit more slippery, and beautifully warmer, as I let every drop fall into her.

"God it's so sexy, you're the sexiest woman ever."

"Mmm, thank you."

We collapsed together, melting in our sweat, revelling in the scent of each other and giving, giving, until there was nothing left. She wriggled and folded her legs around me, pulling me close as she could, wanting more to flow between us.

"Mmmm, thank you Cal, that was so lovely. I'm glad we did it, otherwise we would have just stayed friends forever. Now we're lovers...you're my wonderful lover, my man."

"I am. I love you."

"Good, I love you to bits too."

Then we did it again.

\*\*\*\*

## CHAPTER TEN: "JUST ANOTHER MANIC MONDAY"

The working week started like any other for Keith. He rose early, about 5.45 and quietly got dressed and shaved in the spare room at Sylvia's, so as not to wake her. After some breakfast he made her a cup of tea and once he'd packed his stuff and parked his black leather weekend holdall next to the front door, he padded upstairs in his socks – no shoes allowed – to give her a kiss and hug goodbye.

"Have a good week love," mumbled Sylvia, still drowsy with sleep, "text me later mmmm, bye...bye."

He kissed her forehead tenderly and watched her as she rolled onto her left side and drifted back to sleep. Her heavy breast moved beneath her arm and for a second her nipple stood out. He wanted to kiss it, but held back, because work was already in his head; things to do, people to phone, stuff that needed sorting out.

He set off in the car, humming a fragment of some tune and feeling the warmth of the heated seats. All was right with his world. He switched on the radio and set it to receive traffic updates.

"Just avoid the M60 if you can today, massive queues building already, due to a two-lorry pile-up and lane closures. Police say it's likely to be after 9.30 before vehicles can be moved." said the traffic girl on a local station, sounding far too pleased with herself, as they always did.

"Great, bloody great..."

\*\*\*\*

Penny leaned over and kissed Trev, as softly as she could, full on his lips. He still tasted of red wine from last night, but that was OK.

"Don't forget Trev, the men are coming today to do the driveway, so make sure the cars are moved and everything hun."

"Ok love, no worries...I'm on the case."

"Right, I'll chat later, love you Trev the Rev."

"Love you Lady Penelope."

Incredibly, after just another hour of dozing in bed, and enjoying a bizarre dream where he met Helen Mirren whilst working as a stunt driver on a gangster movie, Trev eventually got up, put the kettle on and had moved one car just before the driveway blokes and their massive cement mixer lorry arrived.

"Morning chaps – fancy a brew?" enquired Trev. The chief driveway layer looked askance at Trev's slightly Sherlock Holmes style embroidered dressing gown, then exchanged a look with his mate, as if to say 'we've got a right pillock here.'

"No ta boss, we just have to get this laid and swept flat soon as really, we've got another job on this afternoon near Widnes, if the weather holds."

"Oh right, bear with me, I shall find the keys to mighty beast that is the Alfa."

"OK pal, ta."

The cement churned like grey porridge in the back of the lorry, as its diesel engine growled and spluttered. The chief layer pulled at some levers and released the long delivery funnel from its holder. Great clanking noises rang around the turning circle area at the end of the street, wakening everyone up, old and young, night shift nurse and benefits mum.

**\*\*\*\***

Angie stepped out of the shower and dried herself as rapidly as she could. Standing in her towel, she quickly dabbed some foundation cream onto her face, then flicked a little mascara onto her lashes. She smiled and sang along the old Bangles song, *Manic Monday* as it played on Wish FM. She remembered it from the 80s and it made her feel young, feel frisky again.

After giving her hair another two minutes of half power on the hair dryer, she brushed it into some kind of sense and surveyed herself in the mirror.

"Well, it'll have to do."

Some days you felt young inside again, exactly the same as you felt decades before; full of hopes and dreams, energy pouring through your body, ready to face the world and take it on. Then you caught a glance of this old person in the mirror, with flesh like crumpled gift wrapping, and you wonder, `what the hell happened, and how did all those years just whizz by like that?'

Angie opened her knicker drawer and chose a beige and gold set. The bra had a lovely silky, satin bit on the side of each boob holder, with lace detail stitched in the middle, where the cleavage could show. It was posh underwear really, but she felt like starting the week with a bit of class in her life.

She eased on her knickers and then began checking her wardrobe for a nice top to match her new blue jeans. Her phone pinged as a message came in.

**Hi sexy, so good talking to you last night. I woke up with a massive hard-on today just thinking about you, R U ready for me babe? I'm on my way xx**

She smiled, like a cat that's got the cream – or soon would be getting it – and texted back;

**Come and get me Rahim, come and fuck me good and hard. Xxx**

Coffee with Vera and Trish was suddenly cancelled. Angie texted her excuses and threw a sickie instead. Monday had just become a bit brighter, and a whole lot younger. She changed her underwear immediately.

****

The blue Vauxhall in front was beginning to really annoy Keith now. Why didn't the driver just pull up close to the van in front, why leave a gap? Oh great, now another car has sneaked up the side of the queue and yes…that's right, just let him into our lane as well. Great, flipping marvellous.

"People like you shouldn't have a licence mate." muttered Keith, glancing down at his wristwatch, just to double check the time. It was just after nine, he was going to be late, probably too late, for his ten o'clock team meeting. Damn.

Then he noticed the engine light was on. Strange. The traffic inched forwards, and the light went off, then came back on again. Very odd. Then a scary light, with a gloomy message, appeared on the little screen between the clocks;

`Engine malfunction.'

"Brilliant. The day just gets better and better."

The car was still going though, even though it had slipped into limp mode and only seemed to be running on two cylinders. Keith nursed the Mondeo off the motorway, down a slip road and then parked it in field gateway. He popped the bonnet and sniffed at the engine, trying to detect oil sizzling, or electrical stuff about the burst into flames. But everything seemed normal. He tried the engine again and it started, although tick over seemed rough, it wouldn't idle properly, and then it stalled as he stood listening to the engine.

He weighed the options for moment. Would the RAC come out to recover the car in under two hours? Unlikely, given the traffic chaos that was still evident. He could abandon the car at a nearby retail park and get a taxi into work, which was only five miles away now, but that could take quite a while too. On the other hand, his house was just ten minutes drive away, so he could go home, do a conference call instead of the ten a.m. meeting and then call the local garage and get them to pick up the car.

Yep, job's a good 'un, let's try that, he said to himself.

\*\*\*\*

After a few seconds, the realisation suddenly hit Trev, just as he poured the milk into a bowl for Romeo the cat. The massive lorry at the end of the driveway, which was merrily gurgling a gravelly gruel onto his land, whilst the two underpants-flashing fellas used lumps of wood to lay it flat, was effectively making him a temporary prisoner for the day.

Now that was OK, even though there was no milk left for a brew, except for the stuff in the cat's bowl - that was a minor inconvenience. The bigger problem was the shed, the new shed, which was being delivered later this afternoon as part of Trevor's autumn home makeover. It had originally been a new summer house project and before that, a spring spruce-up for the patio and drive, but well...these things get delayed somehow.

Hmmm, how would this shed get into the back garden, now that the second half of the driveway was being coated in creamy gloop, just as the back half had been clagged up about half an hour ago? As Trev pondered on this problem, his mobile rang.

"Penny baby, how goes it?"

"Alright hun, just out of a tutors meeting, usual boring stuff. What's happening then, are they there, is it being done OK?"

"Yes it's all going swimmingly my love. Half is done and setting already, they're just doing the front half now, looks good."

"Right, and you're sure they can do the top bit today as well?"

"Well, apparently they have another job on, so that will be done tomorrow."

"What? So what if it's raining tomorrow, which it is according to the forecast? I hope you haven't paid them already Trev...please tell me you haven't."

Trev stirred his black coffee thoughtfully.

"I paid half, as they were mithering about material, like these work people do, y'know how it is love. They can get the other half of the dosh tomorrow, I'm being very firm with them."

You could cut Penny's heavy veil of disappointment, frustration and brooding annoyance, with a knife. Silence pulled them apart slowly, irrevocably, like setting concrete.

"At least tell me you haven't let the cat out this morning."

"Ah. Er no, Romeo's here...sipping some milk with me, so don't worry."

"Trevor, you are the world's worst liar. You've let the cat out haven't you?"

"Yes, technically he escaped through a window, I did not *let* him out, but there we are."

There was another moment of silence, whilst Penny digested this information, as teachers do and then weigh up the likely verity of the statement, given the past crimes of the child involved.

"Is that because you had the window open whilst smoking, instead of going out onto the patio, as agreed?"

."It was just half a cigar...the workmen were smoking first thing when they arrived, so it got to me...I'm sorry my love."

"Oh Trev, just take the milk out into the back garden and call the cat in. Tell the workmen they've agreed to get all the work today, and if they don't, then they won't get paid. I'll be home a bit early, I can't leave you in charge of anything can I?"

"Well, I'm OK with a barbecue and a few beers…"

"That's not remotely funny. See you later."

Trev took the bowl of milk outside as instructed and began calling the cat. Nil response. He then took the other half of his cheroot style cigar out of his dressing gown pocket and lit it up. Time for a Hamlet moment, he mused to himself, whilst also pondering that nobody under 50 years of age would know what a Hamlet moment actually was.

Just then there was a shout over the fence. It was the chief concrete stirrer.

"Hoi mate, there's a black and white cat wading through your driveway, not yours it?"

"Oh fuck."

Trev closed the back door, went to the front of the living room and opened the window. There was Romeo, cowering near the shrubs on next door's garden, his paws coated in thick globs of concrete sludge. He took a lick of one paw, and then pulled a face as he spat the stuff out again. There were lovely trails of cat paw-prints setting nicely into the first half of the driveway.

"Hold on, I'll come and get the cat."

"Whoa, you can't walk on it mate."

"Right, yes, I know…erm, I was going to inch along the front door step and then jump onto next door's driveway."

"OK mate, yeah that should work, go for it.

Trev carefully opened the front door and set the very tip of his big toe onto the tiny ledge that jutted out onto the drive. He squirmed his body against the wall and reached the corner of the ledge, braced himself and then jumped, like a broken Slinky toy tumbling down rickety stairs. Failing to meet the distance requirement, Trev's left foot landed – no let's say planted itself – into the fresh, wet concrete mire at the edge of the drive. His slipper came off and was left marooned. Trev's dressing gown flew open, as he fell forwards and barrel rolled onto next door's property. Luckily he had pants on. Unluckily, they were a comedy pair that Penny bought him for Christmas, with the words `Sexy and I Know It' emblazoned on the bum side.

The workmen fell about with laughter. The front door caught the airflow from the open living room window and slammed shut, locking Trev out of his abode for the day. He sat on next door's driveway, examining a wound on his knee. It looked a nasty scrape, bits of grit in it.

Romeo the cat watched the proceedings with wide-eyed detachment, and then delicately pitter-pattered his way across the wet concrete once again and leapt, with the grace of a mountain cougar, in through the living room window. Romeo then paddled concrete all over the carpet, before settling down in the kitchen near the wood-burner.

Happy, contented, ignoring the world's frantic Monday morning.

**\*\*\*\***

Rahim parked on Angie's driveway and texted her to say he had arrived.

**Come round the back, the conservatory door is open, lock it by pulling the handle up and then come upstairs…I'm ready for you. Xx**

He followed her instructions, a smile on his lips and a heavy stirring happening in his trousers. He was so ready for her too, after two weeks or so of sulking and trying to forget. But there was something addictive about Angie's body, the wetness that poured from her when she came, the feel of her breasts in his face, the power in her hips. She really liked sex, she let herself go completely…and he wanted that, he needed that.

It only took seconds for him to peel away her underwear, exploring her skin with a real urgency, almost an animalistic pawing, as he stripped her, enjoyed every inch of her, kissing her, absorbing her…

Angie was lost in the moment too; letting herself be totally taken by him, bent over from behind, pulled on top for a while so that she could come a sweet, sticky load onto his dick and balls, telling him to go faster when she needed him to. She loved that about Rahim, his hard stick of rock between her legs, pulsing up and down for her, just at the perfect speed. Magic.

So magic that she didn't notice, neither of them noticed, the two pings as messages came in from Keith, just letting Angie know that he would be home to do some work as the car was playing up.

Keith arrived and parked on the street, looking twice at the strange car parked right behind Angie's Audi. Maybe her friend Sue had bought a newish BMW?

Keith let himself in and shouted `hello' from the hallway, but the only answer was the unmistakeable sound of mattress springs being pummelled and a woman starting to come, with some force, and a few choice swear words thrown in too. Knowing his wife had a boyfriend was one thing, but hearing her being fucked stupid by him was another. Keith was having a very bad Monday morning indeed.

He stomped upstairs, hearing the noises all the more clearly.

"Go on...fuck me, yes...fuck me harder...ohhhhh, I'm coming...I'm coming for you babe."

The door was already open, so Keith could see all the action from the landing. There they were, in *his* bed. The bed he'd bought from John Lewis in the Sale last Christmas. Bastards. Angie's face was flushed red, glistening with sweat and her hair a riot of tousled blondeness as she came on Rahim's light brown skin. His hands were touching her belly and breasts, caressing her nipples as she shook with pleasure. Keith couldn't recall the last time she had shaken like that for him. It had been maybe 20 years ago, more perhaps.

"Pack your stuff and get the fuck out!" Keith exploded. Angie and Rahim froze in mid-thrust. Then collapsed and parted in shock and embarrassment. Keith saw the size of Rahim's erection; it's tanned thickness, smooth circumcised head, and he was overwhelmed by anger.

"And take your fucking Paki lover with you. Get out!"

"Hey, I'm no Paki, I'm Iranian OK mate?" said Rahim grabbing his underwear hurriedly.

"I don't care if you're the Shah of Persia, and you're not my mate. You've got ten seconds to get out of my house or I will kill you – and in Britain, husbands can kill the blokes fucking their wives and get a suspended sentence...the jails are full you see. So fuck off back to burqaland before I cut your throat."

"Keith I'm sorry...I was meant to go out, but he called...oh God, I'm so sorry."

Angie wrapped a dressing gown around her body and reached towards Keith but he turned smartly and ran downstairs. Angie ran after him, Rahim continued to get dressed as quickly as possible. Keith grabbed a knife from the block and Angie recoiled as she saw it in his hand.

"No, don't hurt him...no!"

He pushed her against the wall in a powerful sweep of his arm and pinned her there for a second, pulling his contorted face close to hers. She smelt the corn flakes on his breath and saw the vehemence in his eyes.

"We had an arrangement. No other people having sex in our bed! That was the arrangement. But you couldn't stick to it could you Angela?"

"I'm sorry, I usually see him at hotels, but he came over...it's never happened before Keith."

"It won't happen again, because I'm going to cut his cock off, and then you're going to fucking eat it...with bacon and eggs, like a full English breakfast! You fucking bitch!"

Keith marched upstairs, head swirling with quiet, determined anger.

"Rahim get out, he's got a knife!" screamed Angie. Rahim had got his trousers and shirt on, but abandoned his socks and shoes as he opened the bedroom window and quickly dropped onto the roof of the conservatory. Luckily, the roof panel only cracked, it held his weight, and he scuttled down the side of the building, unscathed except for a bruised knee.

Keith watched him from the bedroom window, as Angie grappled with him, trying to grab the knife from his hand.

"Please Keith...come on, stop it, he's gone, it's over, it's over...I'll never see him again."

On that score, Angie was right. But if she thought it was over, she was wrong. Everything had changed the very moment she had orgasmed with Rahim in front of Keith. Everything was different now. Her world had turned upon its axis and she would feel its force for the rest of her life. The music had stopped.

****

# CHAPTER ELEVEN: "ON WHITE HORSES, SNOWY WHITE HORSES"

Sue stirred softly, her body clock anticipating the alarm clock by about ten minutes. She pressed the button to silence the alarm before it went off and walked, hazy-headed to the bathroom. The light was blinding for a second as she switched it on, she groped for the shower dial and turned on the water. She stepped in hesitantly, then once she was sure it was nice and hot, she immersed herself within its embracing spray. The droplets mixed with shower gel over her skin, washing away flakes of sleep from her eyes. She began to feel awake, human and ready for the horses.

One was called Polo, after the mints, because he was white, well a kind of white-ish grey truth be told. Polo was her horse, but she also looked after Tamarind, which belonged to her friend Janice. Jan still worked, but Sue had retired a year ago when she'd just turned 62. The lump sum and pension offer from the council was good, so why not?

She checked her breasts for any suspicious lumps or bumps while she showered and then gave her hair a quick rinse. She would shampoo and condition it later today, once she'd had time mucking out, grooming and riding Polo in the autumn sunshine. She dried herself off carefully, and then got dressed, glancing out of the window to see if the roads were dry. The ebbing tide of night made it hard to tell, it was still only twenty to six. Sue liked to rise early, ride early and occasionally make love early in the morning too.

But not today, Kevin was over at his place and she was off to ride her horse, which was always, ultimately, more satisfying than riding any man.

When she got to the stables and parked, she could hear Polo whinny at her as she shouted `Morning Polo, morning Tammy' at the animals. There were five horses in the stables at the moment, with Polo being the only stallion but as he was a gelding, he was nice and calm around the lady horses. Sue went into his stall and said hello, nuzzling his handsome face and whispering into his flicking ears. Polo leaned forward and tipped his head in towards Sue, making little neighing noises and then just looking at her soulfully.

She checked his water and food, handed him some hay to munch on and then set about gathering her grooming brushes, cloths and hoof picking tools. She tried to ride each day, as it was good for Polo and her to have the exercise, the sheer routine of it all. Plus Sue liked to ride him in show-jumping competitions and there was one coming up in two weeks, so the more practice she could get in on a good day like today, the better.

She stroked Polo and pressed the hard, bristly brush stalks into his flesh, easing away any bits of dung or dirt that might be stuck there. She used the comb on his tail and mane, teasing out knots gently, as a mum would do with a child. Then she checked his hooves for any stones, tweaking at the shoes with her hoof-pick, like a patient dentist, digging for fragments of sweets between teeth. His hooves were perfect, she smiled and patted his flanks.

"Good boy Polo, now let's go for a ride, the daylight is wasting away."

She gathered together Polo's saddle, saddle pad, his bridle, bit and reins, lumping the whole lot from the tack room at the end of the stables. Then she carefully set everything on him, following her usual routine to the letter, so Polo wouldn't be unsettled in any way. Once he was in the reins and ready, she took him out of his stall and walked around in circles for a bit, letting him get used to the feel of the tack and get some air out of his system, so she could maybe tighten the girth on him a tad. Everything had to be right, it all had to be perfect, or Sue wouldn't ride him. Polo had to be happy so that she in turn, could be happy.

The day was lovely now, a pale October light kissing the clouds and the dim roar of traffic in the middle distance in full flow as people hammered their weary way to work. Penny passed by, just three fields away on the M62, as Sue put her riding hat on and mounted up from the steps in the yard. Friends, who were invisible to each other, yet close by.

Sue swung her right leg across Polo and settled into the saddle. She squeezed her legs gently around his hefty frame, signalling him that it was time to walk on. He started off down the lane and they both breathed in the morning air, caught the freshness of the day in their lungs, and were invigorated by its promise. Once in the field, Sue gradually built up speed, trying a few laps just cantering around, getting the feel of Polo's weight and strength between her legs as she told him what to do with a little press of one thigh, or a gentle pull on the reins.

"Right then Polo, let's jump, come on lad! Go!"

She swung him around, as if she were making a tight turn in a competition and gave him a mighty squeeze to build a sudden gallop. Off he went, filled with power, each muscle defined as he drummed his hooves hard against the earth. Polo snorted as he saw the jump and his ears moved as he focused on it.

Sue shouted another `go on' in encouragement and then they were both airborne, floating in space for a sweet second or two, Polo's back arching and Sue rising forward, holding tight as they took the fence beautifully. She felt the thump as they landed, her clitoris bumping into the pommel of saddle, her buttocks smacked by the smooth leather lip, near the back of the saddle. She loved this energy, this power, this beautiful partnership.

"Again Polo, again."

They jumped, they cantered and galloped a little bit, and all the while she bumped her sex against the front of the saddle, feeling the tingling, getting lost in the primeval pleasure. It was better than sex had ever been in 30 years of marriage, more satisfying than the miserable box-ticking jobs she'd had at the council for over two decades. When she rode Polo, Sue felt truly free, as she bathed in the adrenaline, sweat and the smell of horse and leather.

She felt more alive now, in her sixties, than when she was in her thirties, a harassed mum dreading the return of a mithering husband from his work. She slowed down to a walk again and let Polo catch his breath after their work-out together. He nodded his head as she tweaked the reins left and right, walking him in circles again. She patted his neck in gratitude and admiration.

"Good boy, good boy Polo, you're the best my friend, the very best."

\*\*\*\*

## MR DOOLEY RODE INTO TOWN

Kevin pressed the button and the steel shutter grad-grinded its way upwards. Another day, another 20-odd sets of tyres sold and fitted, hopefully.

The business was something he'd inherited from his Dad over 15 years ago, but lately, it wasn't the steady breadwinner that it been back in the glory times, before the internet. Nowadays, people Googled the cheapest tyre deals on their phones, and if they could get a Pirelli £5 cheaper elsewhere, then off they'd go, not caring that some untrained monkey with an air ratchet was going to chew up their wheel nuts.

Kev unset the alarm, flicked all the lights on and went into the office. There were bills lying morosely in the in-tray and a series of scribbled notes on the main part of the desk, some held in place by a half-full tea mug. Dave, who had locked up last night as Thursdays were late night opening, had also left a half-eaten Greggs sausage roll on top of a copy of the Daily Star. Kev was tempted to eat the sausage roll and just read the paper, but somehow, the show had to go on.

The morning started well, with a few phone call enquiries and a nice job on a Range Rover Evoque, which had some profit in it. But then a stuck wheel on a Peugeot 407 and a call from the accountant soon put a dampener on the job for Kev.

Young Tony and `Big' Dave worked hard for Kev, and worked well, but the reality was that the business couldn't really make enough profit to pay three living wages, plus its overheads each month. Something would have to give in about a months' time, when the last four grand or so of overdraft left in the business account had to be passed onto HMRC to pay the VAT bill. What then?

Sell up, or work for no wages, live on his savings for a year or so. Then that would all be gone too. It was all a bit grim after so many years of oily, dirty work. So bloody unfair too, thought Kev.

Then a black Mercedes S350 pulled into the car park and out stepped a man in a grey suit, carrying one of those daft satchels that bearded students like to sport whilst cycling between coffee shops.

"Hi mate, how can we help you today?" said Kev, smiling at the thought of a few tyres fitted to a beefy Merc BlueTec.

"My name is Martin Dooley and I'd like to talk to you about your property, if I'm speaking to Mr Kevin Jones?"

"Yes that's me. Do mean the shop, or my house?"

"Your shop, the car park, the bit where you're storing used tyres waiting for pick-up, the whole site. I work for a property development company, here's my card. Can you spare the time for a quick word?"

They went into the office and Kev shut the door, and then stuck the kettle on. Mr Dooley carefully set his satchel down on a threadbare chair and took out an iPad, firing it up immediately. His eyes took in the details, the clues all around; last year's calendar still on the wall, bills stacked up unpaid, clapped out HP computer gathering dust by the second desk, which was groaning under boxes of spare wheel nuts, assorted bolts, spanners, hammers, Swarfega tins and a hundred other fragments of a failing business.

"The company I work for does social housing projects, well a mix of things really, but the short story is that we are interested in acquiring the entire site, so we can build flats, plus some starter homes here."

"Oh right." said Kev, pouring some semi-skimmed into two mugs of tea. "Do you take sugar, yes..?"

"Er no thanks." smiled Mr Dooley, who wasn't a full sugar, full fat kinda bloke. His accent was also tricky to pin down, a strange mix of south-of-England and something else, a kind of broad Irish, which had been carefully honed through travel and business meetings, to disguise his social roots. The younger guy opened his bidding by asking Kev to tell him a bit about the business.

"Well, it's my place, as you obviously know and my Dad paid off the mortgage on the buildings many years ago, so we own it outright. That's a rare thing in business – no rent to pay. Bonus!"

But Dooley was used to playing poker with bigger fish than Kev Jones.

"Indeed it is. But rent is just one overhead isn't it? Insurance, VAT, Corporation Tax, wages, providing pensions for your workers now the law's changing...it never ends does it?"

Kev sat down opposite Dooley and looked him in the eye.

"Fair point. It's tough. Let's cut to the chase then, what's your offer Mr Doily?"

"It's Dooley." He said, irked a tad and blowing on his tea with a mix of contempt and suspicion.

"Yeah sorry, Mr Dooley, what is your company's offer then?"

"I like round numbers Mr Jones, so let's say a cool £800,000 for the lot and you get to retire in the sun. How does that sound?"

Kev thought about it, pictured lounging on a beach somewhere, sipping a cold beer and watching hot women walk past in ridiculously small bikinis. That was OK for the first week or two, but then what? What would he do to keep busy, feel like getting up in the mornings?

"Hmmm, I'm only fifty-three Mr Dooley, so 800K isn't really enough to retire on. It would be all pissed away in perhaps 15, maybe 20 years. As you know, the banks aren't paying any interest on savings, so you can't live on capital. That means I have to start all over again, build another business – then my 800 grand could be gone in two years."

Mr Dooley took a sip of tea and digested this information.

"My client is very keen to start building early next year, which means we need to buy the site, or another site close by, in the next few months. My final offer is another round number, £830,000 and you have a month to think it over, then it expires – forever. Don't make the mistake of thinking you have a future here selling tyres to scrotes and pensioners driving old Vauxhall Corsas. Britain is being divided into haves and have-nots Mr Jones. Sad to say, I don't see many haves living around these parts."

"So the future is property, not cars eh?"

"Assets Mr Jones: There's gold in bricks and mortar, no big profits in tyres. Britain is a crowded place, so that means we have to squeeze more housing onto the same land. People will soon have to pay so much to have a roof over their heads, that they won't be able to buy cars, only rent them – and why buy decent tyres for a car you rent?"

"OK Mr Dooley, let me think about it for a week or two, and I'll get back to you. I will have a serious think about it all." Kev saw Dave approaching the office with a query and didn't want the meeting to get too public. He stood up to indicate that Dooley's time was up.

Mr Dooley took one more sip of tea, just to be polite. Then he stood up and packed away his iPad, like an actor folding his favourite stage prop away.

"Goodbye then, speak soon."

The two men nodded at each other and shook hands firmly, like prize fighters before the opening round bell.

\*\*\*\*

### MEET THE PARENTS

It had been a great night at the Peppermint. I had the lovely Lisa on my arm, wearing a tight white dress and pale blue shoes. She looked beautiful and I was so proud as I introduced her to my friends at our usual table. Everyone was polite and warm to her, asking her a dozen questions about work, children, past relationships, all the usual things. She batted away most of the enquiries deftly, just talking about her daughter, how we met on the disco boat and the vomiting incident.

She was such good company and she danced with me to Roxy Music, Bruno Mars, The Temptations...anything really. We looked and sounded like love struck teenagers and people said we `made a great couple.'

I was happy.

We left the club about midnight and drove back to my flat, chatting and singing along to songs on Smooth Radio. I touched her leg and she squeezed mine, we flirted as I drove. When we got home, I asked her if she was hungry and she randomly asked for muesli, with some sultanas on top. It sounded good so I had some as well, and after a strange late night breakfast, we brushed our teeth and went to bed, slowly caressing each other until we made love. We were really tired, aching from the dancing, but still longing for each other. We both needed the echo of another's heartbeat to lull us into sleep.

"Love you Lisa, thank you for meeting my friends, it means a lot to me."

"Ah, love you too Cal. Your friends are wonderful, I'm so glad you have them – don't ever lose them because of me."

It was only later, when I thought about it, that I realised what an odd thing that was to say.

\*\*\*\*

## CHAPTER TWELVE: "WE'RE SMILING BUT WE'RE CLOSE TO TEARS, EVEN AFTER ALL THESE YEARS"

It was a bleak November evening, with a raw edge to the wind that broke the skin on your lips and ice-picked tears from the corners of your eyes. Not great for a night out, but this Wednesday was the first time that tickets for the fancy dress Christmas party went on sale, so plenty of the regulars turned out at the Peppermint.

Trish asked me what my costume was going to be, but I had no real plan. I'd been toying with the idea of being Mr Darcy, with a top hat, boots, frock coat and riding crop. But I wondered if Lisa would be Miss Bennett – fancy dress wasn't her thing.

"I don't know yet Trish, I will speak to Lisa first, see if she fancies doing a couple type theme maybe. Travolta and Olivia from Grease, maybe a pair of trolley dollies from an airline. How about you?"

"Well, it's a trade secret right now, but there's a great deal of work involved, that's all I can say. Anyway, where is your lovely girlfriend tonight?"

"Oh she's here, but having a girlie night with her friend Karen, and then when Karen has a late dance with her bloke Barry, we're meeting up later on."

Trish looked sideways at Vera, who was doing the honours and pouring out a refreshing brew for her, Trish and Angie.

"So let me get this straight Cal," noted Vera, stirring her tea thoughtfully, "you're dating, but you're having a separate dance here tonight and then meeting up after midnight?"

"Well yeah...I don't want her to lose her friend because of me, I mean her and Karen have been dancing once a week for years. Not here, but over near Wigan, salsa classes or something."

"Well bring them over here, they can sit with us." interjected Angie. Vera shot her a withering look, as she hated `incomers' on the top table, unless they were invited with her royal assent.

"Ooh are you sure?" noted Vera, kicking Angie's leg under the table, "I mean that Barry has very odd-looking eyebrows, they seem to wander off in different directions, like brown leylandii on his face. Weird."

We laughed at Vera's fear of facial topiary and then I changed the subject, asking Vera how things were with her mum at the minute.

"Oh not so bad. She's had a few bad days, but still hale and hearty, watching Corrie on the telly and asking for fish finger sandwiches. There's no stopping her!"

"Ahh good, I'm glad."

\*\*\*\*

## MOVING ON

Next day Angie woke up feeling hungover and fuzzy-headed. It had been nice seeing Gary again, but staying on at the Peppermint after hours for a staff lock-in was a bridge too far. Marco was funny though and anyway, what did she have to come home to?

Keith had packed his bags, his shed contents, lawnmower, shirts, shoes, old wristwatches, photos and god knows what else, and moved it to Sylvia's garage. On the upside, Angie had the house to herself, but on the downside Keith had told her bluntly that he wasn't paying the mortgage anymore and all he wanted in terms of assets was the caravan in the Lake District, plus his own car and savings. Mind you, all that probably added up to over £150,000, so she wasn't much better off than him, assuming she could finish the mortgage off in eight years and keep the house. What was it worth, £200K, maybe £220?

The more she pondered on things, the worse it looked. Speaking to a solicitor for half an hour only confused her even more about the complicated process of divorce and splitting assets. In truth, the whole thing bored her rigid and she considered selling the house cheap, taking about 140K equity out of it and buggering off to Spain. In a way, she missed Keith and the stodgy pie dinners he liked, his dull reliability – he also kept the garden nice, so who would do that work now?

Oh yeah, she remembered offering Gorgeous Gary that job last night.

She stood by the kitchen window and looked out at the garden, which was soaked in the clammy November rain, bare branches twisted skywards, hedges looking anaemic. She flicked the TV on and tried watching *This Morning*, but gave up after ten minutes. There was something about buying old houses on BBC, sod that one…what else? Angry phone-in shows, style makeovers, history documentaries, nope, none of it could interest her. Her son Steven texted her, asking `what is all this going on between you and Dad?'

It wouldn't be nice explaining things to the kids, especially if Keith was busy doing the explaining already.

She walked slowly back upstairs, took off her jeans and got into bed in her underwear and T-shirt. Then the sobs overwhelmed her. The loneliness ate into her soul like a wet Sunday afternoon in the 1960s. Everything closed, deserted, silent, like a country frozen in the past, trapped by its own faded glory. She was fading away too, a sixty-something sex kitten who wasn't wanted anymore, who was reduced to paying a boy to fix up her garden, so that she could pounce on him after an hour's hedge-strimming. God help her.

She cried, and then slept away half the day. There was a weight upon her soul that would not ease, a sudden grief for her old life. As she missed the sureness, the comfort of it all, the pain settled like a cold mantle over her shoulders.

****

## HOLDING ON

Jim's text was blunt and delivered a heavy kick in Vera's guts. The sort of blow that stopped you dead, made you catch your breath and wait for the pain to grow, until you wanted to go numb, just to forget it happened.

**It's Mum sis, she looks funny. You'd better come quick. X**

The taxi journey was perhaps ten minutes but Vera wished it away a hundred times, said silent prayers, made deals with God while the driver chatted about 'keeping positive' and how everything would be alright. But when she arrived her legs went weak. She stumbled on the path when she saw Jim's face at the door. It was washed away, empty and crumbling like parched crags of limestone in the Pennines.

"The ambulance is on its way. I called them again, just now." rattled Jim, holding Vera by the shoulder, as he guided her into the living room.

And there she was. Folded up like a forgotten rag doll, with limbs set at strange angles and a look upon her face that formed a bridge to somewhere else. Her mouth hung slack, a trace of spittle easing its way out onto her waxen skin. The flesh pulled itself, this way and that, forming ashen pleats as she spoke, mumbling a litany of confusion.

"The sprouts are wasted...wasting away there, look nobody wants them...do you want them love?" said Vera's Mum.

"No I'm OK thanks Mum, how are you feeling eh?"

Her eyes stared back, vacant and bereft. She really had no idea who this person was, or what was happening. All she felt was something strange building inside her, a leaden weight pulling her to the earth.

Vera placed her hand on Mum's straggly hair, picking a little bit of vomit from the end of a few strands.

"Did she eat anything today Jim?"

"I tried her on soup, bit of bread dunked in it, but she brought it back in minutes. She's so tired, so tired bless her...hardly slept last night."

"Thanks for staying with her, I couldn't do another night with her. I had to go out. Jesus I feel awful for leaving her Jim...I'm sorry."

Vera leaned forward and began to let sobs puncture the air, release the pain that ebbed and flowed in her heart each day and had done so for the last three years, ever since this slow, soul-emptying illness had started to claim her Mum's life. Bit by bit, name by name, memory by memory, she'd faded from view, a ship sailing aimlessly out to sea.

Then, just a few months ago, they'd done some more tests at the hospital and found cancer in her colon and despite the drugs, there wasn't much anyone could do to stop the daisy chain of dying cells from joining up inside her. Mum was leaving Vera, and it wouldn't be long now.

Jim heard the sirens first as the ambulance approached and after the initial burst of activity, as they monitored and poked and asked her name about seventeen times, Mum kind of slipped into a semi-coma. She made noises akin to a calf in pain, lowing forlornly, trapped in barbed wire.

"We're admitting her, there's no way she can stay here any longer." said the older Paramedic, then placed a hand on Vera's arm, "You've done a great thing for your Mum here, but she needs more care, she needs looking after. Let us do it now."

"I don't want her to go. I want her to stay with me...'til the end. I said I would...I promised her that, last year."

"Sis, let them look after her now. We can go to the hospital with her, come on love."

Vera let warm tears fall on her Mum's shoulder. She pressed her face close, smelling her Mother's hair and skin, trying to absorb it, and make it become a part of her, so that she'd never forget it, never. She clutched her Mum's hand and whispered to her.

"I love you so much, I love you Mum. Don't leave me yet, please don't. Not yet, just stay another day here with me."

Her Mum made a drawn out noise from her throat. It could have been words, or just a cry of pain. No one in the room was sure anymore, sure of anything, except this suffering had to end for now. The Paramedics worked their magic, calmed her, and then carefully wrapped her onto a stretcher, gingerly easing her through her old front door, for the last time. Jim held Vera, both of them holding the other person up.

****

## SAVE THE LAST DANCE FOR ME

The black Mercedes slinked and jinked its way over the pot-holes in the Peppermint's car park. It drew to a halt opposite the main entrance and the engine ran, turbine smooth, for a few seconds as the driver finished off a phone call. Inside, Marco got up from the reception desk and unlocked the double doors, ready to receive his visitor.

A lean man, wearing a business suit from Next, Samuel Windsor Dealer boots and carrying a small, but expensive Italian leather bag, walked briskly towards Marco. He looked about 30, maybe 35 years old. Too young to be so wealthy, thought Marco, a bit too cocky really.

"Good morning Mr Camilleri. Lovely day isn't it?"

"It is Mr Dooley, it is. Come on in, welcome to the Peppermint Lounge."

Marco showed Mr Dooley into the back office, a cramped room with a basic desk, two chairs and a vintage metal filing cabinet that stood nearly six feet high. It was clunky, but had the advantage of having locks on the drawers that needed a crowbar to open, and Marco liked to keep secrets. The Peppermint was built on secrets, and he never forgot that, which was why this early morning meeting was just between the two of them. Even the cleaner was due in later today, so that Marco had a clear hour with Mr Dooley.

It was worth the courtesy, as Mr Dooley opened his fancy pants computer and showed Marco a virtual reality slideshow, depicting the row of shops near the busy main road, the three cul-de-sacs of semi-detached houses that would be built behind them, plus the brace of three-storey apartment buildings that would flank the posher houses, shielding the better off people from the busy crossroads junction nearby.

"So, OK, this looks fantastic and everything but you still haven't told me who is behind all this – who is putting the money in, it isn't your money is it?"

"You're very perceptive Mr Camilleri. No, the company I represent is a developer, headquarted in Douglas, who is keen to acquire this site and proceed next year. They see massive demand for housing in this part of the North, and they want to supply it. It's that simple."

"Hmmm, England...it's never simple Mr Dooley. Planning laws, local objections...councillors wanting kickbacks...blah blah, I've seen it all in my time."

"I'll bet you have." Noted Dooley, letting his eyes wander to the four image CCTV screen in the corner of the office. "This club has an amazing history I believe."

"It does. Georgie Best, Peter Stringfellow, Oliver Reed, all the hellraisers came here in the 70s and 80s."

Mr Dooley looked baffled. He had no idea who Peter Stringfellow or Oliver Reed might be, although he knew George Best. Marco was warming to his nostalgic theme now and painting a picture for Dooley.

"You had to be here at eight pm, sharp, to join the queue to get in at weekends. Even the Wednesday disco nights were full by nine o'clock. This place was *THE* place to be seen back then. Stars from TV, top comedians, singers, famous bands like Hermans Hermits and The Sweet – they all played here, on this stage. Page Three girls used to come here to meet all the Manchester agents, it was a fanny festival, let me tell you."

"OK. Right then, amazeballs." agreed Mr Dooley smiling in bemused sympathy, as he sipped his tea. He glanced sideways and noted the paperwork on Marco's desk.

"Well, times change. Maybe it's time to think about retiring, selling up and moving on? We can make a very strong offer on the site, within days – money's all in place."

Marco took a long, slow drink of his tea, then placed the cup down gently and looked Dooley straight in the eye.

"Let me tell you something about me. There are no flies on me Mr Dooley. I came over from Malta back in the Sixties with a suit, a smile, and fuck all else. But I learned fast that information has a value, in every business deal. So, do you want to be honest about your `development' company, or do you want to keep pulling my cock all day?"

Dooley blinked, shrugged a little and leaned back in his chair. This was a more serious opponent than Kevin the tyre fitter.

"OK, so we are actually an Isle of Man based casino operation, and property development is a new venture for us. Let's just say that online gambling has a short shelf-life, we can see regulatory problems ahead, but housing...well, it's steady profit."

"Anything else you want to admit to, whilst we're being so open about everything?"

"No that's all really, I guess you've done some homework on us."

"Yes, I have my friend and I've been told you're looking at three or four other sites in this area. So I ask myself, are they *really* going to build these rabbit hutches on all of them, or are they going to try and play off one seller against the other?"

Dooley's face reddened visibly, he was busted and he knew it. Marco had a network of business contacts locally that fed him all kinds of information. He should have realised that.

"OK, here's the deal." said Marco, taking charge of the meeting as easily as a fly fisherman casting his line into a lazy river. "You can buy this place for £2.2 million, which is exactly what it's worth. You will also pay some money into a Bank of Malta account, as a deposit, in case things get a little fucked up in translation. That deposit is non-refundable by the way. In return, I will assist your friends in the Isle of Man with some local planning problems, do some PR...schmoozing. Because you see...I'm a nice guy. We are all nice guys in Malta – it's just like the Isle of Man, but with sunny weather - and less inbreeding." joked Marco, winking at Dooley.

Dooley, who was born in Ramsey, flinched a little at the insult, but held his tongue. Marco was nothing if not thorough in his research.

\*\*\*\*

## CHAPTER THIRTEEN: "KISS ME UNDER THE LIGHT OF A THOUSAND STARS"

It had been a strange night at the Peppermint. People kept coming to the table and asking where Vera was, as she hadn't missed a Wednesday in about two years. Trish and Angie broke the news that Vera's Mum was in a pretty poorly way and they were moving her into a hospice. It gave the night a heavy heart for most of the usual crew, and few felt like dancing.

I was sitting out the Motown and Northern Soul section, as I couldn't hack dancing every week to the same songs, usually played in the same order, but Sue and Kev were having a real rocksteady time out there. Sue flicked her blonde mane over her shoulders and smiled broadly, wiggling her hips as she shimmied sideways, then back again. Kev threw in a few little turns and spins, which wasn't like him at all. The two of them seemed to have the magnets on for each other and he reached out and grabbed her waist a couple of times, setting her off in a little spin.

"They seem extra happy tonight." I noted to Trish who was sipping her drink and weighing up a dapper looking man standing by the bar. Despite his goatee, he looked kinda handsome.

"Always nice when someone's getting a bit." observed Trish, winking at me.

"Amen to that." threw in Angie, knocking back a double vodka and coke.

Gorgeous Gary breezed by, clearing up glasses and bottles and letting his tanned arm dangle near Angie for a few seconds. He placed his hand on her empty vodka glass.

"Finished with this one Ange, can I get you another one?" asked Gary, giving her an all-too-obvious look. Trish and I exchanged a pair of arched eyebrows.

"Yep, it's dead Gary, might be tempted by a cocktail."

"Right, is it a large one you want?"

"Oh fuck yes, a large stiff one."

"OK, ice and a slice?"

"Yeah why not? Bit of fruit in there. I like to get five portions a day."

Gary laughed as he gathered all our empties onto his little round tray, bending his body across the table, stretching to reach a bottle that Kev had left standing. Gary gave it a little shake to check the bottle was empty and Angie let her eyes caress his taut bum cheeks, peel away the material of his tight black trousers and visualise the smooth, tanned, and tiny buttocks that lay beneath the cotton.

"I'll bring it over in a bit – anyone else fancy a drink?" asked Gary.

"Will you behave woman?" chided Trish, but with just enough humour in her tone to defuse any conflict. Angie shrugged back at her, already half-cut after three big drinks and no food since four this afternoon.

"Trish, let me give you a bit of advice hun; leave the judging the God…and let the rest of us just play the cards, wherever they fall."

"Good words Ange, I'll drink to that when Gary gets back."

"Cool. You know what Cal, you're a diamond mate and I'm happy you've found love with that Lisa. She's like a Sugarbabe, a real cutie, you make a lovely couple. Where is she tonight?"

"She's along later, we're meeting up for a dance, then it's home time about midnight – got an early start at work."

Angie smiled conspiratorially at Trish as Gary arrived back with our drinks. She raised her glass and clinked it against mine.

"As Trish said before hun, it's nice to see someone's getting some. Cheers everyone, here's to the Peppermint and all who cop off in her, and here's to Vera…sadly missed tonight, the Queen Mother of the disco - long may she reign over us!"

"To Vera." I took a long cold drink and then checked my phone. Lisa was late and there was no text from her. But she'd come, I knew she would be with me soon and we would light up the dancefloor like Sue and Kev were doing right now. It wouldn't be long now.

\*\*\*\*

## FUTURE DREAMS

Sue opened her mouth and let her lips swirl against Kevin's mouth. She could feel the heat from beneath his shirt, smell the scent of work mixed with aftershave drift from his warm, bare skin. She felt a trickle of wetness between her leg and instinctively reached sideways for a tissue to mop up the come.

"Ooh there was a lot of it tonight, been saving it for me darling?"

"I have, been dreaming about you Sue. It was lovely tonght wasn't it; dancing, looking at each other, cuddling in the car and then coming home to make love? Just felt great. Thnks for loving me."

Sue smiled at his words and snuggled back under the duvet with him. She didn't usually bother making love after their Wednesday night disco session, as she preferred a cup of hot chocolate and then bed, but there was a difference about Kevin tonight, he seemed full of life, optimism, hope…fizzing with ideas. It was the old Kevin, the guy she'd met two years before, when he was keen to be her toyboy and make her cry out with delight as he took her from behind in the stables. What a night that was; the horses snorting in the pitch dark...the smell of leather, saddle soap...muck. It was animalistic, almost brutal. She loved it. Shame those days had gone somehow.

"What would you like to do if I retired early?" asked Kev, right out of the blue.

Sue lifted her head from his chest and rolled over away from him, to look him in the eye, as best she could in the 30 watt gloom of the low energy bedside lamp.

"Retire?" But you're not even fifty-five yet, never mind 60-odd. Anyway, what would you retire on? You told me that pension you have is a crock of shit."

"Yeah it is. But just supposing...let's say, I sold the tye business, just got out of it altogether, paid the bank overdrd off, and sold my house. What would your dream be; go on a big cruise, buy a villa in Spain maybe?"

Sue pondered on this question for a second or two, looking at him with a mixture of curiosity and exasperation. She would rather sleep and get five hours shuteye in the ba before she had to rise to see to the horses.

"Erm...neither really. I think if I had the money then would open a horse sanctuary in the middle of France. The French are cruel to horses, well some of them are, so I'd lov to set up a rescue centre and give a few ponies a decent life give them love."

"Ah, you're a big softy under it all aren't you?"

Sue wriggled down into her pillow, lay sideways facing away from Kev and then folded her bum cheeks against him, spooning his body. She let out a sigh.

"Lovely idea, I shall dream of it. Night hun, love you."

"Love you too, night night sexy rider."

But Kev lay awake for another hour, replaying the call from his accountant this afternoon. The fine details of the tyre business, from nuts to ramps, spanners to spare Dunlops, had all been totted up and emailed to Mr Dooley. Copies of the deeds had been posted via recorded delivery. Everything was set; all he had to do now was wait for a formal offer. The bedside clock ticked silently, its second hand counting down the hours. The world was turning on its axis; unstoppable, subtle and beautiful. Kevin could taste the future.

\*\*\*\*

## THE ECHO OF ANOTHER LIFE

It had been worth the wait. Lisa arrived with her mate Karen and said hello at the bar to me. We kissed and I smelled her shampoo and perfume. She smiled at me warmly.

"I love that shirt on you Cal, you are such a handsome man. I will be watching you on the dancefloor."

"And I will watch you too lovely Lisa."

Our eyes kept meeting in the swaying crowd as the music played. Some classic Chic filled the floor, then we had a taste of Taylor Swift's *Shake It Off* and a lovely shimmy to *Get Happy*. Lisa had a beautiful little hip action and I couldn't take my eyes off her. It soon ticked past midnight and she kissed Karen and Barry bye-bye and came over to say hello, then we danced together, chatting and laughing. We had a slow dance to Pink's *Try* and then I said goodbye to my gang, half of whom had already gone home.

I walked her to my car and opened the door for her. She settled in and then fidgeted a little bit as I joined her. I started the engine and began slowly easing my slightly aged VW Golf out of the Peppermint's motocross car park.

"Nice tonight wasn't it?" I asked her, switching on the CD player and picking up track 4 on a Santana greatest hits disc.

"It was, it always is hun. Sorry I was late arriving tonight by the way, I had a stack of emails to look at before I got ready, poor Karen was sat in my lounge for half an hour fluffing up her make-up and texting Barry." she explained, squeezing my hand as I changed gear.

"Can't wait to snuggle up in bed, I'm tired now, been a long day." I said.

"We can't make love tonight my darling, something odd happened today."

A strange feeling welled up inside me, all kinds of scenarios flooded my mind; an old boyfriend had got in touch, she had received bad news about a relative, or some terrible illness had suddenly appeared within her body.

"Why, what's happened?"

"Well, I started a period...my first one in nearly two years, I really thought they'd finished altogether. You must have reached the parts that other willies cannot reach!"

Relief swept over me, I squeezed her hand.

"Ooh that is kind of wonderful, slightly inconvenient...but a wondrous thing nevertheless. Maybe we should start using protection."

"God no, I hate the smell of condoms. Like some kind of stretchy cheese made in a tyre factory."

Then she paused for a moment to think about things we had chatted about in the past.

"I wish I'd met you years ago, and then I could have had your baby. All those years you tried when you were married, it's all so sad. Would you have one now if you could?"

It was a hard question to answer, because all those emotions had been buried inside me for nearly a decade, after the pain of trying for over six years with my ex-wife. In the end, childless sex had become a millstone, this baffling project, a puzzle that no doctor could solve and no magic potion could cure. I'd stopped thinking about it and lost my head in work, drinking and buying things...toys for older boys.

"It's all too late, that ship has sailed for me. But if you fall pregnant my darling I shall stand by you. It would be a miracle."

"Well at 52 I'd be in the BMJ, and frankly I don't need that!"

"BMJ..?"

"British Medical Journal Cal, kind of a trade magazine we have at work. I don't fancy being a star attraction in there. So you shall just have to pull out my dear...how old fashioned eh?"

"I know, kinda sexy though."

When we got to her house, we both had a bit of muesli, and then got ready for bed. After I'd brushed my teeth I left her to her own devices in the bathroom and she emerged a few minutes later wearing a T-shirt and little blue knickers. I could see the bulge of the sanitary towel in her pants as she clambered into bed next to me. It was an image that took me back to my married life, another time, another place.

We kissed and caressed, said goodnight to each other and I fell asleep with her spooning against me. A tiny fragment of life flowed between us, an echo of vanishing youth, fertility and a last roll of the dice with God. I hugged her and dreamed of babies that never were...

****

## CHAPTER FOURTEEN: "HAD A LITTLE TIME, TO THINK THINGS OVER"

Angie stood stock still for a minute, and then sat down at the foot of her stairs. She read the letter gain, slower this time, silently mouthing some of the words as she digested them. Her solicitor tended to ramble a bit, but the gist of it was clear; she would be unlikely to win a monthly allowance to maintain a lifestyle and there was no way that the caravan in France, Keith's classic E-Type or his Swiss watch collection could be regarded as assets of the marriage without some bank records to prove he, or Angie, or indeed both of them, had bought them in the first place.

The solicitor's letter had a depressing, familiar tone running through it, like a thread dripping with slow poison; according to the DVLA and Companies House, Sylvia and Keith's brother were both directors of a holding company which in turn owned both the E-Type and the caravan in the South of France. Complicated. The sneaky git had also set up a trust, placing his share of the house, plus some shares, premium bonds and ISAs in there, so that their children could inherit it all one day, but Angie couldn't get at it.

"Basically, I'm fucked love...that's what you're saying." said Angie, as she reached the final wishy-washy paragraphs suggesting ways she could claim this and that, contest blah-blah in court, so long as she threw another 2K into the solicitor's coffers as payment by instalments. Sod that, she thought and went into the kitchen to make a strong coffee and have a long, hard think.

On the upside, she could stay in the house for now and refuse to sell it, although Keith's legal eagle had already filed a petition and listed the house as an asset to be sold, soon as possible. The process might take a year, maybe two...at a push three, but sooner or later, she would have to leave this wonderful home. Move on...but to where, and what? Some poxy little apartment, full of doll's house furniture, or worse still, sheltered accommodation where the bathroom had a panic pull-cord and steel rails the size of baguettes on the walls of the shower? No thanks.

She sipped her coffee and ate lightly buttered toast, her brain whirring away, trying to think of ways that she could get back at the bastard.

Just then the doorbell rang. It was Gorgeous Gary, here to mow the lawn, trim the borders, weed the patio, empty the bins and generally do the things that blokes were useful for. Angie opened the side gate for him and he swaggered through the entry, carrying his strimmer like John Wayne holding a shotgun. His tanned legs poked out of canvas style shorts. Despite the raw November weather, Gary didn't seem to feel the cold that much. There was that wild bloom of youth still covering his skin in a roseate glow.

She gave him a list of jobs to do and then went to take a shower. She wanted to be ready for him later; clean and inviting, pink and wet.

## ISLE OF MAMMON

The landing at Ronaldsway was choppy, but Dooley wasn't fazed by it at all. He'd been hopping over to the mainland for seven years now, in all kinds of weird weather; foggy nights, cross-winds, rainstorms, it was all part of the Isle of Man experience. You just got on with it.

The taxi ride was short and sweet, with the driver dropping him off at what looked like a nondescript 1970s boarding house type hotel. In fact, it had been a guest house back in the day, but financial services, not tourist services, were the engine that greased the wheels on the Island, so now, the anonymous white paint and cobalt blue painted front door hid a suite of offices, spread over four floors.

Dooley was buzzed in and took the lift to the top floor, where Helen was still at her desk, even though it was well after 6.30pm.

"Evening Martin, they're waiting for you."

"Cheers m'dear, you go on now, get yourself home."

"Will do, soon as I've finished up these emails." she smiled back, amused that Marti thought he had the power to send her home, when the real power sat inside the boardroom.

Dooley went into the skylit room. The mood lighting was switched on, illuminating the two paintings on the walls, plus the antique map of the Island. Ray and Billy were seated at the table, but Ivan was sipping a drink and ensconced in the folds of a big leather settee. Nobody had yet touched the buffet that Helen had organised. Ivan was sinking his second beer, whilst Billy nursed a tumbler of Glenfiddich, with a wee drop of water. Ray was on still water, doctor's orders after his heart scare last year.

The three of them waited for Dooley to plug in his laptop to the big 50 inch screen and get the right files lined up in order. Ivan began to steam into the buffet, attacking the sausage rolls with a Viking style hunger. The trio made small talk about daft punters betting on Elvis making a comeback on X Factor, the gambling potential of the TT races next year and so on, until Dooley signalled to the older men that he was ready, by grabbing a bottle of 1664 lager from the buffet table and cracking it open.

"Gentlemen, we have two front-runners in terms of development in the North-West, and one very decent in the Midlands to look at this month. All offer great long term rental revenues, with a relatively high rate of employment in their respective catchment areas, plus the land is already pre-approved for housing, with a particular bias towards of social housing by the local Labour and Lib Dem councils. So we have some people locally who are on side, always a blessing."

"It's a help, but we don't want a re-run of that fiasco in Manchester where the idiots at the council wanted half of the flats let to fucking migrants. Where are these two sites in the North-West?" asked Ray, who hated wasting time trying to sell houses to anyone except buy-to-let landlords. Housing Associations always took an ice age to tick boxes before handing over the cash.

Dooley brought up photos of Kevin's Tyre Depot, starting with an exterior pic of the gates, security fencing, the units from the back, the storage unit areas that Kev sub-let and finally and aerial shot, with a thick red line indicating the entire plot owned by Kevin.

"This tyre fitting business is on its arse basically, owned by a guy in his 50s, wants out before the bank and HMRC pull the plug. He wants a mill, but I've stuck at 900K – which in my view is more than generous. You guys have been emailed a full plan of how the housing estate would look, but basically, we are talking 18 apartments, three sets of six semis and a row of eight townhouse units. Gross sales revenue would be about five million. After overheads, marketing costs blah-blah, I reckon it's a net profit of 1.4 to 1.7 million."

Ivan studied the aerial photo carefully.

"What's that water behind the plot then?"

"Part of an old canal, and then widened into a little lake after the local mine closed about 30 years ago."

"Mine areas...nightmare." observed Ray, chewing on his Mont Blanc fountain pen thoughtfully, and then stopping suddenly as he remembered how much the pen cost.

"On the upside that water feature adds about 20K each to the apartments that feature a decent view of the pond." noted Billy, who could already visualise the apartment block being called Waterside Park, or some-such nonsense.

"It's decent enough but just a tad small – is there land next door we can buy maybe?"

"Some private housing, a Co-Op shop and an old Methodist chapel."

"Can we buy the chapel and make that into some upmarket flats maybe, bolt them on with a shared car par between the chapel and the new units?"

"Yes we could do that, but the chapel isn't that historic looking, in fact it's plug ugly. Best option in my view is that demolishing the chapel would make a handy new entrance to the estate, so we could then squeeze in another apartment block of say 8-12 apartments alongside the road." said Dooley, who had studied the area carefully, snapping photos and video clips with his iPad.

"Get onto the church then, see what they'll take. If the numbers make sense, buy it soon as possible. Get back to us in two weeks or so. Right what's the next one?" demanded Ivan.

Dooley closed down the tyre depot file and opened the folder marked `Peppermint.' As soon as the first three or four exterior photos appeared on screen Ray almost fell off his chair laughing.

"What the fuck..?? That place, Jesus H Christ on a bike."

"You know it?" said Dooley. Billy looked at Ivan in a baffled way.

"Hell yes, that's the place my brother and me went to years ago, to pick up women before internet dating was invented. How the hell is it still going?"

"Well, it survives on a mix of funeral teas, dinner dances Saturday nights and a Singles Night disco on Wednesday." explained Dooley, and then added, "There's a Maltese guy called Marco who owns most of it, he's pretty sharp, so I reckon he's got a cash sideline coming in somehow that doesn't show up in the accounts."

Ivan smiled approvingly at the aerial pic of the Peppermint site. It was big, a fair bit bigger than the tyre place, although its location near a dual carriageway was a downside – people didn't like paying over 200K for a noisy house where lorries rumbling past woke you up in the night. Dooley began to scroll through his collection of site photos and street map images

"This project could have a small eight-til-late type shop, maybe a bookies, set near the road, with a dedicated lay-by, plus traffic lights are already in situ at a nearby junction, so people will stop anyway and see the new shops. Good shop rental revenue potential with over 30K vehicles a day going past. Now then, we can get 20 semis on this site, plus 15-18 apartments. It can make us nearly eight mill gross, but costs are higher in terms of building the units and there's a bit of road laying we have to do to keep the council sweet as regards access." noted Dooley, flicking his biro across various computer generated graphics of the proposed housing units.

"This Marco, how much does he want?"

""Two point two mill, plus a 250K bribe placed in an offshore account...for his `local schmoozing' assistance."

"Cheeky git isn't he?" spat Billy, who hated bent deals with cash under the table. Those days had gone, with the electronic trail of texts, phone calls, emails, bank transfers etc. making it all too easy for the Taxman to trace `funny money' nowadays.

"Bigger money...but more hassle. That's my take on it, what do you think lads?" enquired Ray, scoffing a ham sandwich.

"Let's see if the tyre thing works out first, put pressure on the owner. See if he'll take 750K soon as we get a green light from the Methodists. You know how I feel about nightclubs...always dodgy in my view, a can of worms." said Ivan, Billy nodded in agreement, then acidly observed;

"Nightclubs are like graves, or old flames, they're best left undisturbed. Walk away, that's my advice." The other three men smiled in broad agreement.

Dooley then moved on to the last plot on the list, a former car dealership and a deserted pub next door, just outside Solihull.

****

## LETTING GO

Vera sat patiently, glancing at the travel clock on the bedside cabinet. The second hand swept smoothly, effortlessly, past the Seiko logo. Her mum's breathing rattled briefly, and then settled back into a drifting, almost seashore-like rhythm, like a windless tide lapping the strand.

Pain, like a muggy cloud, emanated from her poor, fading body and hung in the hospice room's disinfected atmosphere. Jim had gone to work, driving groceries to dark supermarkets and warehouses, in the dead of night, where the poor and single – those who couldn't claim tax credits because they had no kids – were shuttered away, toiling out of sight, out of mind. The Britain that Vera's mum had known, of corner sweet shops, men in vans delivering fizzy pop, sacks of potatoes, or boxes of meat, fish or tinned veg and puddings, had vanished into the ether. That was a black and white, sepia toned memory now, a dream that Vera's mum had as her body slowly shut itself down, broken by pockets of cancer inside her, tiny black holes taking the atoms of life and reassembling them in some other corner of the universe. She was leaving, even as her eyes opened a little and she tried to focus one final time, on something familiar, something real, a person she remembered.

"Vera."

It was the first word she spoken in two days. Everything else had been strange mumblings, fragments that made no sense. Vera took her mum's hand and squeezed it as hard as she dared, feeling the white, bird-like bones through her withered, spotted skin.

"Mum. I love you mum."

"Vera, why me, why does it have to be me? What have I done wrong?"

Tears blobbed on Vera's cheeks and she stifled a terrible succession of sobs deep inside her soul. She ran her fingers through her mum's straggly hair, feeling the waxiness of her skin, the looseness of it, like her flesh was ready to peel away from the skeleton trying to escape from within.

"Nothing Mum, you've done nothing wrong. And if you have then all is forgiven, all of it. Rest now, try and sleep."

Joan drifted away, and her breathing sank back to a kind of slow tick, like a great old mantelpiece clock; an uneven rhythm that broke the silence. Inside Vera thought, God make it end, make it stop soon.

\*\*\*\*

## CARRYING ON

Trev came plodding upstairs, carrying two mugs of hot chocolate for him and Penny. She was in bed, watching

*Poldark* on DVD and pausing the best bits. Trev paddled his way around the bed, catching his toe in the duvet cover and spilling a little bit of the choccy brew, before making a stylish recovery. He placed the hot mug down, kissed Penny's head and then pad-padded to his side of the bed. He carefully removed his rakish dressing gown and then eased his body beneath the quilt, dressed simply in a scruffy T-shirt, old boxer shorts, featuring lots of red lip-shaped kisses, plus well-worn grey socks. Well, it was a cold night, this was no time for fashion considerations.

"What are going to wear for the Christmas bash my love, any ideas?"

"You can be Poldark, I'll be Demelza...might have to lose five stone or so, but hey, there's four weeks to go."

"You must never diet my darling, I love your boobs the way they are, big 'n' bouncy, so losing weight would shrink 'em. Don't risk it!"

He playfully tweaked one nipple and winked as he delivered this advice, just to emphasise the point. Penny giggled and pulled the top of her nightie down so he could make himself at home.

"Ooh, take your pleasure Captain Poldark." she said seductively. Trev needed no further encouragement and was soon removing his kissy boxers, feeling Penny's expert hands caressing his hardness. She pulled him inside her, lifting one leg and cupping his balls with her hand, just the way he liked it. They knew each other's bodies so intimately now, that it only took a few minutes to ding each other's bells. But that was OK, in fact it was wonderful. It worked for both of them and sometimes that's what love is; an invisible wire which can transmit something electric with the very slightest touch, a single look.

Afterwards, as they cuddled and enjoyed slurping their hot choccy beverages, Trev pondered on the future now that the last of their children was about to get his own place and fly the nest.

"I was chatting with Kev earlier today, well texting you know, about the Christmas Party 'n' that. He and Sue are going as Sonny and Cher by the way."

"Oh she'll make an ace Cher, that's a good one. But hang on, nobody knows who Sonny is though, except us old farts. Anyway, what's the news?" she knew Trev's way of rambling around the fringes of an anecdote before getting to the heart of the matter. Tonight she didn't have time, she needed sleep, and soon.

"He was saying that he's thinking of selling his business, and buying a place in France. Sue is going to open some stables, or a riding school or something. He says he's going to fix old scooters part-time and drink lots of wine."

"Wow, that is big news. Sell the business? I really thought he was chained up to that Kwik-Fit shop he's got forever. So when did all this happen, who's buying it?"

"Says there's a company making an offer on the place very soon, so he plans to go to France over Christmas and start looking for property. I mean, it's a big step, but what a move eh? Live the dream."

"Amazing. What does Sue think about all this?"

"I didn't ask, I expect she's all for it." soothed Trev, failing to notice Penny raising her eyebrows in astonishment. Men never asked important questions.

"Mmmm, yes most likely she is mad keen, if there are horses involved. Night night Trev the Rev, sleep tight."

They kissed and then Penny switched the lamp off and they both fell sound asleep within minutes. Happy, so blissfully happy, in their own little world.

\*\*\*\*

## CHAPTER FIFTEEN: "YOU GOT TO ROLL ME, AND CALL ME THE TUMBLING DICE"

I was lounging in bed with Lisa, resting my head on her bosom. My mind was full of that `all is right with the world' feeling. Smooth Radio was on in the background, the duvet was nicely messed up from our lovemaking at 5.30 this morning and the dog snoozed at our feet. Life was good.

While I dozed, in that blurry-eyed Sunday morning bliss, Lisa tapped away at her phone.

"Ahh, my mate Diane has got in touch on Facebook, God I haven't seen here in ages, years and years."

"Oh that's good." I mumbled.

"Friend request…accepted. I can't believe that we aren't friends already, I must have missed adding her when I opened my FB account. Annoying."

"Hey, remember when people used to use *Friends Reunited*? Let's go for a drink with all the people who bullied us in PE lessons or stole our dinner money? What a great idea."

"Oh my God yes, do you know, I think I'm still on that Reunited thing. Did you ever join Twatter, or whatever it's called?"

"Shamefully yes, I did Twitter for a bit. Packed it in now, it's become a lynch mob."

Lisa sat up slightly in bed, adjusting her pillows. I moved off her chest as she scrolled through her FB pages.

"Ooh, she's divorced now...lost weight too."

I took a glance at Diane's photos. She looked in good nick for someone who'd just turned fifty.

"We will have to get her along to the Peppermint, have a boogie, and let her meet some new people." I suggested.

"Yeah, let's do that. I'd love to catch up with Diane. Be fun." she rolled over onto her side, kissed me on the neck, and then the lips, smiled a beautiful smile. Irresistible Lisa, with her tangled hair and warm scented skin.

"Are you making me some breakfast then Mr Disco?"

"For you, anything."

I was bathed in her glow, completely addicted to her.

\*\*\*\*

## DESIRE WITHOUT NAME

Youth is a strange contradiction. A beautiful blend of energy, love and hope, buoyed by innocence and misplaced trust in lovers and friends. Life has yet to teach you all its bittersweet lessons, and so you charge headlong onwards, making it up as you go along, overwhelmed by the sheer, seemingly endless promise that the future holds. You can almost taste the myriad possibilities, picture all the future lovers that will touch you, teach you things and change your life forever.

That was how Gorgeous Gary felt as he walked down the street towards the railway station. It was a bitterly cold November day, but his jacket was unzipped as he strolled past the bookies, then catching a whiff of manky peppers and onions as he passed the pizza parlour. Darkness was already closing in, even though it only about four o'clock. Cars swooshed by with their lights blazing bluey-white in the gloom.

Gary dug his hands deeper into his jeans pockets for the warmth and traced the outline of a £2 coin with his fingertips. There wasn't much else in his pockets, as bar work at the Peppermint, plus some gardening jobs in the summer didn't really cover all his bills. Never mind, Angie would `lend' him twenty quid after he'd given her another good seeing to – hey maybe he could make a living as an escort for these older birds? It was a rough job but...

Just then an unfamiliar face loomed up towards him, with a grim, stone-set expression stretched taut upon the older man's dark skin. Without any debate, or warning, the man pulled an extendable metal rod from his coat pocket and whacked it neatly into Gary's scrotum. The pain jolted him stock still and convulsed his body in a kind of foetal shape, a curling, mewling agony, as he fell to the pavement.

As Gary fell, the hard-faced man placed his gloved hand across Gary's mouth to stifle the noise. A passing van driver glanced at the scene but continued yakking on his mobile and ignored the painful exchange.

Rahim put his face close to Gary's eyes and held the metal rod in front of Gary's face. He waited for a few seconds until Gary could open his watering eyes properly and the pain began to subside in his tackle area.

"Listen boy, you stay away from Angie OK? Are we clear on that score?

"Yeah...OK, whatever mate."

Rahim tapped the cold metal against Gary's forehead to emphasise the point of their conversation;

"You tell the Police and people will hurt you, understand? You go to Angie's house again and you get hurt, badly hurt. You may lose a bollock next time. Stay away from her, got it bar boy?"

"Yeah, yeah, no problem, come on mate...I don't want any trouble."

"You've got trouble. You'll get more if I see you near her again, so get a job at another club and do it soon. Fucking rent boy!"

Rahim drew himself up and glanced around the street. A woman pushing a buggy had stopped on the opposite pavement and was staring at him. He folded away his metal rod and smiled at her.

"Owes me some money, the little fucker." he explained to the woman, who shrugged and carried on walking.

Rahim pulled up the hood on his jacket and walked casually around the corner, ducking down an alleyway which led to a car park. He flicked the key, opening the door locks, glanced behind to see if Gary was attempting to follow, and then slid into the driver's seat and thrummed away at a steady speed. Rahim felt his heart racing with jealousy, rage and the need for Angie. His fingers tingled, from the violent thump he'd delivered into Gary's groin. But on the outside his dark brown eyes stared, blank as a Rothko canvas, into the gathering rush hour traffic.

He drove slowly home, ate food with his family, watched TV and then went to bed with Maryam. He slept soundly.

\*\*\*\*

## THE DOUR SLEEP OF WINTER

It had been a long slog at work for Kev. Winter time was a good time to sell tyres and other bits 'n' pieces, as the cold mornings exacted a bitter price on aged metal, oil and rubber. But it meant you worked flat out, grabbed a greasy bacon barm for lunch and hacked away at wheel nuts and seized on exhausts with frozen fingers, skinning your knuckles on rusty wheel-arch screws. He felt like he'd had enough when the cold seeped inside his bones and made everything a big effort.

Joints creaking with tiredness, Kev drove home, then slunk into Sue's kitchen and dinged a ready meal in the microwave. While it was spinning Kev fired up Sue's tablet computer and checked his emails. Nothing new from Dooley, or the accountant, but to be fair, it was just two days since the last update on the land registry, boundaries and planning application stuff. The deal should be completed by Christmas with luck, thought Kev, but he'd been in business long enough to know that all kinds of last minute snags could cause problems.

His chicken and cashew nuts microwave meal dinged and he sat down at the table, flicking to his favourite French property guide websites, to check on the latest farmhouses with land attached.

"Limoges area...so much land for your money, perfect for horses, or scooters." said Kev, not caring that he was thinking out loud, as the hazy dream began to look closer, more achievable, by the day.

Sue came in from the stables, smiled at him and his basic meal, then kissed him. She smelled of Polo's sweat, the leather of the saddle and bridle, plus there was a dash of winter frost about her cheeks, a raw redness that lingered on her skin, despite the car heater working overtime as she drove the three miles back from the stables.

They chatted about their respective days as she prepped up some beef casserole for tomorrow and set a chicken and vegetable lattice bake in the oven. She liked to cook from scratch and eat little and often, whereas Kev often wanted a big sit-down meal at the end of a grease-monkey kinda day. They'd agreed to differ on the routine of daily meals over a year ago – it saved having the same fractious conversations when meals went uneaten.

"So, what news on France then?" asked Sue, munching on a parsnip crisp as she waited for her food to heat up.

"Found two amazing places in the Limoges area. One's a five bedroom farmhouse, two of which are inside an outbuilding, old barn kinda thing, but there's also storage/workshop space in another building. Loads of potential. Plus there's about two acres of land included, all for just over 100K."

"Oh my giddy aunt, it's so cheap. You'd have to pay about three times that to get somewhere that nice round here. How lovely. Show me the other one hun."

They scrolled through photos of another wonderful farmhouse, with ivy on its crumbly stone walls, wooden shutters on the windows and beautifully bowed-in tiled roof. There was less land, but this one was just £95,000 or near offer. Sue imagined herself inside the pine kitchen, laying the big table, entertaining friends and family in the summer, teaching English kids to ride in the holidays and rescuing horses in the winter months. She kissed Kev on the cheek as they checked out details like the electricity supply for the properties they liked and then Sue had an idea.

"Let's go on Ryanair's site and see if there are any cheap flights over Christmas, I want to look around these houses. Do you want to Kev?"

"Well, we did say we'd go to see my sister and her mob, plus there's your son's big get together on Boxing Day."

"I know, but you close up for four days and it's a great chance to see some places. We could do the relatives over the New Year, couldn't we?" Sue gave Kev a look, the kind of look she used to give him when they first met two years previously, that was sexy, pleading and shining with happiness.

"Yes, go on then, let's check some flight times out and just do it. I just want to go right now to be honest."

"Me too, it looks so fantastic over there. A new life, a new start for us." mused Sue, then added; "You know everything will be all different, even the food – they don't do ding meals in France Kev, so you can learn to cook once you're semi-retired. You'll have to shape up boy!"

"That ain't gonna happen love, I'm telling you now. I'll live on jambon baguettes, dribbly cheese and red wine. I'm gonna be a fat man on an old Vespa."

"You bloody won't y'know," said Sue, sliding out of her chair and parking her Jodhpur clad bum on his lap, "you'll be my stable boy...and I shall work you like a dog, to keep you fit for action."

"Mmmm, action...a la Francais eh?" smoothed Kev, warming up his hands under her checked shirt.

"Oui. Le grande action m'sieu..."

They kissed and melted into each other, Sue letting her hands wander down into the folds of his jeans, squeezing his tackle through the material. The prospect of real change, a new chapter, had got inside her soul. Now, she wanted to escape Britain and its rain-sodden sense of disappointment, of endless struggles with traffic and cramped little houses. She wanted a final hurrah, a last ride into a different kind of sunset.

And what Sue wanted, she usually got.

****

## A TIME TO KISS GOODBYE

It was unusually quiet at the Peppermint, with small pockets of regulars gathered around their tables, chatting, watching, and waiting for an unspoken signal to dance.

Lisa was giving the Peppermint a miss tonight. She was at a conference in the morning, doing a Powerpoint presentation on new techniques for inserting stents, how to scan them, different materials used etc.

I liked it that she was so brilliant at her job and her department had put her forward to do the presentation. She'd shown me the slides a few nights previously, and I loved the way she explained the procedure, the gadgetry, the risks and more. I loved that quality within her, the thirst she had for the breadcrumb trail of knowledge. She fascinated me.

Vera was also missing that week, as her Mum was not very well and deep down, we all knew it was just a matter of time, maybe weeks, maybe days. Nobody discussed it in detail, but Trish had been to see her, give her some comfort, have a chat, and take her mind off things for an hour or so. Friends showed their true colours when the chips were down, and that was why I liked my group – they had good hearts.

Sue and Kev breezed in, looking super happy and dishing out Christmas cards early, as they were going away – a spur of the moment thing, explained Sue. A few minutes later, Trev and Penny joined the crew, with Trev arriving half-plastered on cheap booze and full of pre-Christmas spirit. He danced like a banshee, flicking his pointy 60s Beatle boots in all directions as Penny watched from the table. She smiled, as an indulgent mum might do at a gruelling Christmas Nativity play, revelling in Trev's frantic energy and comical dance moves. He was a true one-off, and she loved him for that ability he had to dance as if nobody was watching.

Angie seemed distant, slightly upset.

"No sign of Gary tonight, not like him to miss a Wednesday night." she noted, as Trish and Sue exchanged a coded look.

"Maybe he's busy tonight, or just tired from all the gardening work he's been doing lately?" hinted Sue, kicking Kev under the table to emphasise the banter.

"Well he hasn't dug over my borders in ages, I can tell you that for nothing." batted back Angie, scrunching her lips up in disappointment. She missed Gary's sheer stamina, even if his technique was a bit rough and ready.

"So you two are off on holidays over Christmas then, going somewhere sunny?" enquired Trish. Sue leaned closer to her ear;

"No, we're going house-hunting in France, as we're thinking of retiring there next year. I'm after a lovely barn conversion place, with stables."

Trish looked stunned for a moment, as she hadn't heard this news yet and she couldn't imagine Sue emigrating and leaving her beloved horse.

"But what about Polo...and the Peppermint? You'll miss this Wednesday disco Sue, and the Motown nights in Urmston. Aw, don't leave us all. Penny did you know about this?"

Penny nodded that she did. Trish looked slightly annoyed that once again, she seemed to be the last to know what was going on.

"I will miss this place Trish," explained Sue, staring briefly across the dancefloor as some of the regulars started throwing a few shapes, "and I'll miss the odd night at the Motown discos too. Polo will have to come with me, that's why I need a farm, or somewhere with a field and stables. It's a dream Trish, and I can't let this dream slip away without doing something about it."

"Well good for you, good luck to both of you. Ah, this could be our last Christmas as a group here. How sad...but let's make the most of it. Cheers and good luck house-hunting you two."

Trish gave Sue a massive hug, kissed her cheek and then hugged Kevin too, wishing him all the best and telling him to look after Sue. The DJ put on Bruno Mars *Uptown Funk* and they all jumped up to join Trev on the dancefloor. It was time to smile, live in the moment, and dance like the last 20 years had never etched their heavy toll onto creaking knees and worn calf muscles.

Vive le disco, au revoir Peppermint.

\*\*\*\*

## CHAPTER SIXTEEN: CHRISTMAS PARTY NITE

Angie, Vera and Trish eased themselves carefully out of the taxi, as the rain steeple-chased down outside the Peppermint's neon pink frontage. Vera adjusted the conical, pointy boob bits on her Madonna outfit, as she walked along the red carpet that the Peppermint had provided for the fancy dress Christmas bash. There were extra strings of lights around the double door entrance, plus a decorated tree next to the reception desk. Marco had really splashed out this year, even the food tickets were properly printed items, not the usual raffle number tickets from the pound shop.

Trish had dressed as a cowgirl, complete with hat and a pair of pistols, slung low on a leather belt. Trish had tied a checked shirt in a knot beneath her fabulous bosomage and Terry the bouncer asked her `Is there room in your holster for my six shot?' Oh he was smooth and, for a bouncer, quite witty.

This was always a happy night at the Peppermint; so many people made the effort to win the £25 Argos voucher fancy dress competition prize, there was an extraordinary amount of drinking, a bun fight at the buffet and all manner of people copped off with someone they shouldn't, as what could be better at Christmas than a little bonk/snog on the side?

Angie tip-toed along the red carpet after Vera and Trish, as she'd struggled to get out of the taxi without damaging her wings. Truly, Angie's sexy Christmas tree fairy outfit was a work of art, with a green bustier as the centrepiece, glittery white stockings, suspenders, red heels, a red heart shaped, cubic zirconia bracelet on one wrist and a magic wand in her other hand. Plus, she had a diamante tiara set upon her hair extensions. Angie really did look impressive, with her mighty cleavage spilling out over the lace-trimmed bustier, like perky presents inside a Santa sack at a company charity event.

Marco surveyed the trio as they checked in and collected their food and drink vouchers.

"Ladies, ladies...you look fantastic! Amazing outfits...and so, so sexy! I think all of you will be fighting off legions of men tonight."

"Probably not be fighting `em," said Vera philosophically, "but as I've got white knickers on at least I can always wave a surrender flag."

Marco laughed at Vera's sauciness and then looked Angie up and down appreciatively,

"Angie baby, great outfit, but a Christmas angel needs a tree and you don't have one. Never mind, you can sit on my piece of wood later."

"That would look wrong Marco - a Christmas fairy perched on top of a pencil, no good! Anyway you dirty bastard, that'll cost you an extra drinks voucher." quipped Angie. Marco laughed at her smutty reply and blew her a kiss, and gave her three drinks vouchers, just because he loved her saucy banter so much. She really was a no-nonsense woman and he liked that about her.

****

### RELATIONSHIPS ARE GIVE AND TAKE

I dialled Lisa's number and she answered on the second ring.

"Hi hun, how are you?"

"I'm fine, just getting ready for the Christmas do, so I thought I'd have a chat before I joined the gang later. Are you working?"

"I am," she replied, her voice heavy-lidded with tiredness, "and I shall have a bath later and then get my PJs on for an early night, I feel shattered."

We talked about work for a while, the weather, Christmas shopping and other everyday stuff. Then I got to the heart of things.

"I'm going to miss you tonight, really miss dancing with you. It's such a shame you couldn't come, it's a brilliant night - the outfits are always amazing."

"I bet they are, do take tons of photos for me won't you?"

I felt my heart rate bump up a little bit, as I struggled to communicate what I really felt. For the life of me, I really could not understand why it was impossible for Lisa to be with me at the Christmas party, especially as I'd bought her a spare ticket almost three weeks ago.

"I know work is manic for you this time of year, but I can't help thinking about how you said you'd make it to the party tonight, but then you've changed your mind last minute. Is it something I've said or done? Please tell me?"

There was a pause as she marshalled her thoughts,

"No, no no, of course not, it's just work, too much bloody work. I'm sorry. You're brilliant my darling, you make me very happy and I can't wait to see you over Christmas, it will be magic to have some days off with you, exchange our gifts...and see in the New Year together as well, our very first! How wonderful will that be?"

Her voice was shining with excitement and love, and I couldn't resist the beauty of her dreams, her hopes for the year ahead, as they weaved a spell inside my head, and heart.

"I don't want to go tonight. I'd rather be with you, chatting in the bathroom whilst you have a nice relaxing bath, soaping your beautiful body, touching you..."

"You must go, I don't want to take you away from your friends hun. You will look so handsome in your Prince Charming costume, send me a photo before you set off – promise?"

"I promise."

So I applied some make-up, a dash of lipstick and gelled my hair up. I was painting on the ghost of 1980s pop star Adam Ant across my ageing face, plastering on a smile. I pulled in my blue belt until it felt snug, and then slipped on the beautiful gold, red and blue trimmed top coat – this was a superb outfit I had to admit. The finishing touch was a pair of dandy highwayman boots, with folded down tops. I stood straight and took a selfie in the wardrobe mirror. I tried to smile as broadly as I could, but it wasn't quite convincing.

I missed my Lisa and I really didn't want to looking for glass slippers tonight.

****

## HAVE YOURSELF A MERRY LITTLE CHRISTMAS

The room was already filling up nicely, with Trev and Penny dressed as matching Batman and Catwoman, Sue was wearing a French Maid costume and Kev looked dapper in a yellow zoot suit, plus green-painted face as The Mask. I arrived dressed as Adam Ant and three forty-something ladies asked if I was wearing a Mr Darcy costume. Anyone under fifty had absolutely no idea who Adam and The Ants were. But there were photos on the red carpet for me anyway.

After buying a drink and dodging a man-hungry divorcee from Essex at the bar, I joined my group and we all exchanged Christmas cards and hugs. I felt lucky to have such close friends and there was a joy in knowing the details of their lives; sharing plans for Christmas Day, talking about families meeting up, the people we missed.

We danced in a circle to 70s disco classics, Motown sounds and cheesy Christmas songs. Trev encouraged Penny to use her Catwoman whip on him when they played Aguilera's *Dirrty* track and I did a few salsa steps to J Lo's *On The Floor* with Vera to make her feel life still had the promise of joy, of fun. Vera needed a break from watching her Mum slip away and everyone at our table knew it. We all put on a brave face, danced with extra verve, just for Vera and shook our bodies like kids at a school disco.

It was Christmas. We air-kissed strangers, admired all the fancy dress outfits and let pushy people get served first at the bar. There was a ripple of goodwill towards everyone at the Peppermint that night; marriage wreckers, wife-swappers, STI transmitters, ugly men with tattoos, annoying dad-dancers or beefy shouldered women who started fights over rich men. We forgave them all their sins. Even Monkey Man and his ever-wandering hands. We wished them all well.

Forgive and forget, for life is short.

\*\*\*\*

## A PLEASUREDOME DID BENDY WENDY ERECT

The scent of alcohol, perfume and latex mingled in Wendy's kitchen. Her guests had nearly all settled in now; some downstairs in the basement, already finding partners, or voyeurs, for the night, whilst others were taking longer to become at ease in the company of masked strangers, or casual acquaintances. They spoke in hushed, clipped sentences, giving away very little about their real lives.

"Actually, I just work in local government, very boring really, nothing worth talking about." said one podgy middle-aged man to a couple of swingers from Swinton.

"Well, I work in a dull job too, so I understand. We all need a little release now and then..." replied the swinger wife, running a fingertip across the government guy's latex shorts and checking out his package.

In the lounge, Florence and Machine's *You've Got The Love* video played on the 50 inch TV screen and two bisexual women, Claire and Katie from Burnley, got nice and comfortable on the three-seater leather settee. A trio of men sat opposite, sipping some of Wendy's Christmas punch and thoroughly enjoying the show, especially the `how much food can you retrieve from my bra' game. The punch bowl contained peaches, raspberries, orange segments, plenty of vodka, a dab of Disaronno, pink champagne, a mugful of Malibu and a gargle of Marlborough Estates white wine. It was alcohol blue touch paper - light it and stand well clear.

"This is my kinda Christmas party." observed one of the trio, winking beneath his Venetian ball type eye mask.

"Y'know it's just great being somewhere where all the fucking phones are switched off and no fool's uploading pictures to Facebook." added the tallest of the three guys, leaning forwards as the chubbier of the two bi-girls let her breasts be lifted clear of her underwear by the expert lips of her close friend.

"Makes a change from the section Christmas do that's for sure." noted the oldest of the local Lotharios, "Listening to people moaning about not getting promoted, some new planning regulations, the latest government cutbacks…all that crap."

Mr Dooley, who had been loitering discreetly near the basement stairs, wearing a red devil facemask and nursing a still water, leaned close to the sweaty, middle-aged bureaucrat and offered a few words of advice into his ear, because drink could loosen tongues all too easily.

"Listen, best not mention where you live, or work, at a place like this. Everything's arranged you know, as we discussed, but use a fake name…and a condom. Enjoy the night sir and I'll leave you to it, merry Christmas to all of you. Bye now."

Dooley patted the man on the shoulder, finished his drink and headed upstairs for a look at what was going on in Wendy's kitchen and living room before he left. His curiosity had got the better of him, even though he was here strictly on business. In the blue, mood lighting gloom, he could see a local councillor, bending over a marble work surface, being spanked by a Wendy, who was wearing her thigh length boots, black underwear and a circus ringmaster's coat. The man's arse cheeks shook like pink jelly as she laid into him with a wooden paddle. He made pig-like squeals of delight as she increased the force gradually. A small crowd were watching and offering various instructions as regards speed and severity;

"More on the left cheek, it needs to match the other one."

"I think he'd like a butt plug later."

"Go lower Wendy, aim for his balls! Hurt him!" egged on the spanking victim's wife of 23 years, who was drinking Prosecco at a rate of knots and tapping a riding crop against her leather boot.

"It's like the UKIP party conference down there. Listen, thanks and everything, but I'm on my way." muttered Dooley to Wendy, as he clocked a woman in the dentist's chair being pleasured by four hands simultaneously. Feeling his job was more than done, he took a final swig of his drink, and paid Wendy the balance of the agreed amount in cash for her services. They did the deal in her downstairs loo, so that nobody could see. Wendy folded the £5250 up, hid it inside her knickers, and then dashed upstairs to get it tucked away in her bedroom safe immediately.

"Always a pleasure, let me know if there's anything special your friends would like to see, or do." said Wendy as she jogged upstairs. Dooley shrugged back at her;

"They're all living the dream down there, it's just what we wanted – you're a star Miss W, a true star."

"We aim to please here." She shouted from the landing.

"We'll talk again in the New Year, all the best."

And after taking off his Satanic mask around the side of the house, Dooley smoothed back his hair, got inside his car and texted his boss to let them know the right people were getting what they wanted. Then he drove home, played some music on his iPod and tried to erase the image of a wobbling, well-smacked, strawberry jelly arse, which was now forever burnt into his memory. Dammit.

Like many people, he could never listen to Madonna's *Hanky Panky* again, for the rest of his life. Not just because it was a rubbish song, but there were all the terrible flashbacks.

****

**IN THE WEE SMALL HOURS**

Trish swung her bra around to the front and unclipped it, then stepped into the shower. It had been a great night and the dancing was so much fun, even though the floor was packed out. She needed a shower before bedtime, even though it was after one a.m.

Whilst she got clean her phone pinged.

**So good to dance tonight and thanks for the kiss Trish. Really like you and hope we can meet up for that drink soon. Would be great, merry xmas hun xx**

She dried herself off and then read the message from her friend Laurence. She'd known him for a few years, but tonight he made it clear he wanted a bit more and they'd talked outside whilst waiting for taxis. He was growing on her, so what the heck, why not she thought?

**That drink would be very welcome Laurence, so good chatting this evening too, hugs, nite nite x**

****

I drove home, make-up smudged away from my lips and cheeks, boots scuffed from dancing on the crowded floor. It had been a great night and I was looking forward to this Christmas. Inside my flat the lights twinkled on the tree and flickered around the edge of the Juliette window.

I pulled off my boots and had a couple of biscuits, while I checked my phone. There was no message from Lisa. I knew that she would probably be asleep now as it was after one in the morning, but love got the better of me.

**Hi babe, just letting you know I'm home, safe n sound. Missing your lips against mine, the warmth of your skin wrapped around me. Sleep well and have a brill day tomorrow. Don't work too hard. Love you xxx**

I played some music on my iTunes as I stripped off and had a quick shower, washing the heat of the Peppermint from me. Then I carefully folded away the Prince Charming fancy dress costume in its cover, put the boots inside their box and got into bed.

I switched the music off. There was no reply to my text. She would be asleep, her head turned sideways into the pillow, blonde hairs coming adrift, her arm sticking out from the duvet at some odd angle. I missed her, I pictured her outline, the soft, sweet curve of her and then I sought out the kiss of dreams to speed the day towards us both.

****

Vera eased herself out of the taxi as its diesel engine clattered and echoed around the street, as if someone had dropped a set of cymbals against an old washing machine.

"Goodnight love, merry crimbo – don't spend too much luv!" said the driver, as she gave him an 80p tip. Well, charging an extra £2 just because it was Christmas time was taking the piss frankly, thought Vera. She rummaged in her voluminous handbag for her house keys and swore quietly as she dropped her packet of headache tablets in the search.

"Fuck-to-buggery, how do these keys hide so well, they're the size of a cobbler's toolbag?"

She bent down and felt the booze catch in her throat as she retrieved her paracetamol from the step. She'd had a skinful tonight, but people had been so kind buying her drinks - it would be silly to refuse. Anyway, it was Christmas. Once inside, she swayed into the kitchen and put the kettle on, as it most definitely time for a brew.

She hung her keys on the hook near the chopping board and considered the idea of some toast, possibly with jam and butter on top. Vera began to unpick various components of her fancy dress costume apart. Then her phone pinged in a message.

"Who the hell is that at nearly two a.m?"

She picked up the phone and swiped it alive, then sat down, her suddenly body folding in upon itself as the kettle built up a head of steam and cried a lonely whistle.

**Hi Sis, I know you've been out with your friends tonight and I'm so glad. Mum passed away peacefully about midnight and I held her hand as she went. There was a glow about her, she didn't look as waxy as before, it was as if all the pain had vanished from her somehow. I said goodbye from you many times, and told Mum she should go to the next place and we would see her there one day. Take care love and I will be round first thing tomorrow xx**

"Mum."

The word hung like a night light in a nursery, faint and almost candle-like. Then Vera said it softly again, repeating it and building up the `Mums' like a litany, a piece of ancient music, a prayer for the chimney at Christmas, a soft fragment of comfort and warm memory. Then Vera went into the lounge, lay down on the sofa and let grief overwhelm her, until the cushion lay wet beneath her head. An ache that was ages old, cried out from her soul and there was nothing else to say, no words were left.

Only time could chime inside her.

****

Angie hadn't heard anything back from Gary, despite sending him a selfie of her fairy costume and a string of Whatsapp messages. Where was he? She stood shivering outside the Peppermint waiting for the taxi that she'd booked to arrive, but all she got was an engaged tone when she called the cab company. Christmas: Taxi drivers all became Dick Turpin...

Angie began tapping her beautifully manicured pink fingernails on her phone screen.

**Hi babe, I know that I'm not supposed to text you but just saying happy crimbo. Hope the trade show in Manc was ace. Missing u Xxx**

It only took a few minutes for a reply to ping back from Rahim's phone.

**Where are u hun? Peppermint tonight?**

**Yes, Xmas party. I'm all dressed up as a Christmas fairy...wanna kiss under my mistletoe?**

She stepped away from the club entrance, where the smoking shelter was located and took a quick selfie of some mistletoe draped across her mighty boobage.

**Just got into bed now tbh, fancy joining me? Xx**

**Soon as I can get a cab, yeah, why not? It's Christmas xxx**

It took another hour, and an extortionate 45 quid to get Angie into the city centre and dropped off at Malmaison. Rahim would be ready for her and Angie was more than ready for him. She ached for his touch, wanted him to take her, bend her over the edge of the bed, and force her apart. She texted him, as she travelled through the twinkling light suburbs, tapping out a morse code of desire, describing the things she wanted him to do. There was a quiet fire in her smile.

****

## CHAPTER SEVENTEEN: "DREAMING OF MERCY STREET"

The feeling had been gnawing at Maryam all week. She felt a kind of hunger in her guts, a need to know what was going on. Her instincts told her that something was still happening between Rahim and that foul old hag. Maryam had already memorised his email password and phone PIN code, just by glancing at his fingers, and then taking her own phone into the loo to write down the few letters or numbers she had gleaned with a sly, sideways glance. She checked his finger taps a few times before entering her passwords, as she didn't want him to get an email alert saying failed attempts had been made.

But once she was into his phone, and furiously scrolling through the text message archive, the bloom of fire welled up within her. There they were, still texting, Angie asking about Christmas plans, the trade event in Manchester, asking if they could meet up and Rahim being evasive. Her saying `I miss you' two days ago, how she `still had the horn' for him.

It hurt so deep. Maryam shook with rage and jealousy, but all that showed on the outside was a kind of icy tremor. Her senses told Maryam that her husband was distracted, lost within himself sometimes, looking at the television but not seeing anything on the screen – his mind was elsewhere. And in her experience, when a man's mind was concentrated upon another woman, his dick usually tried to follow...

So Maryam contacted her mother and arranged childcare for the night of the trade show. She drove slowly to the hotel and parked nearby, then moved to a safer area near when a space became free, as some of the back streets near the Malmaison were full of urinating drunks, whores and drug dealers. Maryam despised Manchester, she looked in pity at the sluts walking by, knickers on show, boobs bouncing out of their tops, nipples hard against the night air. It was no way for any decent woman to live, she thought.

She chatted to Rahim and said goodnight to him. He seemed slightly drunk and just as distant as he'd been for the last few months. She told him to sleep well and that she would see him soon.

****

### NEW FROM K-TEL – BRUSH-O-MATIC

Vera opened the bottom layer of the battered pine chest of drawers in her Mum's old room. The room she had stayed in for a year, just before things took a turn for the worse and she'd had to relocate downstairs. Carefully, as if unwrapping a china wedding gift, she took out a handful of old photo albums. The three neat folders, with their shiny red, embossed covers smelled of cellulose, plastic and the ghosts of Christmas past. She took another hit from the brandy bottle before opening the first album.

There she was, faded, panda eye-shadow etched across her young face, snapped at her engagement party. She had a frumpy green dress on and thick brown tights or stockings, she couldn't recall which. The dress and shoes were probably bought weekly, on the `never-never' from Mum's John Myers catalogue, something like 4/6 a week for 20-odd weeks. A fortune back then.

There was Mum, sat between Vera and her husband to be, Brian, resplendent in his Burton's suit and quiffed up hair. That hair soon fell out after their second child arrived in the 70s and they struggled by on a three day week wage, recalled Vera. She sighed and let her finger touch the big daft hat that Mum was wearing that evening. It had seemed such a posh do at the Masonic Hall back then, but leafing through the photos, everything looked so worn out, moth-eaten and Spartan.

It was as if the war was still on; bare wooden tables, the odd plate of fish paste sandwiches, balding men in shirt sleeves and braces, grimacing for the camera, so as not to show their lack of teeth in their head. There was a picture of Vera and Brian dancing to the twist, her legs looked so skinny, pale as school milk bottles.

There was a photo of Mum, taken later in the evening when a couple of Gin and Tonics had got the better of her. The hat had gone and her bouffant hair-do had collapsed slightly on one side. Her smile was wonky, but genuine, as she raised a glass for the photographer, in a toast to the happy couple.

Tears rolled across the pink folds of Vera's face, as she remembered the details of her wedding night; the band were called `The Morning Papers' or something artsy and played bad covers of Beatles, Stones and Kinks songs, before older relatives insisted on hearing lousy renditions of classic waltzes or foxtrots. Vera's sister, Lesley, had nipped round the back of the Hall for a snog with some lad and then been collared by Mum just as things were getting steamy. There was hell to pay. Vera recalled Mum actually swearing at the boy, saying something like `Get your filthy paws off my daughter, you horrible little ginger turd!'

Vera laughed to herself at the mixture of memories; Mum's leonine rage, Lesley's red-faced shame, the boy's pasty-faced fear and skulking walk down the road. Those were the days, those were great times...

She took another sip of brandy and pulled a cushion beneath her weary head and creaking neck, as she skimmed through the yellowy-tinged, Max Spielman envelopes of her past. The bundles of photos spilling out onto the carpet; the dead mixed up with the living, lovers long vanished, and relatives made almost unrecognisable by the rosy bloom of a younger time.

She paused and stared into her Dad's scrunched up eyes, as he sat, arms folded defensively, stubbornly wearing a vest on Southport beach in the roasting summer of `76, his skin turning shades of nougat pink. It was a rare photo of the man that Mum used to call `your Father,' as if he was akin to God, a deity to be served with endless darning, washing, ironing, food set on the table like clockwork at 6.10 every weekday evening. He was a hard man to love, even at this distance.

Vera shuffled the deck of photographic cards and moved on, finding another picture of her Mum, posing on a wall near the funfair, her dress hoiked up just above the knee, her headscarf despatched to her shopping bag as she let her frazzled dark brown hair catch the breeze. She looked happy. Carefree for a day, having escaped the drudgery of running the house, the endless washing and arm-wrenching mangling of clothes, and chasing after her four children. It was a beautiful photo.

Vera picked it out of its cellophane wrapper in the album, unpeeling it gently, so she could use it on the funeral service booklet. People should remember her as a happy woman; everyone should see the beauty she once had, in all its summery glory.

Vera checked inside the drawer, in case there were more pictures that she had missed. But there were just a few boxes of old knitting patterns, thimbles, needles, bits of spare material, curtain hooks and so on. Then she spotted a shoe box and opened it, expecting some sensible brown flats inside. Instead, there was a gadget from the 1970s; a K-Tel Brush-o-Matic, which people used to brush dog hairs, dandruff and assorted fag-ash from their Val Doonican jumpers.

Vera smiled as she removed it from the box and looked at the useless brush from all those years ago. She swivelled its head and it still clicked into place. Mum had kept it all this time, God only knows why...

Vera held the brush close to her face and examined the hairs stuck on the Velcro-like surface of the gadget. The strands of hair were dark brown and the faint scent of Mum breathed its Harmony hairspray way into Vera's lungs. She started to sob and shake, feeling grief strike a heavy bell within her soul; a mournful tolling note.

The sadness of years weighed upon Vera. The stark fact that both her parents had now gone, and she had become this sudden waif and stray, an orphan in her sixties, so utterly alone, overwhelmed her. Although she'd lost a dozen friends, plus a sister to cancer, in the last decade, there was no preparation for this aching gulf, this churning pain that stared back at her from frozen photographs. Age doesn't take the sting away from losing a parent, experience never truly salves the wound. Instead, you look for meaning in the tiny things, the fragments left behind. There are moments that remind you how a simple love, an unspoken bond, was once the anchor that held you to this place, this home, and all its beautiful swirling, chaotic life.

So you clutch those moments close to your heart. Like dust from a bedside drawer, the smell of the past in the paper lining, or a single hair pressed like a crucifix upon your clothing. In the deep of the night, that's all you have.

****

## THE BUTTERFLY UPON A WHEEL

Angie stepped from the taxi with a sense of resentment and relief. The driver adjusted his position in his seat, so he could catch an up-the-skirt glimpse as she emerged from the back of the Toyota Avensis. He smiled a cheeky grin and thanked her for the tip;

"Cheers love, you have a great Christmas yeah?"

"I intend to, cheers." grunted Angie, barely looking in his sweaty direction. In truth, all that she had upon her mind was Rahim and touching his caramel soft skin, running her nails over his shoulders, digging them in deep as he eased his way inside her, opening her slowly. She paused to text Rahim briefly and then trotted on her heels towards the hotel, attracting an appreciative wolf whistle from a lairy, drunken bald man. Raindrops and glitter sparkled on her face as she walked through the doors and nodded at the security staff as they welcomed her in, asking if she was a guest, as only guests could drink now.

"Yes I'm with my boyfriend, he's staying here love, in fact he's just over there."

Rahim was waiting at the end of the bar, holding a soft drink in his hand and smiling at her spectacular costume, beckoning her to come over.

"The Christmas Fairy has come to grant you a wish." giggled Angie, as she wiggled her way to him and jiggled her mighty boobs in front of him.

"Just the one? I've been a good boy all year though." shrugged Rahim, curling his arm around her waist and kissing her. She pulled back a little and there was a spark of fire in her eyes;

"No you haven't, you've been a bit of a bugger sometimes...but I forgive you, I'm too soft aren't I?"

"You are hun," cajoled Rahim, letting his hand drop from her waist and skim the bare flesh of her thigh under her frilly skirt hem, "but I'm not soft, I'm quite hard actually...and I know what my wish is now."

"No Rahim, I've told you before, I'm not taking it up the arse. Not even at Christmas, but everything else is on the wish list."

"Awesome. Let's go to my room, I need to be inside you Angie baby."

\*\*\*\*

Outside, in the grim Manchester rain, Maryam watched Angie totter inside the hotel and imagined their meeting from the warmth of her car. The words they spoke, possibly the gifts they exchanged too. The images burned into her eyes and ignited her emotions. She almost vomited with emotion, and then composed herself and texted Rahim;

**Hi darling. Missing you and I can't wait to see you soon. It will be such a good Christmas for us this year and I want you home, where you belong.** Big hugs from your wife M xxx

There was no reply, of course, but she didn't expect one. She knew what was going on. Again. A quiet anger started to build inside her and underneath its cold, clammy embrace, she felt a sort of hopeless grief. She had lost her husband, he was never coming back to her. Not truly, not like he'd used to be, a kind, dedicated, loving man. Somehow, he had become a stranger, someone she didn't know, or trust.

She texted her mother.

**Mum it's me, Thanks again for looking after the kids. You've been so good to me, and them, and I won't forget it. Please don't worry too much, as I'm at the hotel now with my friends, safe n sound. Hugs xxx**

Maryam turned the engine on and moved the car into a parking space that had become free, just a few metres from the hotel entrance. It was only a little bit closer to the hotel, but she needed to be nearer the doorway, she had to see the bitch leaving.

She texted Rahim again.

**Something is going on isn't it? It's that woman again, I know it is. Call me back please.**

No answer. An hour went by. She ran the engine a little bit to stay warm, but switched off the interior light, so that nobody took much notice of a single woman inside a car. Just watching, waiting, surrounded by the stillness that only a lifetime of patience can bring.

She texted Rahim one last time.

**I'm on my way. See you soon. She better had NOT be there. That's all I'm saying.**

Then she saw them both. He was in his shirt and trousers, shoes on but no socks, and she had wrecked hair, a tangled mass hanging over her shoulders. Angie turned around, flustered as revellers hooted at the sight of her loose breasts in the costume. Rahim pulled her close and did the top button up on her fairy dress, making some kind of crude joke as he did so. Angie giggled, like a pathetic schoolgirl.

Maryam turned the key, heard the engine growl into life and engaged Drive with the gear dial. Then she checked her mirror before setting off and accelerated as rapidly as she could towards the pair of them.

At the very last second Rahim spotted the dark outline of the Volvo X90 rushing into his field of vision and thought it must be a drunk driver, as there were no headlights dazzling blue-white on the car. Then he saw Maryam's eyes staring directly at him, unflinching, completely fixed. He instinctively jumped backwards towards the doorway of the hotel and felt the brush of air, heat and tyre noise as the car flew past.

Falling on a wet step, he banged his elbow and a jolt of pain made him swear. Rahim sat up and watched the car swerve slightly to the left as it crossed the main road, and then, with a graceful, almost ice skater, slow motion beauty, it collided with a panic-braking minibus. There was a bang that sounded like an explosion. The Volvo lifted onto two wheels, and the airbags deployed, with the steering wheel boss cannoning into Maryam's face, knocking her out. Her foot still pushed forward on the accelerator as she moved forwards inexorably, for just over 2 seconds, gathering another 11mph as the Volvo clipped the kerb, became airborne for around seventeen feet, before crunching head-on into the frozen, harsh stonework of a shopfront support wall.

The bodywork folded in twisted origami shapes, the windscreen became a crazy paving mosaic in miniature, bursting into plasticky icicles that scattered like jewels. The radiator spewed its brackish, green water onto the pavement, hissing steam in sudden pain. On this second impact, Maryam's torso moved slightly to the left, but still caught the steering column and her kneecaps broke like seashells beneath her skin, as she came to a jarring, thumping halt inside the concertina cabin of the vehicle. Maryam's brain collided with the fragile dome of skull tissue, breaking the sac of fluid around her brain, detaching retinas. Three teeth were lost as her head whipped in a perfect arc onto the dashboard that rushed up to greet her. There was a terrific blue-white flash in her mind and then nothingness; just peace and silence.

For a second Rahim thought `poor driver' and then the realisation that Maryam was driving hit him. He got up and ran across the road, failing to notice Angie lying unconscious, with a strange, awkward new joint in her lower leg, where the car had crunched bone and tissue, then turned the snapped femur about 90 degrees beneath the skin. Inside Angie, blood began to pool in one lung, as a jagged edge of a broken rib skewered her breathing capacity. Her brain started to swell in quick reaction to the glancing, spinning blow that the pavement delivered to her head as the Volvo skittled, and lifted her, completely off her feet.

Rahim reached the car and tried to open the driver's door but it was buckled by the impact. He saw Maryam lolling inside, her head resting against the ruptured airbag. She looked peacefully asleep, coated in a fine white dust, like bizarre Halloween make-up.

She was already dead, her aorta torn away by the sudden, folding, twisting thud into the minibus, and the twin blows to her brain as the car hit the wall. She'd forgotten to wear a seatbelt before gunning the car straight at the two traitorous lovers, determined to split them apart, once and for all. Rahim banged his fists on the window, but Mariam didn't move. He ran around the other side of the car and pulled on the door, which opened easily.

"Maryam, Maryam! Can you hear me?"

There was only an awful silence, just for a few seconds, before a terrible scream of shock erupted from a young woman, staggering drunkenly from a nightclub, woke the witnesses from their suspended lives. Men came forward and dragged Rahim away. A sober man checked Maryam's pulse, and then placed his jacket over her face and shoulders. Rahim sat on the wet pavement, collapsing within himself, feeling his soul press deep into the earth. He began searching out somewhere dark, alone, beyond pity and comfort.

It was another twelve minutes before a Police car arrived and they used a metal battering ram to smash a rear window in the car and crawl inside. A young officer checked her pulse had utterly vanished, her breathing had stopped forever. Then the policeman walked Rahim over to the steps of a shop nearby, made him sit down and told him, slowly, quietly, that his wife was gone.

Only then, did the policeman ask if he knew the older lady lying in the road, the woman coughing blood and making odd, disjointed, fractured moans of pain. Rahim looked the copper in the eye and said;

"No, I don't know her, sorry."

\*\*\*\*

## CHAPTER EIGHTEEN: "THE ROAD IS LONG, WITH MANY A WINDING TURN"

The policeman gently ushered Rahim into the passenger seat of the Vauxhall patrol car, took out his notebook and flicked the volume down on his radio a tad. The copper nodded at a SOCO officer who had just arrived, yawning with Christmas road crash fatigue. The SOCO guy nodded back and began the painful process of setting up yellow tape and ushering phone-filming, drunken bystanders well away from the scene, so that he could glean for the wheat and chaff of clues.

Rahim gave his full name and address again and stared ahead down the busy street. Blue lights danced back into his eyes from empty office windows, shadows played in doorways.

"So this lady with the blonde hair, you're sure that you don't know her then sir, not at all?"

"No. I feel sorry for her, but I don't know who she is. Sorry." The words stumbled from Rahim's mouth, with the melancholy, lumpen weight of lies, the hesitancy of deception.

"It's just that the security guard at the Malmaison said you were kissing her, just before the car driven by your wife, crashed into her. I'm just trying to clear that up y'see."

Rahim continued to stare straight ahead. He was closed in on himself, a wooden box forming around his mind, blotting out aspects of the recent past. He pictured his children, their children, and wondered how he would break the news to them.

"My family is all that matters to me now, my children. All their days must be made better somehow. Better than this mess. It is down to me to make amends as best I can. So, I cannot say anything else until I speak to a lawyer, I'm sorry. That's all I will say. Take me home when you're ready, or arrest me...or let me go, I don't care."

The copper could see the exhaustion and grief on Rahim's face and although he knew that he was lying, and had quickly worked out what had been going on that night, reasoned that there was little to be gained by muck-raking through the fine details tonight. It would keep for another time.

"There, for the grace of God, go a few more of us sir. I understand. Stay here a while and I'll get you a cup of tea from somewhere, how's that?"

"Kind of you. Thanks."

\*\*\*\*

The Paramedics slotted a board beneath Angie with the slow, precise skill of a watchmaker setting a balance wheel and hairspring in situ, feeling the every little twitch of tension, gazing at the delicate, fluttering dance of movement that showed a hesitant spark of life.

"OK Angie, we're on our way now, hold that mask close by and take a breath of gas if you need it. We'll soon have you comfortable hun." said the bigger of the two guys, a bearded, gruff-voiced giant called Dave.

They made sure that the fluids line wasn't kinked or pulled free from her scrawped and bloodied arm, as they cajoled her broken body into the back of the ambulance. A dressing absorbed blood seeping from her shattered leg. But the race was on to get her into hospital and fix the jagged, invisible, broken rib, that punctured her lung tissue, filling that beautiful sponge with blood, eating away at its capacity to fill with air and filter it effectively. Angie was slowly drowning and as the ambulance moved off she could feel something terribly wrong happening inside her, now that the adrenaline had dissipated. A dismal, heavy blackness seemed to press inside her chest, numbing her every thought and action. Her leg was now throbbing with an awful, violent cacophony of pain and shredded nerve-endings.

"Rahim. Is he OK?" she whispered. Paramedic Daniel checked the oxygen mask was secure upon her face, held her hand and smiled at her.

"Yes he's fine Angie, he's OK. Just rest for a bit now and we'll soon be there."

They drove over a whacking great pot-hole on Oxford Road and a gobbet of blood erupted from Angie's throat. She felt an awful choking, then spat out another mouthful into the mask, noting its bright, vivid red hue in the strange, bright light that filled the ambulance. Daniel stuck a rubber finger in her throat and cleared her airway, watching the pupils of her eyes enlarge in raw fear and pain. And then she was gone, settling suddenly into unconsciousness, overwhelmed by pain, blood and drugs.

"Get the drain kit, it's there." said Dan tersely at the other, less experienced crew member.

"Is that it, is she dead?" asked other Paramedic, with an eerie lack of interest. Some people are in the wrong job, and you wonder at their true motives.

"Nope, I'm putting a line in her to drain off the blood and keep the lung from collapsing completely. Better she loses a bit of blood for ten mins than drowns in it."

So Dan worked his magic and shoved a needle into Angie's chest cavity, piercing the soft envelope of fluid that surrounds the lungs and then finding the puddle of blood near the bent and cracked ribs. A few drops sputtered out onto the floor before Dave got the line attached properly, but then it flowed smoothly into the bag and he reached over to re-apply the oxygen mask to her face. Angie's eyes were half open, she was on the brink of consciousness and Dave knew she could probably hear what they were saying.

Dan asked the driver how long it was to Wythenshawe A&E and received an estimate. The driver radioed an update on Angie's condition to the triage nurse.

"Ten minutes Angie, that's all. Hang on kidda, hang on."

\*\*\*\*


## WHO NEEDS CHRISTMAS?

The touchdown at Tours was wet, with a scary crosswind that made the wings flutter and dip on the Airbus, like a bird awkwardly skeetering in to land on a choppy winter lake. Kev held Sue's hand as they dropped the final few hundred feet to earth, the wheels whumping into the runway, then the fuselage shuddering as the brakes kicked in. They looked at each other with childlike, excitable smiles as the plane slowed on the apron, and then halted.

"Let the house-hunter see the stable!" joked Sue, as she surveyed the pouring rain outside the window. Kev squeezed her hand tenderly;

"We will find the house of our dreams hun, and if not, well, we'll drink some great wines and have an ace Christmas together."

They gathered their things and traipsed through security, queued up patiently for their luggage, and then went through the tedious rigmarole of the car hire desk. None of the bureaucratic bullshit could dampen their enthusiasm and even after a stodgy meal in a café style restaurant, they were still on a cloud when they arrived at a small hotel in Saumur.

The room was nothing special, with a tiny TV perched in the corner of the ceiling, a slightly lumpy bed and the usual pointless chair blocking easy access to the bathroom. But once they snuggled down, and Kev set his phone alarm for 6.30am, they were as happy as could be. Drifting to sleep, his body folded sweetly behind Sue, one arm caressing her breasts beneath her nightie, Kev felt they were starting something new, the old year was fading away. Vanishing like a distant headache.

****

The next day crept over the horizon, grizzled grey, with stubble clouds promising rain hanging heavy in the sky. Breakfast was the mandatory selection of croissants, with super sweet jams and preserves, hopeless attempts at tea and random slices of cheese.

"Who has cheese for breakfast?" moaned Kev, piling more strawberry jam inside a croissant to create a kind of jammy Cornish pastie, "I miss my Shredded Wheat with honey drizzled on top, magic stuff."

"Try some muesli, it's nice." observed Sue.

"Nah, it's like bedding for hamster cages that stuff, pot pourri with rogue orange peel."

"You do realise if we move here that you'll have to get used to different food. They don't do sausage `n' beans in a can at the Hypermarche y'know."

"Heathens. What's wrong with `em?"

They finished breakfast, took their phones off charge and then threw their anoraks in the back of the hired Clio. Sue fired up the Sat Nav on her phone. It took a while, but eventually a map appeared and a familiar blue dot showing their location. Sue donned her reading specs as she typed in their first destination.

"Right, estimated time is twenty-eight minutes, so plenty to time to get lost as we don't have to meet the agent until nine thirty." noted Sue, using her schoolteacher type voice, as she made sure Kev knew his day was now being ruthlessly organised. He needed organising, most men did.

"OK hun. Let's go."

"Drive on the right."

"I knowww, I know. God's sakes..."

There was a little more carping as they traversed the quiet back lanes and narrow roads leading towards Cholet. Occasionally a Peugeot van would hurtle at them from the gloomy landscape, lights blazing, and then narrowly avoid an impact at the very last second. Kev switched the radio on at one point, but Sue immediately turned it off again without saying a word.

"Ok, slow down, we are nearly here. Yep, go about 500 metres, then take a left. Yes, just here, by these houses. Now go steady it's down this lane about half a mile or so."

There was tension as Kev let the Clio bumble along in third gear at about 25mph, then Sue lit up as she saw the roof tiles through the trees.

"There it is, on the right, here's the gateway Kev. Oooh, look at that! Wow!"

They drove into a mildly pot-holed driveway, past an abandoned milk crate near the broken five bar gate at the front of the place. The remains of a bonfire, stained brown and black by yesterday's rain, sat upon what should have been a beautiful garden at the front of the house. As they parked in the courtyard, Sue could see the size of the old stable on the right. The sales agent's purple Citroen DS3 was slotted to the left of the front door on the main house, which had white shuttered windows, red tiles playing rag-tag on the roof and the air of a faintly drunk, down-at-heel uncle. A curious chicken lurched at Kev as he stepped out of the car, cluck-clucking a mournful greeting.

"This is so wonderful, I love it. It's huge!" said Sue, beaming as she strode to the front door. The sales agent emerged from her car and waved cheerily.

"Yeah, I'll bet the renovation bills will be huge too." mumbled Kev under his breath, then fixing a smile as he shook hands with the prissy, scarf-fondling sales agent lady.

"Bonjour, bonjour, sa va aujourd'hui?"

"Oui, tres bon." replied Sue, then added, "Pardon, nous parlez un petit  Francais, tres mal."

"Oh, it's OK, no problem...we can speak English." soothed the agent, shaking hands with both of them and beckoning at the sky expansively, "You brought the weather with you I think? Well, never mind, it's still a beautiful place, even in winter. Do you know the area, perhaps through friends living locally?"

"No, we just want a place we can settle, ride horses, escape from the hectic world."

"Ah perfect. This place it fits the bill I think, but anyway, come inside and look around and I will answer any questions you have. Welcome."

So they toured the house slowly, breathing in the smell of old wooden block floors, damp carpets and sagging curtains. The light switches were a mish-mash of electrical accessories from the 80s to the late 90s and the kitchen had a wonky, stone-slabbed floor that was as dangerous as it was charming. Spiders viewed them with suspicion from dark corners and the vintage fridge was best dumped in a skip.

On the upside, every ceiling beam, each slightly skewed door frame, oozed character and history. The old cast iron range cooker in the kitchen was an oil-fired, great jewel of a thing, that Sue could visualise glowing, like the embers of a camp fire, as friends gathered around the massive oak table for cheese, biscuits and thick, sticky red wine.

Upstairs, the main bedroom was a lovely size, with views towards the town through the trees. It smelled of polished wood, faded roses and linen sheets washed and folded a thousand times by a busy farmer's wife. There were three other bedrooms and a huge family bathroom, that someone had chucked money at with crazy abandon; roll-top vintage bath, massive two-person shower unit, bidet and loo, all surrounded with pale blue and white patterned tiles. It even had a heated towel rail, silver edged, baroque style mirror too.

"Amazing yes?" enquired the agent, knowing this room was a real plus point. Sue glanced at Kev, who turned on a chrome tap on the wash basin and felt a decent flow of water come spluttering out, clear water too.

"It's very nice." he stalled, not wanting to sound too keen. He wanted to make a low offer if possible, pick a few faults.

They went around the stable block outbuildings with Sue in a kind of daydream, as she pictured her horses and tack in particular spots. She checked the bolts on the doors for strength and ease of movement, she flicked the lights and grimaced when nothing happened. Darkness remained steadfast.

"There is a problem with the electrical wires in `ere." Explained the agent tersely, flicking her scarf over her shoulder, "but this will be solved before the sale, and agreed in writing of course."

Kev put the light app on his phone and peered at the fuse box near the main doorway of the stable block. It all looked like vintage Bakelite stuff from god-knows-when.

"Hmmm, OK then..." he noted, shooting a look at Sue. She shrugged with Gallic aplomb;

"Well, so long as it's working before purchase, that's the main thing."

"Yes, yes, of course, this can be done."

The pair of them wandered around the land near the back of the farm, muddying their shoes and taking phone photos of the views, and the back of the house. There was a good sized patio, all block paved, with a rusty BBQ parked up under a wooden lean-to building. You could see the potential, picture the summer evenings. It was a million miles from the roaring traffic on the gridlocked M62, the grim little semis with doll's house sized bedrooms, and the general hemmed-in feeling of clapped-out northern towns. Here, there was space, great scudding skies of empty space and fields ripe with promise.

A blank canvas for a new life.

****

## NEWS FROM HOME

Sue and Kev viewed another wonderful place, and in truth, it was slightly disappointing to see the third house on their list, because the first two had been so full of space and brimming with endless possibilities. But Kev and Sue persevered, mainly because Sue wouldn't have anything less than a thorough, detailed examination of all the facts when it came to big decisions. She hated Kev's carefree, `oh it'll be alright' attitude. She wanted certainty that things were right, correct.

The last house on this opening day was smaller, but it was the most beautifully modernised one. An English couple had spent a fortune on it, over a ten year stretch and then packed up and gone back to Blighty. The agent told them that it was for `family reasons.' In truth, it was because the husband had been diagnosed with cancer and had but months to live. French policy was to stall on medical care for `foreigners,' no matter what the EU health treaty said, so the couple went back to the NHS, to beg for help after fifteen years of living in France.

But the agent didn't tell buyers stuff like that, it was off-putting; it spoilt the dream.

The living room smelled faintly of pine disinfectant, which Sue thought a bit odd, but she was impressed with the solid oak dining table and matching chairs, plus the heavy dark wooden bookcase.

"All deese items are included in the price by ze way." explained the bored, forty-something, male property agent, waving his arm towards the furniture and the mirror on the wall in the living room. The fireplace was stunning, with a large, brick chimney, plus a railway sleeper support set across its welcoming mouth. Sue let her hand trail along the pleasing, crinkly lines and notches in the wood, feeling its great age, its strength, seep into her bones. She liked that feature.

Just then her phone rang. It was Vera, so she answered it, in case it bad news about her Mum. Of course, it was terrible news, the worst, and so Sue sat down on the wooden floorboards, next to the patio doors, as Vera told her how her mum had just `conked out really, and gone to a better place.'

"I'm so sorry hun, really sorry to hear that, especially at Christmas time too. We will be back for the service of course, just let us know and we can get a flight organised."

"No don't be daft, anyway as it's Christmas it will probably be in the New Year now anyway. But listen Sue, I have some more bad news babe – are you sitting down?"

"Yes, but what is it, what's happened?"

"It's Angie, she's been run over by Rahim's wife, in Manchester after the Christmas party at the Peppermint. She went over to meet him apparently, and his wife was waiting outside when Angie left the hotel about three in the morning."

"Oh dear God, is she alright?"

"She's alive yes, but badly hurt, internal injuries they think. Anyway, I'm going to see her tonight, if they'll let me see her. It's all a terrible to-do really, because Rahim's wife is dead, she drove the car into a wall after hitting Angie. It was featured on the local TV news tonight, Granada Reports were there - I just saw it - but they never mentioned Angie." summarised Vera, who was an expert when it came to relaying big news in staccato bursts.

Kev could see by Sue's expression that something awful had happened and he sat down next to her, draping his arm around her shoulder as Sue's eyes welled with tears. Sue listened as Vera described more details and then told them to stay in France and have a romantic time together. It was an odd thing to say maybe, but just Vera's way of coping with her grief; caring about others took her mind off things, gave her another subject to talk and think about. Life keeps spinning by, no matter how much you want it to stop dead in its tracks sometimes.

The sales agent hovered in the doorway leading to the kitchen, looking glum and confused. Why were these English all so crazy? He asked himself. And why didn't they just go home for Christmas like normal people, after all it was

Christmas Eve tomorrow? Who needs all this property searching at Christmas time? Crazy dreamers.

****

## CHAPTER NINETEEN: CHRISTMAS EVE

I drove over to Lisa's place with my bag of gifts set carefully in the footwell, on the passenger side of my car. I had chosen a 60s style hat for her, something I just bought on impulse because I thought it might put a smile on her face. Then there was the scent, her favourite one, which she had told me to buy. If you don't learn the rules with women over gift buying then it all goes horribly wrong at Christmas, that's my experience – always ask, don't fanny about. Never buy underwear, ever. It basically says, `I fancy a good, hard filthy bonk this Christmas, so please wear this prostitute's outfit.'

The most lovingly wrapped item was a new handbag, again something she'd pointed out two weeks ago on Amazon. But I bought it from John Lewis instead, even though it cost more. Women often to want to return things sometimes after just one evening out, especially if a friend has exactly the same accessory, so always make it easy for them to quietly exchange your expensive gift for something they actually love, or an item which simply outshines whatever their friend is bragging about on Facebook.

Traffic was a nightmare, so I texted her.

**Hi hun, running late as there are queues everywhere. Can't wait to cuddle up with you on that sofa**

**later, I've bought a bottle of Malbec as well, so we can unwind this afternoon. Love ya Miss L, see you soon xxx**

The traffic grunted and grappled forwards slowly. A text came back about ten minutes later.

**OK hun, see you soon. Xx**

That was it, just a curt acknowledgement. Something was wrong, but I couldn't quite put my finger on it. Since the Peppermint party night she'd sounded very different; a bit distant, preoccupied. Maybe it was work, or her family? Christmas was awkward for her, as her ex-husband was due to pop round and see his daughter, exchange gifts, probably bring his new woman along too I guessed. Awkward.

I parked half on the pavement and walked with a festive feeling to her front door. She opened it wearing a dressing gown and slippers, looking whey-faced and tired, without a scrap of make-up on. Her hair was scrunched back in a bobble, but I didn't care, as it was great to see her after a week or so apart.

"I'm full of lurgi, or something. Sorry hun, it's not good at Christmas is it? Typical of me." she excused herself and kissed me on both cheeks.

We chatted in the kitchen for a while and I said hello to Sarah, as she breezed into the kitchen to take her phone off charge, before heading out to meet friends. There was a big night on the lash in Manchester city centre on Sarah's horizon, anticipation glowed upon her skin.

"Have fun you two, behave yourself Mother." she joked, Lisa opened her mouth in mock shock at her;

"We are always good, aren't we Cal, perfectly respectable?"

"People our age don't have love lives Sarah, we get our kicks watching cookery shows on TV or building new sheds."

"Ooh I love a man with a big tool shed, they're so handy." bantered Lisa, as Sarah pulled a face and gathered her things together. There was a beep outside from the taxi driver.

"I'll be back late Mum, I've got a key, don't worry."

"Stay safe love, don't drink too much, please."

Mother and daughter exchanged a look that said they understood each other, and cared enough to always worry. Then they hugged and Sarah was gone, a whirlwind of clacking high heels, blow-waved hair and Rihanna scent, vanishing into the gathering dusk.

I opened the red wine and Lisa settled into her favourite niche on the sofa, the dog lounging at her feet, as she drew up a cushion beneath her ribcage and lolled on the arm of the sofa. I sat back and gazed at her as she flicked through the TV channels.

"Is everything OK, have I done something wrong?" I asked, leaning towards her and holding her hand. It took about a minute of dreadful, aching silence to pass, as she summoned up the courage to look me in the eye. She let go of my hand and sat upright, staring into my eyes.

"Cal, do you want to tell me anything, anything at all?"

I sat there stunned, trying to work out what past misdemeanour I should to confess to committing, but I really didn't know what she was driving at.

"I don't know, do you mean about how my marriage ended, all the arguments, losing the money? I told you all the worst of it, and the internet dating that came after divorce."

"It's just that, well, someone has told me things, shown me a photo in fact...it is difficult to explain. But I can't stop thinking about it, I just can't. It's like there is this *other* you in the past and after all the hours we talked about children and how you couldn't have any with your wife, it's all got to me somehow. That's all."

"What are you talking about? Is this why you've been acting weird lately, not answering texts and speaking so coldly to me?" I was utterly lost in this conversation.

"I'm not cold Cal. Far from it, I love you, which is why I can't believe what I've heard is true. I thought you were a better man."

I was still confused, and getting angry. For the life of me, I really couldn't figure out what she was going on about. It didn't make sense.

"Right, just tell me straight, what is it that this friend says I've done?"

"OK, I'll show you."

She reached across to the shelf under the coffee table and took out her iPad from its folding cover, firing up the device with a strange, schoolteacher-like efficiency. I felt like I was in detention. The screen peppered itself with icons and she opened Facebook, and then went to her emails, logging in as quickly as she could. The silence between us was crushing, an iron lung inside the room. Even Jess the dog picked up on the tension and scuttled away to her bed in the corner.

She showed me a photo of a boy, aged maybe seventeen, or eighteen, dark haired, with dark eyes and high cheekbones. He was grimacing against the late summer sun as he posed for a holiday photo on a beach.

"My friend Diane is best friends with a lady called Beth, who slept with you a long time ago. This is your son, Oliver. I believe you've never met him, never even asked how he was doing. Is that true Cal? Is he your son?"

I stared into the photo and felt the world stop, take a breath upon its axis, and then press an unholy weight against my chest.

"This cannot be...this cannot be real."

\*\*\*\*

## QUIET NIGHT IN AT TREV AND PENNY'S

The unmistakeable smell of burning cakes emanated from Penny's kitchen, wafting through the house, until Trev finally became aware of it, as the acrid scent penetrated his pleasantly alcohol-induced stupor. Penny was in the summer house, chatting merrily with her two grown up children, Dan and Joanna. They were reliving the spirit of Christmas past and full of news about life after Uni, boyfriend troubles, girlfriend shenanigans, new jobs and wonky old banger cars.

Trev sluggishly leapt into action and headed out of the lounge at a reasonably brisk pace, to try and salvage the less singed cakes. However, his sudden burst of speed upset the cat, which neatly jumped for cover into the Christmas tree, pulling several baubles, plus a few lights down, as the animal battled with fake green branches which refused to offer any real purchase, even for a master mountaineer.

"Oh for fuck's sake Romeo!" exclaimed Trev, as his sock-clad foot stepped on a bauble, crushed it like a large duck egg and sent a painful splinter into the arch of his foot. He hopped onwards, swearing profusely, and then opened the oven door, grabbing a tea towel to help eject the cake tray as quickly as possible. The heat still managed to burn one finger and he yelped in pain again as he dropped the lot onto the floor.

Once again, the cat showed its cowardly yellow streak in the face of a domestic crisis and jumped on top of the kitchen work surface, sending a half consumed bottle of Jacob's Creek completely horizontal. The remaining contents glugged onto the floor and Trev stepped into the mess, mixing blood, wine and cakes, in his own personal pagan sacrifice to the winter solstice.

"Fuck, fuck, fuckity-fuck! Owwww!"

Penny came scampering in, hearing the almighty racket and surveyed the scene with a resigned air. She instructed Trev to get his finger under the cold tap and then eased off his sock to inspect the foot wound. Her son Dan almost pissed his skinny jeans laughing at the scene, as the cat greedily licked up wine-flavoured bits of fairy cakes.

"You two are the nuttiest people that I know. I knew I could count on you both for Christmas entertainment. Brilliant stuff."

"Yes well thanks for helping Dan." observed Trev, who was in quite a bit of pain now. Penny made an `oohhhh' noise as she took a close look at Trev's pierced flesh.

"Hmmm, Trev there's a bit of it in there still. Hang on, I'll get a sewing needle and dig it out."

"Whoa, wait a minute." protested Trev, hop-skipping across the kitchen floor and settling onto a high chair near the breakfast bar. He wasn't keen on having a minor operation performed, unless more drink was consumed by way of liquid painkiller.

"It's got to come out hun, and you can't go to A&E on Christmas Eve – you'd still be waiting on a trolley on Boxing Day. Just relax and I'll operate on it, here have a drink of whisky." Penny poured him a double helping of Bells, spilling a bit.

"Penny baby, come on, you're a bit pissed to be doing this. I mean we've both been drinking since lunchtime. Let's stick a plaster on it. See how it feels tomorrow."

Dan poured himself a large whisky and dropped in two ice cubes from the bucket, smiling broadly.

"I'll do it Trev, this is only my second drink and I've got A level biology, so I should miss all your tendons OK mate." He said with a twist of sarcasm.

"Dan, the day I trust you to deal with wounds is the day hell freezes over. Remember the poorly hamster incident?"

"Oh fuck off, I was ten years old, you pisshead old wanker!" spat Dan, who had never taken to Trev as his step-dad in over a decade.

"No stop it please, it's Christmas." begged Penny, cleaning Trev's foot with a sterile dressing from the first aid kit. But Trev's usual laidback insouciance was distorted by the twin peaks of pain that collided inside his nervous system. Adrenaline flowed within.

"Dan, I may well be an old pisshead, but I'm happily retired, on a decent pension, with a second home in Spain and I own half this house. Whereas you are a 2:2 graduate working in a call centre on fuck all wages, living in a slum flat and playing X-Box games half the night. You've done nothing and been nothing, so shut the fuck up and stop drinking my whisky."

"Fine, fuck you tosser. Mum I'm sorry, I'm going home."

Dan downed the whisky, grabbed his coat from the hallway and drove off into the night, despite Penny tearfully begging him not to. Penny then burst into tears in the living room. Joanna mopped the floor and squidged the winey-cakey residue into the bucket, shooting a mournful glare upwards at both of the grown-ups.

"Well, that went really well didn't it? Merry Crimbo everyone."

\*\*\*\*

Vera had to admit that Jim had one of the most comfortable recliner chairs in Christendom. It moved, no glided, on the touch of a button and had deep folds of heavy brown leather, nicely worn in over the last three or four years. Vera raised a glass and glanced at Jim, who was engrossed in watching a comedy quiz show.

"To absent friends, cheers."

"Aye, I'll drink to that. Mum and Dad both gone sis, it's us up next now. Makes you think eh? Where do all the years go to, they seem to fly away like birds?"

"I know, but the way I feel now I wouldn't mind being next in the queue to go upstairs, I really wouldn't." said Vera sadly, but with a determined smile on her face.

Jim looked at her and pondered for a moment, swilling his beer in his glass thoughtfully.

"It's no use thinking like that though is it? Mum would say `make the best of it, don't do anything daft."

Vera settled back in her chair and chuckled as a comedian did a half decent impression of Boris Johnson crashing Santa's sleigh and humping a chimney.

"No I don't mean top meself. Just that, well, I can accept whatever happens now, do you know what I mean? I feel she's at peace, bless her."

They both missed Mum, and let her image flash across their memories for a few seconds.

"She is, you're right sis." shrugged Jim, taking another sip.

"I usually am Jim, happy Christmas hun, all the best."

"Aye, all the best."

They both drank themselves to sleep, Jim blowing off wind occasionally and Vera snoring like a trooper on a very dull, but cosy, guard duty. They were as happy as they could be under the circumstances and alcohol was a useful, necessary salve for their wounds. Sometimes, just a few precious hours of oblivion, and a chance to forget everything, is a sweeter saviour than any God can muster.

****

### HERE'S TO THE FUTURE

Bendy Wendy dropped her shopping bags in the hallway, shook the last raindrops from her brolly and then locked the front door. She felt the heat fill the house and sighed with pleasure as she took off her coat, kicked away her shoes and dumped her food shopping in the kitchen. Wendy stowed away the milk, bread, frozen veg and some wine in the fridge. Then she grabbed the rest of her purchases and took them upstairs. The carpet folded around her toes as she walked, taking little twinges of tiredness away from her.

She tipped out the jewellery from the bags. Two 18 carat gold bracelets, quite heavy, without any stones in them, gleamed in the light. Wendy didn't want gemstones in them, they were never worth bugger all when you tried to sell the items, it was the gold that counted. The sheer weight, the purity of the metal, was the value to her. Not any notion of beauty, or design.

She unpacked the Cartier watch she'd bought from the Trafford Centre and looked closely at it. It did sparkle with diamonds set around its square cut bezel, and a beautiful white gold bracelet strap added a finishing touch. It was worth the money, it looked utterly stunning on her wrist.

"Not for today though, too nice to wear." she said to herself, carefully placing the watch back inside its luxurious box and slipping that inside its outer packaging once again. She walked over to the corner of the room, pulled open her wardrobe door and leaned down to unlock the safe. It took a moment to recall the combination, but then she was inside, squeezing the Cartier watch in against a Rolex box and a brown envelope stuffed with gold sovereigns, rings and bracelets. She sat on the carpet for a while, taking the envelope off the shelf, then counting out her gold, slowly, methodically, listing her assets, the fruits of her labours.

The last few months of swingers parties, plus entertaining Mr Dooley's VIP friends had gone spectacularly well, but Wendy knew better than pay in large amounts of cash at the bank. Those days were gone now, the banks would snitch on you to HMRC the moment you finished getting the paying-in slip stamped. But gold, well, gold was liquid, untraceable, and something that the Taxman couldn't touch.

Even if you lived on benefits, they didn't count your jewellery as an asset, like a caravan in France, or twenty five grand in the bank. Wendy knew that there would always be a way to turn gold into cash in the future, for two important reasons; Jews and Muslims. No UK government would ever upset those minorities by banning their traditional trade in gold. Gold would always be an alternative currency, a back-up plan, a safety net. Better that she hid her cash in watches, handbags and gold, than left a breadcrumb trail of guilty numbers in bank accounts.

The gold warmed her inside; it illuminated a brighter, more certain future for Wendy. The day would come when she wouldn't be beholden to anyone, she would be rich, independent and free from all the dirty, pawing men. She couldn't wait.

Her phone pinged a text message. It was Mr Dooley.

**Thanks a million for everything, you have a good Xmas and see you for the New Year do. Take care x**

Yes, the New Year's Eve party would be the end of many things, thought Wendy. There had to be a better way to make money, a safer way. Many of Dooley's friends liked to talk too much at her parties. One idiot even tried to take phone photos. People who talked too freely about what was going on in their sex lives were dangerous, unpredictable, and volatile. Wendy liked order, discretion.

She placed the two new 18 carat bracelets on her wrist and admired them in the wardrobe mirror. She smiled back at herself.

"Merry Christmas Wendy."

Then she got changed, went downstairs, made some food and ate alone. She slept alone and spent the whole of

Christmas Day on her own watching TV and pottering around the garden. To her, Christmas was just another day. No more, no less.

\*\*\*\*

## CHAPTER TWENTY: "IN THE MIDNIGHT HOUR"

Rahim's father looked his son straight in the eye and raised a glass.

"I won't wish you merry Christmas of course, that's all bullshit anyway, but I hope next year brings you peace, and peace for your children in some way. All we can do is help them now they have lost their mother. There are hard days ahead, for all of you.

Rahim felt his face flush red with shame. He felt like a schoolboy again, being chided by his father for another failed exam, another mess up in his life.

"Dad I'm sorry I ever got mixed up with that woman, I thought it would just be a fling, you know. Over in a few months."

Rahim's father shrugged and leaned back in his chair.

"You must not blame yourself too much. Maryam was killed by her own anger, she should have accepted that these things happen. Men stray and wives forgive, eventually. It's the way of things and it has been like that forever."

"I suppose so. Thanks Dad."

"You know we are family, so there's no debate, no judgement by me. All I ever wanted to do was help you Rahim." the older man hesitated for a second, then added;

"You would've made a better lawyer than a jeweller I think, if you'd stuck at it and passed your exams when you were younger. Ah well, you could never resist the ladies, and they could rarely resist you."

"It's all a mess, all my fault. I have wrecked my life with this, haven't I? It was on the TV news, for God's sake."

Rahim began to let tears fall from his face and crumpled up inside. His body shook with grief and shame. He was glad that his children were spending Christmas with their grandmother and not here, in this house, surrounded by reminders of Maryam. Her shoes still lay scattered in the hall; she smiled down from photographs on the kitchen noticeboard, and the scent of her lingered on the towel in the bathroom. Her side of the bed still smelled of her and a stray hair or two was draped on her pillow. All this would have to go, be tidied away very soon, if only for the sake of their children.

Rahim's dad placed his arm around his son's shoulder and squeezed him hard.

"Come on, you have to be strong now. Good times or bad, nothing lasts forever."

Rahim's dad stood up and went over to the bookcase. He opened the doors on the cupboard part beneath the shelves and took out the chess set that he had passed onto Rahim some ten years previously. Then he patiently set up the board and pieces as Rahim dabbed his eyes and pulled himself together.

"OK, the game of all games, the game of life. Let us see if you can beat an old man eh? What d'you say, will you try?"

"Yes, I think I can win." smiled Rahim at his dad, who winked back at him.

"Well if you try your best that's good enough for me."

****

## FRIENDS WHEN YOU NEED THEM

"Sorry, are you a relative?" asked the hugely obese woman manning the hospital reception. Gary paused for a second before blurting out,

"Yes, I'm her son."

"Right, OK then." drawled the woman, pushing aside a bag of Haribo as she typed furiously onto the keyboard. "What name is it please?"

Gary gave his middle name and Angie's surname and then explained that he'd been away at Uni, which is why he'd only got the chance to visit now. The woman softened a bit when she saw Gary's `get well soon' card that he was clutching. He also seemed to have the remains of a nasty bruise on his cheekbone, which pulled at the receptionist's softer side.

"It's well out of visiting hours, but as it's Christmas Eve, I'll let you see your mum for a while. She's probably sleeping. Take a seat there and I'll get someone to take you to her ward."

Gary waited for about twenty minutes, which seemed like hours. People shuffled past. Nurses and trainees wandered past, all wearing different ill-fitting uniforms, a random maintenance bloke asking for directions and a steady stream of confused and upset relatives. Nobody seemed to know what was going on and there was absolutely no sense of urgency. Then a porter appeared and the KFC loyalty card holder on reception pointed towards Gary.

"Alright son, just follow me, this place is like a rabbit warren. What's your mum in for?"

"Car crash, pretty bad really."

"Oh right, well she's in the best place, they'll look after her." reassured the older guy, who knew what to say to people to calm any nerves.

They went into a huge lift, which was big enough to take a small car. In fact a car could have done a three point turn inside the lift. There was a semi-silence in the lift, as the porter attempted to half-whistle a cheery scrap of a pop song. They emerged three floors up and walked briskly down a corridor that smelled like toilet cleaning liquid. An old man shouted `Nurse!' as they walked past the doorway to a ward. The porter ignored it.

After a left turn and another long walk, they reached a small reception desk and Gary had to check in once again.

Another beefy woman, this one munching on cheese `n' onion crisps as she typed in details, ticked all the boxes and then showed him into the little side ward where Angie lay.

The lighting was low, but she looked gaunt and pale, her sleepy face stretched by bruising from the impact. A drip fed into her arm and a wire was attached to a gadget that was clipped to her finger. She lay at a slight angle, to take pressure off the wound where they'd been in to mend her smashed ribcage. Her left leg was set inside a plaster cast and it looked a mess of bruised and torn flesh, struggling to cling back onto pinned bones. Gary could see under the hospital gown that she was wearing big paper knickers.

He felt embarrassed and shocked. Angie looked so old, so frail, before his eyes. From some angles, it didn't even look like her. The car had altered the shape of her body somehow, when it spun her around and then thumped her onto the pavement with its solid fury. He placed his card on the bedside cabinet and rested his hand on hers.

She didn't respond. The drugs held her in a beautiful stupor.

"Angie, it's me Gary. I just wanted to see you and tell you to get better. Keep fighting it. One day you'll be back on that dancefloor. Yeah, you'll be back there with all your friends."

Even as the words left his mouth Gary didn't believe it. He knew things had changed forever and he never wanted to go back to the Peppermint. Not after this, all this pain.

Angie barely moved, her breathing was regular and she seemed completely out of it all. Gary leaned down, kissed her on the forehead, as gently as he could, and then nodded to the receptionist as he left the ward. He trudged slowly along the same corridors and the same old man was still shouting for the nurse as he passed by. There was nothing he could do, nothing at all, so Gary kept his head down as he walked.

When he got back to the main reception, Gary mouthed a quick `cheers' to the gatekeeper lady, but oddly enough, she simply stared back at him. It was a long, hard, examining look, as if Gary was carrying some secret contraband, like Thorntons chocolates, pie `n' chips, or a bucket of tasty chicken wings. Gary shrugged and walked out of the front door.

He had only taken about ten steps when a thin woman, with a thin, hard-set, top lip on her face and very piercing eyes approached him. A bulky guy, aged about 45 years old and carrying three cameras, also lunged out of the darkness. The photographer pressed the shutter and a burst of brilliant light erupted as nearly 20 photos were etched on the memory card. The thin-lipped woman shoved a smartphone at Gary's face as she stepped in front of him, blocking his path away from the sickly glare of the hospital entrance.

"Hi Gary, I'm Emma Holland from *Fast News Agency*. Can I ask you how Angie is doing and any thoughts for Maryam's family at Christmas time?"

"What the fuck? No, no comment." said Gary, ducking his head down instinctively, but the journos were not so easily dissuaded and she walked closely alongside as the snapper grabbed more shots of Gary's bruised face.

"Did Angie say anything, is she sorry that her affair with Rahim has cost someone's life?

"Piss off." Gary quickened his pace as the journo loped alongside him, firing more questions at his shocked features.

"Charming. You think it's OK to swear at us when a woman has died do you? Listen, we're running a story on the whole love triangle Gary, can you confirm or deny that you and Angie once did it on a sun lounger in her back garden, in full view of the neighbours?"

"No we didn't, we just fell asleep."

"Well her neighbours are saying different, that's the thing, I mean they told us that they saw you two going at it one night, is that right? We just want to give you the chance to put the record straight."

"Angie is a great woman, leave her alone, leave me the fuck alone too."

"Appreciate you're upset. Is it also a lie that she paid you to do gardening work just wearing your pants?"

Gary stood still for a moment, and let anger rise inside his throat. He hated the way she was degrading everything into some sort of cheap sex game.

"Look, there was one time in summer I did some work in my swimming shorts. It was boiling hot that day. I don't even know why I'm talking to you, just fuck off will you?"

Emma stayed calm and glanced at the snapper, who moved in a bit closer and then changed cameras to one with a wide angle lens. Hopefully Gary would lose it completely and they'd have a photo that would be a page lead story in the tabloids on Boxing Day.

"That was the hot day when Angie rubbed sunscreen on you, and then later on you bonked on the lounger then? That's what the neighbour is telling us and to be fair, we will run with it, unless you say he's a liar. Your call mate."

"That's it. Bye."

Gary pulled his hood over his head and began to jog away across the car park. The photographer took one last set of pics and then checked his playback screen.

"Some winners here: He looks sad, angry, shocked, miserable as Morrissey at a meat pie party. Lots of emotions. Good stuff." noted the photo guy, scratching thoughtfully at his stubbly, jowly cheeks. Emma plugged in an ear bud and listened to her interview with Gary, smiling at the stress in his voice.

"Right, I'll phone a piece through and email the audio clip. No denial on the sun lounger shag – brilliant. See what we get for it all in syndication. Tell you what, it's a proper bonkfest at that nightclub y'know, we should go back on New Year's Eve and get more background – this story's got legs."

****

## GHOSTS OF CHRISTMAS PAST

Lisa sat maybe two feet away from me, but she might as well have been a hundred miles distant. Her voice, her posture, the look in her eyes, had all changed irrevocably. Emotion ebbed and flowed between us.

"Can I see the email from Beth please?"

I thought the least she could do was show me what I was being accused of, from seventeen years ago, but Lisa wanted to keep me out on a limb for a bit longer.

"Cal, you think back over the years and you tell me what really happened, that's the best thing. So go on, when did you meet her?"

The TV was still on, with the volume turned down low, as she interrogated me slowly, methodically, picking apart the sorry jigsaw pieces of my past. It was almost surreal, watching a Christmas carol service being broadcast, with people making those `I'm so holier-than-thou' faces to the camera, as I tried to recall the night I'd slept with Beth.

"I went to one of those corporate Christmas nights out; big marquee, circus performers, disco and three course meal. She was on a table nearby with some work people. She just kept staring at me and later on we danced a bit. I got stupidly drunk and lost my jacket later on. Anyway, my room key was in the jacket and she said I could sleep on the floor of her hotel room. You can guess the rest."

Lisa pulled a face which said `yes, and then what happened?' She didn't need to say anything. I folded my arms as I carried on.

"Next day I tried to forget about it all really. She texted me a few times over that week, but I blocked her number, because it was…well, full on. She wanted more."

"But you couldn't do that, as you were happily married? That's what you told me when we first met Cal; that you didn't cheat on your wife and like an idiot, I believed you. More *fool* me." she accentuated the word `fool' with cobra-like venom. I felt small, insignificant and ashamed of my lying.

Lisa re-arranged the cushion and sat up straight, looked directly at me.

"So that was it, you never heard from her again?"

"Well yes. No doubt she's told you." I took a deep breath and confessed the final, broken fragments of the whole sordid story. There was no way out of it now, it made no difference, I knew we were finished.

"She came to my office months later, met me after work in the car park. Told me she was pregnant. I didn't believe her at first because I was certain that I couldn't come, I actually passed out at one point while I was on top of her, just stupidly drunk. But in any case, she said that she didn't want a child, because she had her career to think about and anyway, we were never going to live together, or get married. So I paid her to have a termination."

"Really? Beth tells it a bit differently. Says you told her to do whatever she wanted and then when she sent photos of scans you just blocked her emails."

Lisa spoke so calmly, so matter-of-fact. Like this discussion was just a routine diagnosis of someone's fatty arteries.

"No, that's not how it was. I paid her, hundreds of pounds...in cash too. Yes it was cash. I never heard from her again after that, so I assumed she'd had the termination. "

"But you never paid any maintenance?"

"Well, I had no idea there was a child! She never approached me about it, never asked for money, any help, nothing. I need to speak to her about this. If she's saying that I walked away from my own son then she's lying, because I'm not like that. This isn't fair. She's using you to fire her bullets, her bitterness at me." I could hear myself almost shouting, feel the raw heat infuse my face. Lisa leaned forward and put her head in her hands.

"Well, I don't know what to believe, or who. But I have to tell you that I met her son and he really, really looks like you. To me, he looks yours, but who's to know?"

"You met him? When?"

Lisa shifted uneasily in her corner of the sofa,

"A few nights ago, at house party. He was there briefly with his mum and then went out. Beth had told me some stuff, but seeing him made it more real and to be honest, it truly shocked me. Out of the blue, I discovered that there was this secret part of your life and then I started to think that you would need to sort things out, maybe see this Beth woman again..? I don't know, I can't explain how mixed up it made me feel. It's a mess though isn't it Cal?"

I had to agree, it was. There was nothing I could do about it over Christmas really, except think about things. Lisa told me she wanted me to go and although she hugged me, there was a strange lightness about her body now, as if it were separate from me, untouchable somehow.

"Can we still talk at least?" I asked, wrapping my coat around my shoulders in the hallway. She looked at the carpet and then gave me a fake smile.

"Let's leave things until after Christmas, probably best. Speak to Beth, speak to your son too. Take some time Cal."

It felt like she was issuing me with a redundancy package; all that was missing was a P45 and a contract forbidding me to work for rival companies in the same sector for 12 months. I didn't know how to deal with all the feelings whirl-pooling around inside me. The Christmas lights around the doorway glimmered and dazzled as I said goodbye to her, waving as I walked down the pathway. I really didn't know if I would ever see her again. She folded her arms across her chest and looked at me as if I were a stranger. The air felt icy cold as I drew it deep into my lungs and the car door creaked with an early evening, breathless gasp of frost, as I slumped into the driver's seat.

I drove a short distance, turned left into a suburban street and parked the car. The interior light faded into darkness and then I cried. Let the sobs erupt from my very being. All that time I was married, all those years of trying for a baby with my wife and the bitter arguments when the fertility treatment didn't work, went on whilst this boy grew up, just a few miles from where I lived. He had measles jabs, went to school with new shoes, read stories, built things from Lego. Fell off his bike. Collected football programmes, or started playing the guitar just after his 13th birthday maybe.

All those moments had been and gone, they were lost to me.

My own stupid fault.

****

## CHAPTER TWENTY ONE: "BACK TO BLACK"

Christmas Day isn't the same when you're all grown up.

Yes, there are gifts, cards, the family gathering round like jackals feasting on an unexpected cargo plane load of food and drink, but it doesn't have the magic, the anticipation, or generate the powerful memories that it once etched into the landscape of your soul. Boxing Day is even worse. It's like an endless beating for your gastric system, already bloated and begging for mercy. Plus, adults don't have lots of new toys to break on Boxing Day, just a paltry stash of gift cards.

For two days, I waited patiently, hoping Beth would reply to my text messages and arrange a meeting, so we could talk about what had happened years ago. I didn't really know what else to do and the questions milled and grinded away in my head. Why hadn't she contacted me in all these years, why drop this bombshell now? Women would always remain an impenetrable mystery to me.

Instead I listened to my family's news, drank their free wine and beer and watched crap TV. All the time thinking back nearly two decades, wondering what if I'd known back then, what would I have done, really? Left my wife? No. But maybe she would have left me.

The sliding doors closed up again in my mind. The possibilities were all fantasy, all imaginary in any case. I drank another glass of Malbec, dampening down the embers of yesterday.

****

## THE LONG HOUR THAT LENGTHENS THE DAY

The funeral of a young mother is never anything less than grim, unfinished pain. A guilt that could not be assuaged, by any number of bear hugs and kind words, draped like a mantle over Rahim's shoulders. There were hard stares and tight-lipped condolences from Maryam's family, and then the sudden shock of a spit upon the ground from her cousin, which almost rent the earth at the graveside. People stood stock still for a split second, expecting the worst, but it didn't come. Wiser heads prevailed and there was no punching, or vengeful wailing, that would salt the wounds of Maryam's children. Instead they looked blankly at the tableaux that unravelled before them, not quite believing that the small box contained their mother, until it was gently lowered, with murmured prayers and tears, into the frost-tipped,  roughly hewn cavern of soil.

Everyone said that she had gone and in truth, Maryam's children didn't believe it. She would appear from behind a tree perhaps, or be waiting for them at home, saying it was all a terrible joke. Cooking for them again, walking them to the school gates, watching over them. That was what they felt, she was watching them all, from somewhere secret, somewhere safe.

Just then, the children noticed a woman standing next to a headstone about 100 metres away. It wasn't their mum, they didn't know who it was. Puzzled, Rahim's son pulled at his Dad's hand and pointed at the woman. Rahim recognised the journalist at once, as she had been hanging around the family home early in the morning, and cursed silently. Then he whispered to his brother to `go and deal with that bitch.'

But as Rahim's brother and two of his male friends strode over, zig-zagging between the headstones, a car began moving and a photographer started to take pictures of them. A fat-faced man with a beard leaned from the window and warned them that they were in a public place and being filmed, so don't do anything stupid.

"Hi," said Emma cheerily, as the men approached her, "we are running a full story tomorrow on Angie seeing both Gary and Rahim – any thoughts on that, is it shameful for your family?"

"You're fucking shameful, fuck off out of here!" shouted Rahim's brother, setting his face in stone as he squared up to the reporter. She was unflinching, this was everyday stuff for her and nobody had a knife or a gun, so it wasn't scary.

"Just doing my job. How about you, do you feel Rahim let your family down seeing a white woman, an older woman, and your sister-in-law has paid with her life?"

Rahim's brother and his friends began to swear, and then shove at Emma, with her photographer jumping out of the car to help her as she tumbled to the solid, unforgiving ground. Rahim's brother held him whilst he vented his anger with the journalist, raging words above her head, then taking his shoe off and whacking her about the head and face. The photographer ushered her away, as a small crowd began to gather – they both knew when to call it quits. The Police were never any help, and so a rapid retreat was the only option sometimes.

"Recorded all his ranting on the phone, plenty of anger there, apparently Maryam's family are blanking Rahim completely, one even spat at him during the funeral." Emma gasped, glancing back at the pursuing pack of mourners.

"Yep," said the snapper, checking his camera playback screen, "I got the shot, no problem."

Job done. If it bleeds, it leads.

****

## NEW BEGINNINGS

Kev and Sue looked at each other across the table, lifting their gaze above their menus and smiling from the corners of their eyes. The deed had been done, the email had been sent and paperwork would be signed next week, at the start of a new year. It was exhilarating.

"Are you sure we're doing the right thing?" asked Sue, letting her menu drop down and reaching over to touch Kev's arm.

"Yes, definitely. I don't want to be flogging my guts changing tyres when I'm sixty-five, chasing up unpaid bills, being mithered by the VAT man. I'd rather be drinking wine and fixing up an old Mobylette instead."

"A what? What's a Mobylette?" quizzed Sue, looking utterly bemused. Kev did a bizarre mime of a man twisting a throttle and pedalling at the same time.

"You know, a Mobylette moped, one that you pedal to get started...makes a noise like a wasp farting in a bean can."

"Good grief. It sounds like a sanitary pad. Mobylette. Ridiculous." Sue shook her head in disbelief at the name, and then went back to studying the menu. Kev could sense her doubts and after another few moments, he offered reassurance;

"Everything will be alright babe. It's the right move for us, and we're getting a top price for the business, well, the land really." soothed Kev, before moving his eyes down the menu and then trying to try and guess why `pasties' were listed under drinks, not mains. Then he realised it was spelled `pastis.'

They talked about the future as they ate and drank, feeling the red wine infuse their hearts with optimism and hope. Kev's steak was excellent too, with a beautiful sauce. He decided that this was the life for them both; less stress, more time together, more horse riding for Sue and the chance for her to branch out and start her own little business venture offering lessons. Summers would be golden, with long lunches in the heat of the day and warm evenings out on the patio. They talked and talked, dreaming of how life would be so different here. So good.

Later on, tucked up in bed, Sue rubbed her hand across Kev's bare chest, and then let it slide down towards his package. She felt it gradually firm up, uncoil a little bit, beneath the stretchy material of his pants. With an expert touch, she pulled the elasticated waistband down and cupped his balls, rolling them this way and that, just the way he liked it. Then she let her finger and thumb meet around his swelling hardness, slide gently up and down, getting him ready.

Sue wriggled her legs free of the quilt, reached under her nightie and peeled away her knickers in a quick scoop of her hands. She kissed him and pulled his willy close to the lips between her legs, letting him feel the wetness within her. Stir her gently.

"Go on, bend me over and give it to me. Fill me up."

"I will, don't worry, I will."

It only took seconds. But they were great seconds.

****

## LORD WON'T YOU BUY ME A MERCEDES BENZ?

Bendy Wendy heard her phone ping again and read the message before it vanished from the home screen. It was Big Phil, wondering if he could come round again over the Christmas holidays and have a sub-dom session; spanking paddle, bum beads...the works.

"Jesus Christ, will I ever get a day off from these horny old gits?" muttered Wendy to herself, and then adding; "whoever invented Viagra has a lot to answer for, these blokes should be potting plants in sheds, not potting their bollocks into every fanny they can find."

But it was work. Lucrative work as it went, so Wendy took out her old school A5 sized diary from the kitchen drawer and looked at what else she had lined up, between now and New Year's Eve. Dooley's soiree, for special invited guests only, was the real money-spinner of the year for her; £1000 per head, which including catering, condoms, `mature' escort girls pretending to be housewives, plus a few packs of the chewy blue gel which older men found beat Wrigleys Spearmint any night of the week.

Wendy put some Calvin Harris on her iPod, placed the device on the big speaker and began some basic yoga stretches. She needed time to think and her body needed to tone up after a few days of lazing around, watching too many movies and eating chocolate. She lay down on the floor and lifted her buttocks off the rug in time to the music, opening her legs wider gradually, feeling bones click as she gently pushed everything to its limit. She took off the small cardigan and let her body relax for a moment in the black leggings and plain blue t-shirt she had on for a `do nothing' kind of day.

It was at the precise point when she closed her eyes that the postman walked past her living room window and glanced in. Thinking she might have fallen, or worse, he paused, and then tapped on the window. She opened her eyes in a start, and then smiled and waved at him. He mouthed; `Everything OK luv?' at her and she got up, to answer the door to him.

He had a small bundle of letters for her, mostly junk but also a bank statement.

"I'm fine, just doing a bit of yoga. Keeping fit."

The postie looked her up and down, noting that her nipples were erect under the t-shirt and she had no bra on.

"Seems to be working out well luv, merry Christmas by the way, did Santa bring you what you wanted?"

Wendy smiled and hesitated for a second before replying;

"Yes, but it's like lots of things in life isn't it? You have to be careful what you wish for. Have a great New Year."

"OK luv, you too." said the perplexed postal operative, before shrugging and strolling briskly away towards next door. He could never fathom these hoity-toity wealthy types in their big houses. What was so godawful about living in a detached house on a quiet estate, where kids didn't murder your cat for fun during the school holidays? Arseholes.

****

## HOMEWARD BOUND

It was almost breakfast time, you could smell the coffee filtering its way upstairs, beneath the door and tickling the nostrils of Sue and Kev as they lay entwined. Sue was in the midst of a strange dream where she was being pushed on a swing, whilst wearing a huge Victorian dress and petticoats. She was next to a big house and swinging over dark, black water, watching people swimming in it.

She awoke, feeling the need to go to the loo press into her abdomen, whilst Kev's erection nudged at her bum cheeks.

"Morning m'sieu." she joked, he grunted something unintelligible back and then his phone pinged a message alert. He read it as Sue headed for the shower.

It was Dooley, letting him know that the agreement had been looked over by their solicitor and things should start moving quickly in the New Year. Kev smiled, leaned back on his pillow, as Sue hummed a bit of Adele in the shower. Life was definitely on the up, he thought, and began googling `best bridging loan deals' as he wanted to give Sue a New Year's Day to remember. He also texted Dave, his right-hand man at the tyre shop;

**Have another day off mate, there's not gonna be much happening as regards trade, so I'll open up tomorrow when we're back. Merry crimbo and ta for looking after the place.**

There wasn't much point in drumming up new business and fretting over bills now. Things were changing fast.

\*\*\*\*

## CHAPTER TWENTY TWO: "ALL WHO LOVE ARE BLIND"

It had been a quiet, claustrophobic Christmas for Vera, draped in a mix of grief, bittersweet memories and the deluge of well-meant messages, cards and flowers from friends and family. People wanted to offer help, but when it came down to it, you always felt utterly bereft, orphaned and alone, without the anchor of knowing a parent was just there, sat next to you, or at the end of a phone line.

Vera got tipsy on Boxing Day evening and actually phoned her Mum's mobile, just to hear the rambling, hypnotic ansaphone message that Mum had recorded some three years previously.

"Hiya, this is Joan speaking. I'm not able to take your call right now, most likely I'm out somewhere like the shops or hospital. Not for long I expect. Anyway, leave a short message and I will try to get back to you soon as. Thank you."

It was the soft lilt of that final `thank you,' the sheer old fashioned politeness of it, which reached into Vera and brought the tears welling and charging to the edges of her eyelids.

So the day after Boxing Day Vera had put some slap on her face, selected a bright red dress from her wardrobe and put on her sparkly `Dorothy' red shoes to match. Very Christmassy, she mused, feeling a ripple of happiness lighten her mood as she added finishing touches and texted Trish, who was meeting Vera for a pub lunch.

**I'm dying to meet this new fella of yours hun, so glad that you've met someone at last. You sound so happy, it's great Trish, really pleased for you. x**

**I am head over heels with Laurence, not sure if that's good or bad thing, but going with my feelings. Will be good to see you later, need a lift? x**

Vera could use a lift, but she thought better about playing gooseberry on the way home with Trish and Laurence and decided to drive instead. On the way she stopped for petrol and as she waited for the grunting, ignorant, man-child behind the counter to serve two people in front of her, she noticed a magazine cover headline on the rack.

`Tragic Mum Dies Trying to Mow Down Cheating Love Rival'

The story was fairly eye-catching of course, but what was shockingly familiar was the photo of Angie, inset next to a crumpled Volvo car. The pic looked like it had been taken from her Facebook feed and showed Angie smiling, glammed up at the Peppermint, drink in hand, jewellery glinting in the camera flash. Vera bought the magazine and skimmed her eyes over the story, which was a double page spread.

Phrases like `Lady Chatterley Bonks With Young Stud Gardener,' and `Devastated Family Split Apart By Affair' sprang out of the pages at her. There was Rahim, looking ashamed at the funeral of his wife, his in-laws yelling at him. Two more photos of Angie portrayed her as a kind of Barbara-Windsor-meets-Joan-Collins, man-eating character, all big cleavage, blonde hair and sexy pout. The feature had a photo of Gorgeous Gary as well, looking tired, and basically very guilty about something, as he left the hospital after visiting Angie. The story made him out to be a rent boy;

`Handyman Gary refused to comment as he left hospital, after giving his best to the lover who is old enough to be his mum. The odd couple met at a notorious `swingers' club near Manchester.'

Vera walked back to her car in a daze. Then she phoned Trish as she drove to the Bricklayers Arms.

"Trish it's me. I've just picked up a copy of that *Real Life – Shameless Special* magazine and Angie is all over it, on the cover and everything, poor woman. They're crucifying her."

"Really? Oh my word, that's awful. Do you think she's seen it?" said Trish, her voice slowing down as she sat down on the bed to take it all in. Trish was still fretting about what to wear for lunch.

"I hope not, she's still in hospital and off her head on drugs last time I visited her." rattled Vera, taking a left turn at a brisk lick in her knackered Fiesta, "I mean whatever you think of her having it away with two blokes at the same time, even banging Gary the barman in the back garden, nobody deserves all that shit." she added, warming to her theme of sympathy, mixed with caustic judgement.

"Poor Angie. Poor Gary too, I suppose they've mentioned him in the article? Are there photos of him?" queried Trish, rummaging for a cream coloured skirt in her wardrobe.

"Yes, they got him leaving the hospital after he went to see her, plus there's a picture from the Peppermint Halloween fancy dress night, where he's dressed as *An Officer and A Gentleman* in that white uniform."

"Oooh yes, I remember that one..." reminisced Trish, as she tried on some beige heels, which didn't quite go with her trousers.

"I mean we've all had a ding-dong with blokes we shouldn't have at one time or another – I had that mad weekend in Majorca with Doug the builder, and he only popped round to slot in my fence panels. But it's awful having it spread all over womens' magazines. People will be talking about it at the hairdressers for months."

"Hmmm, I dare say." mumbled Trish, losing interest slightly as she spotted the perfect shoes n handbag combo.

"Anyway, I'll see you and Laurence soon, I'll save you a couple of seats hun. Laurence can sit next to me and I can get to know him."

"OK Vera love, see you soon. Bye."

You bloody won't be sitting next to him, thought Trish, as she fluffed up her hair with a brush and applied a bit of lippy. It's been two years since I've had a man in my life, so back off Vera. No chance.

****

## THE SOUND OF YOUNG AMERICA

The Motown nights at Urmston Working Mens Club weren't the stellar affairs that they had once been. Sure, there were still outrageous dancers, like Flixton Phil in his handmade suits and fedora hats. Plus a new generation of forty-something women, who had lived and breathed that Mod revival thing about twenty five years ago, and now, after bad marriages, kids and a succession of part-time, dead end jobs, were all ready for action. Good times; dancing, romance, sex. A few laughs before their eggs dried up and the hot flushes made sleep impossible for half the night.

It was unusual to have any type of event on between Christmas and New Year, but as it was a Saturday night and people had generally had enough of chocolate, fractious relatives and the boredom of not working, the place was busy. Vera was there early doors and parked her handbag on one seat, and her coat on another two, as she bagged a booth style table for the duration. Trev and Penny arrived next, keen to shake off some Christmas calories and have a night away from the extremely testing younger generation, who seemed to have taken over the household with tedious XBOX games and music that only made sense if you took legal highs and jumped into a mosh pit.

I rocked up about half an hour later, along with my mate Nicky the Greek, a former pro footballer, who had run restaurants, a bookies, a wedding car business and was now doing taxi driving at night and window cleaning by day. He dressed like a Vegas card sharp and, feeling flush after lots of late night Christmas taxi runs at double rates, he was in the mood for a hot woman.

"Vera, great to see you again, my little Queen of Sheba, how are you – getting any lately?" he teased. Vera giggled and waved him away like a naughty schoolboy after kissing him on both cheeks. Then Nicky said hello to Trish and her new man Laurence.

Laurence shook Nicky's hand with a certain reserve, and a firmer-than-usual grip, which basically said, `stay away from my woman, you old rogue.' I said hello to Larry and asked if he minded being called Larry – he did mind. OK then. I greeted Trish with a hug and whispered `so happy for you' in her ear before she sat down. Trish was a great woman and she deserved a break in her love life.

Nicky said hi to Trev and Penny and then he began scoping out the dancefloor. In fact he made it obvious by nodding in appreciation at two younger women as they breezed past to their table with drinks in hands. What is it about guys from the Med? They are all woman-crazy - must be something in the olive oil.

The place filled up fast after nine thirty and the music cranked up a notch in volume and pace. *Stoned Love, Tainted Love* and plenty of similar classics got people moving and swaying on the L-shaped floor. I danced in a group with Trev, Penny, Larry, Trish and Nicky. It was kinda weird, like we were a gay couple being made to feel overly welcome at a wedding disco. In truth, my heart wasn't in it, my mind was elsewhere, wondering, endlessly pondering on the past. But I didn't want to talk it all through with my friends. It was too raw, too confusing.

"Come on Cal, move those hips my friend, get some women interested for me will you?" encouraged Nicky, but I wasn't keen to be his warm-up man tonight. I went back to the table and had a drink. Trish looked at me and could tell I was more subdued than usual. She asked me if everything was OK between me and Lisa.

"Not really. It's hard to explain, but I don't know...it's different now, she is different somehow." I really didn't want to tell my friends about discovering that I had a son, it was still something I was sorting out via text message and fractured phone calls with Beth.

"Is she away over Christmas?" asked Trish. I told her no, said she was just at home with her family. Nicky and Trish urged me to go get her, fetch her here, have a dance. After all, she lived just down the road, about ten minutes away by car. That was a fair point and in a rush of blood to the head, I decided to go. Even if Lisa didn't want to see me, it was better to call it a night if I wasn't enjoying it, and just talk about things. In fact deep down, that's what I wanted, more than anything.

I said good bye, assured everyone I'd be at the Peppermint NYE party, dressed in some elaborate costume, and then strode across the road to my car. I could have texted Lisa, but I thought, hey, let's surprise her, smile and apologise, see if I could heal the wounds a little bit.

It stopped raining as I pulled up outside her house, behind her hatchback and a big Vauxhall Insignia parked next to it. I could see the glimmer of light between the gap in the curtains. The TV was on, and there was the sound of laughter. Sarah was in the living room, chatterboxing away at 90mph.

I rang the doorbell and rehearsed a few lines in head, hoping Lisa would smile and be happy to see me. Instead the door opened and a stocky guy, in his early 50s, looking worse for wear on cheap supermarket beer and Pringle based snacks, greeted me. He looked me up and down.

"Yeah?"

"Er, is Lisa in please?"

He scrunched up his nose in mock disgust at my winklepicker shoes, purple shirt and tight disco trousers.

"And you are..?"

"Cal, her boyfriend."

"Oh Really? I'm Chris. Her *husband*. Merry fucking Christmas. Now fuck off."

He slammed the door in my face before I could say anything, and then the shouting, the awful shouting, began inside the house. I waited for a while, standing at the end of the path next to my car, not knowing what to do. Within minutes, listening to what was being said, it became obvious what was going on. A terrible realisation overwhelmed me and then I flushed with embarrassment and anger, at being taken in by her, taken for a complete idiot, just a bit on the side.

She came to the door and said `Sorry,' before her husband dragged her back indoors and then ran towards me swinging his beefy fists. He was drunk, wearing slippers and about three stone overweight. I was sober and easily dodged his first punch, twisting his body and shoving him face-first into his own flower beds.

"Calm down, I'm going." I shouted at Chris, then looking back at Lisa as I headed for my car and telling her;

"Not as divorced as you thought then eh? What a dirty trick, you could have fucking said something to me. Been a bit more honest. Have a great New Year."

I got in my car and drove home. There was nothing else to say.

****

## CHAPTER TWENTY THREE: "I CAN FEEL A NEW BEGINNING EVERYWHERE, CAN YOU FEEL THE FORCE?'

Vera was in high dudgeon, even though it was New Year's Eve. For one thing, her mum's funeral service couldn't take place until the 5th of January and Vera felt annoyed that mum was basically resting in a big fridge at the Co-Op for so long. Vera had wanted the service to take place in the few days between Christmas and New Year, but the undertakers said everyone at the Crematoria was on holiday, so there was nothing that could be done.

But the other thing which vexed Vera was that Angie had texted saying she was being discharged from hospital.

"It's far too soon," Vera observed as she updated Trish on the general news, "back in my day we let people recover properly in hospital, especially from things like broken bones. Now they can't wait to turf you out, just to make room for a load of freeloading foreigners and fat bastards who need gastric bands fitting because they can't read food labels."

"Well I suppose times are hard, yes." agreed Trish, with a diplomatic tone, as she sat up in bed, with Laurence lying next to her. Trish casually stroked his manhood and thought of ways to soothe Vera's mood. But it was early, just gone eight a.m. and her mind was on other matters.

"Thing is, I don't feel Angie should be let out yet," observed Vera, " and another thing, they'll probably be a load of journalists waiting to ambush her when she gets home – I don't think that should be allowed, they're bloody vultures the lot of them. Scum." continued Vera, pausing only to take on board a large swig of tea, as she warmed to her general theme.

"Poor Angie, do you think we should go and see if she needs anything – she probably hasn't got any milk in the house...or veg?" noted Trish, playing expertly with Laurence's testicles, feeling them move around inside the skin.

"Well yes, you're right, come to think of it, very practical of you Trish. Right then, I'll text Angie and say that we'll pick her up and take her home, save her the taxi fare, and we can stop off at Tesco on the way." announced Vera, as if she was issuing orders to a team of temporary shop staff. Trish nearly jumped up with a start and Laurence winced as she squeezed his balls slightly too hard.

"Oh no...I mean, I can't do that just now. I've got to have my hair done this morning for the party tonight, and my nails. I've got appointments booked and everything. Tell you what Vera, I can pop over about lunchtime and see if Angie wants for anything."

"Oh I see, well I didn't know you were pushing the boat out that much hun." said Vera, with a razor's edge in her voice. "OK then, I'll pick her up just now and you do the second shift this afternoon, that'll be a big help, I'm sure. OK love, see you later at the Peppermint – unless I'm on News At

Ten!" joked Vera, before hanging up. Trish put the phone down and pulled Laurence a bit closer.

"All your mates are bonkers." said Laurence, smiling as he spoke, and then adding thoughtfully, "But in a nice way." Trish smiled back at him and hugged him tight.

"Can you handle them all tonight at the party? There will be some drinking involved and some of them will probably say some daft things to you. Sadie will get hammered on Breezers and offer you a quick go in the back seat of her Renault Twingo, most likely."

"Yes, it will be fine, don't worry. You're worth it Trish, in fact you're the best of them. The nicest lady I've ever met."

"Ah thanks hun, and you're a nice man too. I'm so glad we've finally got together. This was all meant to be, in fact my psychic lady told me this would happen six months ago. She said a man with grey hair, who I already knew as a friend, would sweep me off my feet."

Laurence eased himself onto his side and placed Trish's hand back onto his thickening willy, before kissing her gently on the lips and touching her breasts.

"Your psychic lady...y'see, utterly bonkers, the lot of you."

\*\*\*\*

Dooley answered the phone after the first ring. It was unusual for Ivan to call from the Island, so it had to be important.

"Just checking it's all arranged with our mutual friends for tonight, at the, er, `house party' I suppose you'd call it?"

"It is. Everyone is paid, Wendy knows who's who and what they need, it's all gonna be gravy." reassured Dooley, tipping a packet of porridge into a bowl.

"Great, great, because this is the last chance with this club thing, we're getting fed up with the owner wanting more sweeteners all the time. That guy is a pain in the arse, even if he is sitting on plenty of land."

"OK, I get the picture. Wendy really knows how to sort these old boys out y'know, and the planning guys, the councillor...all the usual suspects, will be there getting their oats tonight. Should be right."

"Well let me know - by phone call mind - don't text, how it goes tonight, without too much gory detail, and if anyone's still hinting about more freebies etc. then we'll just go with the tyre place instead, as that guy is good to go, plus he's on the bones of his arse financially so we can get a better price at the death. Well, I should say, you can negotiate a better price Dooley...you're my ace card there."

"I do my best. Right, well I'll wish all the best then, are you out tonight?"

"Am I bollocks, paying £80 for a cold roast dinner and listening to some cabaret singer covering Ronan Keating – fuck that."

Ivan hung up and Dooley's porridge dinged in the microwave. He stirred it thoughtfully.

\*\*\*\*

Emma was getting tetchy. Not only had her in-depth feature on Rahim's tangled love life and business interests been spiked by a national paper, as the Editor felt it would 'upset the Muslim community a bit,' but her partner Drew, had moved out over Christmas and gone back to his mum's house. That left Emma with the problem of paying all the rent and bills on the flat. The next quarter's rent was due on the 10th of January. She needed a syndicated story. Quickly.

She texted her Features Ed at the agency;

**Angie is out of hospital today, how about we offer her a couple of grand for an exclusive 'her side' type of thing, go for the New Year, new start angle?**

She rubbed a hole in the condensation building up inside her car. The steamy windscreen obscured her view of the main entrance at the hospital. Em didn't want to miss Angie sneaking out; it was worth a slap in the face if she could get a decent photo of her, keep the story going a bit longer.

"Come on, come on." she muttered at the phone. Minutes ticked by, leaden as Wythenshawe rain.

Finally, a text back;

**Yes OK. Approach her with offer under 2K as she is yesterday's news really. Best we can do. If she bites then write it up from the female angle, kids left without mum, tragic end to affair, lessons learned etc. You know the script. We will arrange a studio photo session for her as well, but get some pics of her leaving hospital today, even if phone shots. Better than sweet FA.**

Em texted back her thanks, argued over the fee and syndication rights for a few minutes and then checked the batteries on her Canon compact camera.

Another dreary hour or so limped by. Frail, creaking old people were decanted from relatives' cars, like unwanted Christmas presents and ushered gently into the main entrance. There were no GP surgeries or pharmacies open today, so A&E was the only option for a breathless grandma, or a great uncle wincing from some unspecified pain. Beefy, pudgy-armed nursing staff and associated uniformed hangers-on skulked outside in the ciggy shelter, puffing their health away, as they watched a bedraggled parade of life grimace its way inside the automatic doors.

Vera arrived by taxi and instructed the driver to wait, which immediately caused and argument as the driver had plenty of other fares today and didn't want to waste money by waiting around for another old bird with a wonky leg to come shuffling down the corridor.

"Listen, just wait, she's just texted me that she's ready. You could get your arse out of the car and help with the luggage, as it's the season of goodwill and all that bollocks!" hectored Vera as she stood next to the open passenger door of the car. Cunningly, she opened the boot of the car before entering the hospital, which meant the driver had to undo his seat belt and get out, just to close it, before driving off.

Which he did. Shouting "You didn't book a return trip Miss Frigging Marple, so I don't have to wait."

Vera muttered obscenities into the collar of her coat, as she storm-trooped her way into the reception area. Angie was sat on a high backed chair, her overnight bag at her feet, her face lined with pain and effort.

"Hiya Vera, ta for coming love. It's so good of you. I've done all the paperwork, signed me life away. They just need someone to sign saying that they're willing to take me away, box ticking thing."

Angie struggled to her feet, balancing precariously against the wall, as she slid her hands onto her aluminium crutches. A bolt of pain from her damaged leg, still swaddled in a plaster cast, arced across her features, eradicating any trace of a brave smile with brutal speed.

Vera bent down and tried to pick up the bag, whilst balancing her own handbag on her shoulders. It was awkward and her handbag slipped down her arm. She looked around for help but the women on reception were hiding behind the wall, chattering away about parties and presents.

Vera marched over and rapped her house keys on the plastic-pretending-to-be-wood desk surface.

"Excuse me, shop! Anyone serving here?"

"Yes, what is it?" enquired a sour-faced, forty-something woman with her hair up in a bun and a few crumbs of mince pie pastry still stick to the corner of her mouth.

"My friend is being discharged today, I need to sign something saying it's OK if she goes with me apparently? Plus, she can't carry her bag, neither can I, so could some kind person please give us a hand outside where we can wait for a taxi? Ta."

"I am sorry." smirked the woman, leaning slightly towards Vera and enunciating each word slowly, "but we can't help for insurance reasons. Would you like me to ring for a porter?"

"Well yes, I suppose so, if you're so busy eating cakes love."

"Well it isn't our job, we are *not trained* to do lifting you see."

Vera exploded.

"Do you know what, you are everything that's gone wrong with this country. You're nothing but a petty-minded, overpaid, pen-pusher who wouldn't know hard work if it slapped you in the face. `Shall I call a porter?' she says. For god's sake, all you have to do is show some common decency and help a human being who cannot carry her bag to the front door, but no, you would all rather hide in the back, tapping at computers and waiting to collect your big fat pension, instead of helping people."

Some of the patients waiting started to chuckle, others, who couldn't speak English every well merely looked slightly alarmed, as this crazy British woman continued her tirade. The hatchet-faced woman's two colleagues emerged from the back room, to see what the commotion was about. The younger one was carrying an open can of Fanta, having been caught mid-slurp.

"The NHS was set up to help those in need, but you lot have turned it into a heartless frigging machine. Shame on you! And shame on all you migrants sat here waiting for free treatment too. Go back home and sort out the mess in your own fucking countries, instead of sponging off us!"

"Right, I'm calling security – that's hate speech." said the younger receptionist, with the firm tone of someone who is aged 24 and knows everything, especially the laws on discrimination. She banged her Fanta down on the desk with some authority.

Vera crunched her face up in disgust, as Angie intervened, feeling adrenaline surge.

"Listen Hitler, she's just lost her Mum about a week ago, so show some decency." interjected Angie, adding a more soothing, "Leave it Vera, let's just go."

But Vera was in an even higher dudgeon than a cycling-mad councillor called Colin, writing to the local paper about dog mess on cycleways, there was no stopping her.

"Hate speech. It's called freedom of speech, you stupid child, you know nothing. Call security? What are they going to do, arrest me for having an opinion? Pathetic. Get some bloody work done love, try tidying up this area or telling those selfish bastards smoking their heads off outside to move away from the door, instead of feeding your face with full sugar drinks and mince pies."

As the younger receptionist dialled the number for security, and Vera headed over to the desk to give her another piece of her mind, Emma arrived at the automatic doors with her Canon camera. She surveyed the scene in an instant and brought the camera close to her eye.

A man from Latvia who had vision problems after imbibing too much hookey vodka stood up and began shouting at Vera in Latvian, telling her he was not a sponger. He worked to buy his counterfeit drinks.

"Look," said the older receptionist, waving at her young assistants to step back a bit, "stay calm everyone and we will sort this out."

Vera stood her ground and continued to list the many instances of gross incompetence she, and her mum, had suffered via the NHS in the last few years. She then turned around to face the Latvian who was shouting at her.

"You are damned racist! Nasty old woman!"

"Listen mate," explained Vera, grabbing the Fanta can and walking over to where the Latvian was sitting, "you're white, and I'm white, so how can I be a racist, you drunken idiot?" asked Vera, and then she poured the contents of the fizzy drinks can all over the Latvian's head, before adding, "Now I'm racist, because you're orange!"

She turned her back on the Latvian, who grabbed her arm in in anger. Then the fight started in earnest, as Vera aimed a perfect kick in his nuts and Angie whacked him with her crutch. The receptionist team of three useless loafers all trundled around the counter to subdue an irate woman in her seventies. Emma snapped away, and then took a few pictures of Angie into the bargain. This was tabloid gold.

"Angie, my paper would like to offer you an exclusive interview, to set the record straight on you and Rahim, can I give you my card?" asked Emma, once things had calmed and Vera and Angie had been ejected from the reception area. Emma placed her card inside Angie's overnight bag zip-up side pocket."

Order was restored, when two security men arrived and separated the warring women from the hospital staff and the EU contingent. Angie and Vera ended up accidentally telling half their life story to Emma, before realising exactly who she was, then when the penny dropped, Vera swore at her and told her she was `total scum.'

All told, it was a lively morning and New Year's Eve had started with a bang.

\*\*\*

# CHAPTER TWENTY FOUR: "I'M RIGHT HERE, 'CAUSE I NEED, A LITTLE LOVE, A LITTLE SYMPATHY"

For three days I did nothing but brood over Lisa, turn over all her words in her mind, recall the closeness, the touch of her, the press of her mouth against mine. To want someone, hunger for them, and then to learn that their lips brush against another's so casually, so easily, is a unique kind of pain. There is a sting in being lied to, being so expertly deceived, that burrows deep beneath the flesh. It seeps bitterness into your soul and poisons a little piece of it.

With a New Year looming, I went for a walk, catching the icy air in my lungs and feeling it clear my head. I just wanted a few words, an explanation, for what it was worth, so I texted her.

**Hi there. Could you spare ten mins to chat to me, face to face? It would mean a lot to me, and I would rather speak than text or phone. It's just better. Give me a ring or text anytime x**

It took her an hour or so to reply.

**Yes you're right, and you deserve my apologies in person. It was wrong of me to do what I did and not tell you that I am still married, on paper at least. In reality, he left me a long, long time ago and he's gone now after seeing**

family members. But I don't think I can face you right now Cal, I suppose I'm a coward deep down. So sorry. Xx

Somehow the two kisses at the end helped ease the kick in the nuts, but still, I wasn't impressed with her.

That time on your sofa, when you said that you would love me until the end of your days. I guess that was something you just told me to make me feel better, or make yourself feel a bit better perhaps? Doesn't mean much now, if you can't even speak to someone, then you haven't got true feelings for them – your actions define you Lisa, not your words. xx

There was another long pause. She guarded her emotions, ring-fenced them somehow and never really let them out. After twenty minutes she replied.

OK let's meet later and talk. I need a friend in my life and I'd rather it was you than any other person. You have made me feel completely loved and cared for these past few months, it has been wonderful. I shall never forget it. Please can we meet at yours as Sarah is home and so it is awkward, say about 2-2.30? xx

I agreed. What else could I do?

\*\*\*\*

In the civilised way that middle-aged people break up, we brewed up in the kitchen, after exchanging general chit-chat about Christmas gifts, family time and the weather. The wall clock tick-tocked a bit too loud, so I put on some music, with the volume low, so that the silences didn't feel too heavy, too laboured. There was something to fill the uncomfortable gaps that were bound to crop up.

Lisa was wearing her jeans with the flower pattern embroidered onto the side of the thigh section, plus brown, knee-length boots. She took her jacket off, but kept a small plum coloured scarf on over her jumper. She looked tired, worn-out, her face paler than I remembered. Her blonde hair was tied back in a short pony-tail.

We sat at either end of my sofa, with just enough space between us so that her knee didn't touch me when she brought it upwards.

"You can kick off your boots if you like. It doesn't mean you're staying or anything." I reassured her, smiling warmly as I blew on my tea.

"Well, I think I have odd socks on, but if you don't mind..."

She did. One stripey, and one plain black sock. It broke the ice a little bit. Maybe that's why she did it. It was obvious that she was far better player at this game of love than I would ever be.

"Lovely tea, you make a brilliant brew hun." she soothed, placing a hand briefly on my arm and squeezing, then withdrawing her touch.

"Why didn't you say, right from the start, that you were married?" I stated, too bruised to let her get away with making this conversation a cosy chat, like some kind-hearted section manager letting me go to explore exciting new opportunities elsewhere.

She tensed up a bit.

"It isn't a marriage anymore, and hasn't been for ages. He met a woman in Eastern Europe three years ago, online of course, and he stays over there for months at a time, doing his boring IT work from her flat in Bratislava. He only came back at Christmas to see his brother's family and Sarah. She is his daughter and for her sake, I put up with it. We haven't slept together for over two years – I can assure you that side of things is finished."

"Really? That's what you're saying, you didn't sleep with him over Christmas?"

I could see in her eyes that she was suddenly on edge, but she hid it with a concerned look and shook her pretty head at me.

"Please believe me Cal, he hasn't had sex with me in years. Honestly."

"But you slept together, at your house over Christmas. Didn't you?"

There was a stony silence. I took out my phone and opened up Facebook Messenger, then showed her the conversation that I'd had with Sarah two nights ago.

Hi Sarah, just wanted to apologise for turning up and spoiling Christmas like that – had no idea that your Mum still saw your Dad, otherwise I would have stayed away from the house and let her sort things out. Sorry if it caused a big argument that night.

It's OK Cal, he only stayed 2 nites. Mum really likes you and you two should work things out. My Dad is a bit of an arse really, take no notice. N E way he's gone back to Bratislava today. Hope Xmas was cool 4 u x

Thanks Sarah, nice of you to say we should work things out. But if she's still got feelings for your Dad then I'm better staying out of it really.

No they both got drunk that night and I could hear them arguing in their room, but second nite she made him sleep on the sofa. Awkward Xmas dinner really! X

I watched Lisa's face as she scrolled down the text conversation.

Oh right. I would feel a bit weird being in bed with your Mum if she's still seeing your Dad, it might be better if we split up. She needs time to think about things maybe? X

Nah she loves being with u Cal. Hey we all get pissed n do things we regret, but give Mum another chance cos she's ace and it's not like she met some random on POF or N E thing. Hey u 2 really go well together hun x

Thanks, we do. I love your Mum. Tell her I said that if you like. It's true. X

Ahh you're a babe aren't u? Hope u get back 2gether soon, hugs x

Lisa absorbed the messages slowly, letting the horror wash over her face as her 22 year old idiot daughter spilled the beans on her Christmas reunion. In the world of the young, a drunken encounter with an ex just wasn't a big deal, and somehow didn't really count as `cheating.' It seemingly could all be forgotten a few days later. God knows what antics Sarah got up to on Snapchat, the mind boggled.

"Fuck's sake Sarah." said Lisa after digesting every detail of the conversation.

"So, would you like to tell me what really went on?" I said quietly, taking a drink of tea and breathing slowly.

"He did sleep next to me. In fact he tried to pull my nightie off me, kept pawing at my knickers...which is why we argued in the night. Yes, I was drunk, but he was drunker and I wasn't having him inside me again. Never again. Not after him being with his Slovakian bit."

Lisa said the word `bit' as if it was an unpleasant thing she had seen on someone's shoe. There was an ancient bitterness in her voice, I imagined that some ugly scenes had happened in her married life, long ago.

"That's it, that's all that happened between you?" I asked.

She put her brew mug down carefully on the floor, let tears well up in her eyes and then snuggled up against me, letting her arm reach around my chest and hold me tight. She said she was so sorry, so very sorry for lying to me. Her words tumbled out, putting the pieces of the past to bed and laying ghosts in my heart to rest. The scent of her hair filled me once again. I stroked her head, told her it was OK. Everything was OK.

What else could I do but forgive her? I still loved her.

\*\*\*\*

Emma had emailed her photos into the office, with some brief bullet point captions, plus a couple of quotes from Angie. Her editor texted `Lolzzz!' back to her, as if he were a 32 year old man-child with learning difficulties. Em texted back asking him directly if he wanted a story or not. Then he phoned her.

"Hi Em, listen the thing is we can't run more of this stuff really, even though it is funny as fuck. Is this Angie woman doing anything like *Loose Women*, or that Matthew Wright thing on Channel 5?"

"Nope, she's trying to keep her head down, but she does want to nail Rahim for doing the dirty on her with other women, she reckons there's loads more to his love life than the `faithful husband who made a mistake' routine he's pulling. He's got a young girl installed in a bedsit flat somewhere and he goes to these swingers club nights too."

There was a pause as boy wonder editor mulled the possibilities.

"The swingers thing is good, but don't go too hard on the `Rahim's a bastard' angle. If you can get in there and get sleazy photos then, I'll take a 1200 word piece, for...say a grand?"

Emma shifted uneasily in her car seat,

"I don't want to visit a swingers night at a strange basement dungeon thanks, can't we-"

"There's a dungeon?" exclaimed the hipster bearded hack, almost spilling his mocha coffee on his red jeans, "why the frig didn't you say? Our readers love dungeons, who doesn't? Please tell me that you can get into this place, when is the next swingers party happening?"

"Well, it's tonight."

"You're booked, the snapper's booked – get pics, get quotes. I mean, just make stuff if you like, who's going to sue us and go to court arguing over which bum cheek got spanked in a dungeon? 1200 words in 48 hours please Em and wear something sparkly, it's New Year's Eve, ha-ha!"

"Very funny, fuck off."

"You'll do it though, yeah?"

"Two grand. I need two...this is above and beyond, come on." Em had a bit of pleading in her voice."

"We'll pay 2K if you get something extra out of it, like a local councillor or a celeb is there, that Foggy bloke is from up North isn't he, the King of the Jungle fella, see if he's having it large there. Anyway gotta go, you know the score love, bye."

Emma took a deep breath and then texted Angie, asking her for Bendy Wendy's number. Nervously she phoned Wendy and pleaded for an invite, saying she was a friend of Angie's and promising to bring double the usual `party fee' for herself and the photographer, who was her `friend' for the evening. Wendy wouldn't normally have agreed, but as the young woman seemed to know Angie, she thought it was OK to add another couple. In any case, these parties were always short of younger women who liked to whip older blokes, so that was a big bonus in Wendy's eyes.

The more the merrier. Let's get lashed.

****

The Peppermint was buzzing with a nervous energy. The band were still sound-checking on stage, as the first of the NYE diners made their way into the bar and bought in great armfuls of booze, so that subsequent trips to the bar would be minimised. Tonight was ticket only, and it was a sell-out.

The theme was Las Vegas, with two showgirls standing shivering in the freezing rain, with drooping head-feathers, as guests arrived. In lieu of genuine paparazzi, Big Tony the semi-retired bouncer took snaps with his nephew's Canon DSLR, the flash unit draining its re-chargeable batteries in the first half hour. Tony didn't have spares, or a charger. So the later photos looked like murky CCTV images.

In the kitchen, Jez, Sharon and Josef ran into each other and dropped cutlery, as they desperately tried to cook for 120 guests. The floor was so coated with spillages and ancient grease that they could have auditioned for *Dancing On Ice*. There was an unexpected strong demand for the tomato soup starter, so the remaining dregs in the giant vat had to be watered down, with a splash of ketchup squeezed in.

Once the meal was underway the cabaret began with a `Top Comic' called Ray Rowlands, who opened with a selection of jokes about his wife's weight and dislike of sex. It went downhill from there, ending with an impression of Adele advertising a fitness DVD, singing `Let the pie-fall, see the weight fall...'

Vera had insisted that Angie come out for the night, even though Angie was still in obvious pain, with her leg in plaster, and she couldn't drink because of the tablets she was taking. Trev and Penny made a fuss of her and helped her onto the dancefloor when the live group, *My Absolute Favourite*, got going with a steady, and entirely predictable, rendition of *Don't Stop Believing*.

Larry and Trish spent most of meal canoodling and touching each other's legs under the table, whilst Kev and Sue danced like strangers almost, a discernible distance between them. It was odd, because the whole group were delighted about their news regarding moving to France in the New Year, making a totally new start. But something was amiss between them.

After four or five songs, the lead singer of the group, a curly-haired van driver called Mark introduced the band, made small talk with the audience, and then asked his `great friend Sonia' to join them on stage and sing a few songs. This didn't go down well with a 40-something lady called Linda, who had been bouncing up and down on Mark's dick for some two months previously. Matters didn't improve after Sonia's first song, when she introduced her second number, *Let's Marvin Gaye and Get It On,* and dedicated it to 'Mark, the sexiest rock star in the North West.'

The lovey-dovey duet made it past eight or nine bars, before Linda leapt onstage and punched Sonia square on the nose, knocking her down instantly and starting a nice trickle of blood running. Mark grabbed at Linda, but she expertly kneed him in the crotch and then smashed his microphone onto the dancefloor as she effed and blinded her obvious disappointed with the show so far.

Caught on the hop, Big Tony, Marco and second bouncer Steve were all in the office counting cash and failing to watch events unfold on the CCTV. It wasn't until one of the bar staff alerted them that there was a small riot on stage, that the bouncers made their way to the front and broke up the Clarksonesque fracas. But the damage was done, one set of keyboards had been toppled over and one microphone had been destroyed. Sadly the keyboard contained all the backing tracks, which meant that the band were utterly lost without a synthesized plinky-plonky beat, plus assorted guitar filler licks, to pad out their songbook. They shrugged and started to pack up their gear, game over.

After a brief but hilarious interlude where Sonia and Linda were decanted outside and carried on brawling until the Police arrived, Dave the DJ got his equipment plugged in and connected to the internet. Disco time, just as the coffees and mints were being served. Phew.

Midnight chimed. Trev and Penny kissed drunkenly and slurred their undying love to one another, clinging onto each other a bit too long. As Laurence and Trish were also loved up, Angie and Vera felt left out of it all and toasted 'good bastard riddance' to the old year.

"Happy New Year Kev." said Sue, holding him close and kissing him slowly, then she broke away and added, "it's so amazing of you to change our lives by selling up and moving, are you sure we're doing the right thing?."

"It's all for you babe, all for you. Wild horses, snowy white horses – that's our year ahead."

**** 

## CHAPTER TWENTY-FIVE: "I TOOK SOMETHING PERFECT AND PAINTED IT RED"

The first dank days of January are always grim. Any festivities, real or imagined, have generally evaporated after the first few days of the New Year. Once people begin taking down decorations and dumping needleless trees in well - known dogging spots, the season of goodwill has definitely ended. For Vera, January 5th was an especially hard day, as her mum was finally being cremated, after a long holiday break for everyone involved in the funeral business and the public sector.

The service was the first of the day and Vera was ready in best coat, black shoes and a black dress on underneath. She had a shiny handbag stuffed with tissues, lippy, bit of make-up and lots of change for the collection plate. Jim stood by the bay window, watching people arrive and park down both sides of the road. The hearse slid, almost silently, to a halt outside the house, with the stretched Volvo behind it. Jim put his arm around Vera as they made their way to the car. Vera paused to pat the hearse, as if it were a faithful shire horse.

"Come on mother, time to say goodbye. Help me through it."

Trev and Penny had given Angie a lift, as their Mercedes estate had plenty of room for Angie's walking stick and legroom in the front. Angie looked a terrible mess. She had read the papers that morning and seen herself plastered over a story about `Soap Star's Swinging Shame.'

In fact it wasn't good news for many regulars at the Peppermint, as details about spanking, bondage sessions, swapping, threesomes, plus free drinks were detailed in all their glory, plus regulars at the club like Bendy Wendy, Angie, Rahim and Monkey Man were all mentioned, alongside a former star of *Brookside,* a once popular soap opera set on a housing estate in Liverpool. The gist of the article was that people met on Wednesdays for a disco at the Peppermint and then a `hardcore posse' of middle-aged swingers made their way to Bendy Wendy's dungeon to get their kicks watching `slaves whipped red raw,' or `a girl in a dentist's chair take on all comers.'

One photo showed Bendy Wendy dressed as a circus ringmaster, whacking a large paddle across the bare bum of a council planning official, with the caption; `Permission granted for a new housing estate – thanks for 20 lashes!'

"I do think it's nice that so many people in the street have turned out to pay their respects." said Vera, who didn't read a daily paper and had no idea of the real reason folk were out gawping, some clutching their hands to their mouths in stunned horror.

Vera was even more surprised to arrive at the Crem to find the car park packed and twenty odd cars down the street.

"This is amazing, Mum would be gobsmacked." said Vera, tears welling up and spilling down her puffy face. Jim said nothing just held her shoulder. A mate had texted him two photos of the story first thing this morning. He just wanted to get through the day.

As Angie emerged, cameras clicked from behind headstones.

"Oh dig a hole and bury yourselves, you sad twats!" she shouted, grabbing her walking stick and heading straight inside.

"Angie love, have you ever charged waiting time for the cabbie from Brookie?" shouted one journo, from behind the safety of a small tree. Newshound Emma sidled forwards and tried to approach Vera as she disembarked from her car.

"Vera, we met at the hospital, sorry to bother-"

But before she could finish, Jim shoved her backwards, spitting out one word, `Vulture!' as he ushered his sister inside the double doors of the Crem. Vera started to rattle off all sorts of questions, but Jim made her concentrate on the job in hand.

Emma wasn't deterred and asked Trev and Penny if they were frequent swingers at `#BendyWendyHouse' as it was being hashtagged on Twitter.

"I've never swung in my life," explained Trev, looking baffled at the question (he too didn't bother reading newspapers), "all I do is dance to *Tainted Love* on Wednesday nights, is that a crime nowadays or something?"

Other mourners were also mithered, until two of the funeral company drivers insisted that the journos and photographers bugger off to the roadside, or the Police would be called. Once everyone was inside and stopped gossiping, the vicar gave a determined `Ahem' and got the show on the road. He did the usual waffle about the deceased's life; lived here, then moved there, raised two children, liked bingo and holidays in Spain. Then, after a hymn, it was Vera's turn to say something.

"Most of you know me, just as well as you knew Mum. We both have no time for BS in this life, or the next I hope, so I'll keep it short and sweet." she opened, there was a ripple of laughter and people warmed to this frail, compacted woman, who wore a smile like a shield against the arrows of the world.

"Mum was one of the wartime generation; she lived on ration books, a lick and a promise. Pay the tallyman next week, she'd say, he'll be back like a bad smell. She took in more washing than Johnsons the Cleaners back in the 50s, and I can still remember the giant boxes of Daz and Omo we used to carry from the shop…well, they seemed giant to me at the time.

God she worked so hard did Mum. I didn't realise what it was like until I had kids meself – then you know what's what in life, it never stops does it? Even though they've gone to Canada and Australia, I know Betty and Sheila will be thinking of us today, saying goodbye to a grafter, a Nana who gave them money for penny chews, knitted them balaclavas for winter, whether they wanted them or not!"

Vera turned to look at the casket one final time, and then rested her hand on the lid for a moment.

"Sleep well Mum, you've earned it luv. I'll see you again one day. Take care."

Applause started slowly, and then swelled around the room. A hundred people blew their noses a minute later.

****

Dooley instinctively knew what to do as soon as he read the lurid story about Bendy Wendy's house of fun. He phoned Ray on the Island and asked him to set up a conference call asap. Once Billy and Ivan were in the room, they got down to business.

"What a total fuck-up, in every sense of the word." said Ray, annoyed at the coverage the planning issue was getting.

"This has bolloxed the whole job up for us, why didn't you go along Dooley, make sure that councillor kept his mouth shut? Now everyone knows that we're offering free rides on auld slappers in return for planning permission. It's a disaster, we could end up getting done under the Bribery Act on this one."

"Hold on, hold on. Wait a sec." cautioned Dooley, who had done his homework thoroughly, "We had outline planning consent BEFORE all this blew up, in fact Marco had permission granted last year, so that he could sell it on. There's no chance that we could face any investigation on that score. But here's the good news; I spoke to Councillor Dimwit earlier today and he's resigned on Twitter about twenty minutes ago – no choice really, as I pointed out."

"You spoke to him?" asked Ivan, letting a bit of fear creep into his voice.

"Yep, on a pay-as-you-go phone, not my own mobile, by the way." explained Dooley, " I told him, and the planning officer involved too, that if they resigned and laid low until the fuss died down we'd look after him, which is bollocks of course - we have to ignore them completely, they're dead to us from now on."

Ivan took a sip of whisky and water and shrugged,

"Got that bit right anyway, OK, go on then, what now?"

"I've already spoken to Marco at the Peppermint and pointed out how slack trade is going to be for the next few months as people – apart from swingers – desert the place. I've set up a meeting tomorrow for all of us to sign a deal to buy the club, the car park, the land, everything for 1.2 mill. He's ready to sign boys, because it's game over and he knows it."

All three of the men suddenly jolted upright in their seats at the news Marco was willing to kiss goodbye to 800 grand just to get out of the sorry mess. This meant he must be trading in debt to someone – someone that they didn't know about – and the last posted accounts at Companies House must have been a crock of shit. Great news indeed, except for one little detail.

"We made that guy Kevin a written offer on his tyre place though, aren't we going to be stuck with that deal as well?" noted Billy. Ivan added that they didn't have enough cash to cover both positions right now.

"It's OK," soothed Dooley, "I put a clause in the paperwork that let us pull out if there are issues like possible flooding of the land, protected species delaying development etc. Lucky for us, my solicitor found an incidence of flooding back in 1978, so we can withdraw at no cost, no compensation – nothing."

"Ha, the power of Google...I just found that flood photo in the local paper." said Ray, delighted at his tablet skills, turning the Samsung around to show Ivan the photo of the tyre depot in two foot of water.

"The canal bank gave way. Oh right. Not likely to happen again though is it?" noted Ivan.

"Doesn't matter," rattled Dooley, "the point is there's a history of flooding, the cause is irrelevant. It's the get-out clause we need, so after we sign with Marco tomorrow we can break the bad news to tyre bloke if you like?"

The three men nodded and shrugged at each other.

"You can do that Dooley, you've got the touch with these types." reassured Ray, warming to the idea of a quick trip in the morning and being back for lunch, "We'll get back to the airport once we conclude business with Marco. Then I want the bulldozers in as soon as we can, I want that place eradicated, *obliterated*, so people forget all this swinger stuff – nobody wants to buy a house where blokes got noshed off in the car park. Let's clear the site, wipe the slate clean."

"You're right there." agreed Ivan.

"OK, see you at the airport, I'll be there to pick you up. If you tell Helen to print off two copies of the contract, then we're away. Leave Kevin the tyre guy to me, I'll sort it in the afternoon."

"Good work Martin, see you then."

Dooley hung up and sat back for a moment. His mind began to turn over an interesting idea. He opened his banking app and checked his balance, and then he sent an email to his business manager. Time waits for no man.

****

Kev came in and brought a blast of icy weather on his coat-tails. Sue was dishing up a lovely bowl of casserole, as he'd texted ten minutes before to say he was on his way. Kev took his coat off, hung it up on the special hook that Sue had reserved for him, and then skirted around two large packing cases in the hallway.

"Wow, you're organised!" he enthused, kissing Sue on the cheek as she opened a bottle of wine for them both.

"Well, I thought as the documents came through the other day technically we own the farmhouse now, so we'd better get a vanload of tools, cleaning stuff and some bedding over there on the ferry as soon as we can."

"I know, crazy isn't it? Our escape to the country, to another country! Cool." said Kev, washing his hands in the sink before talking the crusty French bread Sue had cut for them both. He sat down and tucked into the hot food, relishing the wine – French red of course – which went so well with the meal. He told her that he'd heard from Dooley today and they had a meeting pencilled in for 4pm tomorrow, just before closing time when it was quiet in the shop. They chatted about the swinger story in the paper and Sue noted that it didn't matter now; they wouldn't be going to the

Peppermint anyway, so nobody could tar them with the same brush.

Everything was in place, the world felt right to them, as they relaxed later in front of the telly, wondering if they'd miss Emmerdale or Corrie when the lived in France. Kev didn't tell Sue about the bridging loan that he'd taken out to pay the £25,000 deposit on the French place however, it was just a minor detail, one of those financial things you had to do until Dooley's company paid the asking price on the tyre fitting shop. All in hand. No worries.

They went to bed, warm and fuzzy with wine and dreams, made love and fell asleep before midnight.

\*\*\*\*

Ever since the New Year had chimed, I'd felt uneasy. There was a nagging doubt upon my shoulders and I couldn't shake it off, no matter how many times Lisa sent me nice little text messages, or talked to me at night, just before bedtime.

**I decided to get stuck in New Year's Day and started stripping off the old wallpaper from my room, you should see the place now. It's been plastered by my builder and I've got the painter coming at the weekend, it will look like a new house when you come round for a brew Cal.**

**You didn't have to do all that, I wouldn't have minded the old décor, it was fine.**

**No, no darling, I want it new; a fresh start for us.**

We batted a few more messages back and forth and then I phoned her up, late at night, just because I needed to hear her voice really.

"You seem fed up with me now, the tone of the texts is different." I wanted to give it to her straight, clarify things. She paused and then asked me;

"Have you had a chance to meet your son yet Cal?" she said it with such sympathy, like a relative asking how the funeral went, but not wanting to know the answer in any detail.

It was a question that knocked me sideways, because the answer was no, I couldn't do it over the Christmas holidays, just couldn't bring myself to drag the past up and make it concrete, real, flesh and blood before my eyes. Instead, I'd spent a fair bit of time drinking too much, feeling mixed up and watching box sets of war movies to take my mind off it all.

"I'm supposed to meet him this Sunday." I admitted, which was true enough, as Beth had kept emailing me over the last two weeks demanding I accept some responsibility at long last. It still didn't seem real somehow, that I had this teenage boy in my life. What would I say to him, what would be the first words out of my mouth? `Hi there Olly, I'm the guy that drunkenly bonked your Mum at a works do, never really loved her, but hey, let's all be friends now eh?'

"You should meet him Cal, will you meet him soon? I want you to."

"Yes, yes of course. But why should you care?"

There was a long, three or four second silence while she absorbed the tone of my voice, the volume, every detail.

"Remember we agreed that if we have any future, it's only because we're both honest from now on?" she reminded me, "Well I think one day we can be more than friends, we can be in love again when you've sorted things out with Olly and I've got things sorted out here too. We both need time I feel, to heal a few wounds."

I agreed with her. Deep inside I knew that she'd already decided not to see me again, choosing instead to concentrate on work, her strange married life and her daughter. There was such a sad thing inside me, an understanding that people change so quickly, and that it takes years to know someone, not just a few months of lovemaking and dancing. People often have secret lives and sometimes, they want to retreat back into them.

In the end, it's safer, for love is a dangerous business.

\*\*\*\*

Next morning I texted Lisa and said I'd arranged to meet up with Oliver and his Mum at a Costa Coffee shop in town. It took her an hour to reply,

**Sorry Hun, big meeting first thing. That's great news, good luck x**

I replied straight away, adding a little test for her;

**Thanks, chat later, love you xx**

In truth I could have used a conversation, some actual support, not just a managerial type of text message. But Lisa was putting distance between us each day, and had been doing so since she'd found out about Oliver's existence. Deep down, I felt that I'd become damaged goods in her eyes somehow, not the free spirit, disco lovin' boyfriend that she'd signed up for. I shrugged and put some Roxy Music on as I drove into the city centre later that day, determined to make the best of things. In the end, I had a son in this world, and that was a marvellous, joyful and unexpected thing. An hour or so ticked by and she didn't text back, which spoke volumes about Lisa – in the end, her work came way ahead of any relationship. That was her nature.

Beth and Olly were already seated at a table when I arrived. Beth gave me a half smile and exchanged some small talk about Christmas and New Year. Olly simply stared at me, like I was from another planet.

"Did you get the iPad Air for Christmas Olly, is it as good as the reviews say?" I opened, not really knowing how to begin a conversation with him, despite rehearsing a dozen different scenarios on the drive over.

"Nah, had it a while. It's OK yeah."

This was going to be very hard work. I ordered a hot chocolate for me and asked what they wanted, Beth ordered a coffee for herself and Coke for Olly. He fired up his iPad and began playing with something on screen. It was incredibly rude, but understandable. You retreat within your own self-constructed little world as a teenager, we all do.

Beth asked me about child maintenance straight away, even before the drinks arrived. I explained how things were since being made redundant three years previously and losing my house after the divorce. She grasped the picture and wasn't very pleased about it.

"All those years when you had a nice house in Cheshire, flashy cars and motorbikes, we were living on benefits. It doesn't seem fair somehow."

The waitress arrived with the drinks and quickly scuttled away, she could sense more tension in the air than an exchange of prisoners between Hamas and the Israeli army.

"Well I have a job now, which wasn't easy to get, as nobody wants you when you get past 50, they all think you're finished." I assured Beth, "All I can say is that I will do what I can now, not what I should have done years ago. Is it worth me mentioning that I brought up two step-children for 17 years, maybe you didn't hear about that part?"

She pulled a grim, sarcastic face.

"Maybe you didn't hear about my two other children and my divorce? We all went through a load of crap Cal, don't play the martyr."

I took a sip of the froth on the hot chocolate, it left a caramel coloured `tache on my lip.

"Fair point. I only ever played the fool Beth, I'm sorry. Let's start from the beginning and see how it goes? There's nothing else I can do really."

Beth brightened up. She'd got what she wanted, an admission of guilt. Sometimes, it seemed like that was all that any woman ever wanted from me.

****

## CHAPTER TWENTY-SIX: "BUT IT WOULD BE NOTHING, NOTHING…WITHOUT A WOMAN OR A GIRL"

There was a heavy, frozen winter silence surrounding the Peppermint that morning. Fog slowly cleared, clinging to the edges of the trees at the back of the club. Dooley inched the BMW past the worst of the pot-holes, crunching a few shards of ice as he parked about thirty metres from the front door. Ivan, Billy and Ray eased themselves out and tip-toed, like bloated ballet dancers, across the frosty car park. Billy had brought his Crombie style coat, prepared for the weather, whereas Ray and Ivan just had crumpled suits on. Ray had two days of stubble, plus his old brown Sketcher shoes on. The suit didn't quite raise his game appearance-wise, he looked like a tramp who'd just robbed Burtons.

Inside Marco showed the guys in and sat them in the `VIP' booth that was close to the DJ's pod on stage. It was cold inside the club, the heating had shut off at six in the morning and dissipated through the ill-fitting French windows. A weary faced woman called Tracy brought them some coffees and a selection of fancy little biscuits. Ivan looked pleased that there were two green, foil-wrapped Viscount chocolate items and nabbed them both immediately. Marco shooed Tracy away into the office and they guys got down to brass tacks.

Dooley produced the documents and asked Marco to have a close read through the details. Marco shrugged theatrically at the four men around the red velour seating;

"What's the point? The club is finished and everyone knows it. Let's get this over and done with gentlemen."

Dooley looked at Ray, who gave a tiny inclination of his head. Dooley passed a Mont Blanc fountain pen to Marco who signed with an array of flourishes and twirls.

"Amazing signature Marco, impressive." noted Ivan, as he brushed biscuit crumbs off his Next suit trousers.

"As a young man in Malta, I was an apprentice engraver, at a jewellers shop in Valletta. I learned that first impressions can be deceptive – some people have lots of flash, but they don't know what really matters with jewellery; the craft, the setting, the purity and cutting of stones...and of course, the beauty of the engraving. A man's word can stand the test of time."

"Hmm, true." agreed Ray, checking his copy of the purchase contract, flicking to the sub-section regarding planning permission and the detailed OS map of the plot they were buying. "I never knew you were such a philosopher Marco, or a man of so many talents – maybe you can get another job engraving stuff now eh?" he added, with a sly smirk that cut Marco to the quick.

Marco took a sip of his coffee and leaned back in his chair, looking Ray directly in the eye.

"You know nothing, nothing, about me sir. Nor do you know how to treat people with respect. This place holds many wonderful memories for me, and for other people too. The papers say it's a den of swingers, but I know good people who met here, and are married now. So you're destroying it all, for what? To build little shoe boxes, where people will be slaves to landlords, the betting shops you own, buying shit on Amazon they don't need? That's nothing to be proud of. You're building a prison camp, not housing."

Ray wasn't listening. He was already visualising the location of the main access road, the row of small shops, and the number of flats he could squeeze in behind the screen of trees. Or then again, maybe the trees could go? They might be rotten and have to be pulled down? That might free up another three or four car parking spaces for the flats.

"Well, you've got a few weeks left to organise a nice farewell party night Marco." soothed Ivan, slurping at his coffee and giving the contract a cursory inspection, "Let us know and I'll buy a ticket – I always liked this place back in its glory days, saw The Bee Gees here once, top night."

Marco said nothing. The idea that he might send tickets to them was an insult, and everyone around the table knew it. Dooley decided to lighten things, water down the bitterness a tad.

"There is an ex gratia payment that we are happy to make, right fellas? Think we agreed a nice round 10K on the phone a few days ago. For all your troubles Marco; a little something."

Dooley passed an A4 envelope to Marco, who looked inside at the wad of fifty pound notes neatly elastic-banded up in bundles of one thousand each. Marco shrugged, gave a little smile and then resealed the envelope and raised his cup of coffee.

"To the future then, wherever the chips may fall." he winked at Ray, then took a mouthful of coffee and swallowed hard. Sometimes you had to swallow hard in life, start all over again, that's the way of it.

****

Sue patted Polo's neck as they slowed to a waggling, rhythmic walk. The horse grunted and neighed back at her, happy to get the exercise around the field on a bitterly cold day. Sue watched the sun dissolve in a coppery-yellow sky as they trotted along the frozen-puddle, pock-marked lane, back to the stables. All this beauty, all this joy, would be hard to find in France, yet go she must: New Year, new start and all that.

"Our last ride together in England Polo." said Sue to her beloved horse, "Soon you'll be on your way in that channel tunnel and starting a new life, with lots of new horsey friends too. How good will that be?"

Polo's ears waggled up and down, but he made no noises by way of reply. Instead the horse focused on the distant thud-thud-a-thumpa drone of a quadbike, which was bobbing down the frozen muddy lane towards them. Sue pulled up Polo and waited for the biker to get nearer, then waved her arm at him to slow down. He nodded at her as he approached, backed off the throttle and coasted past the horse and rider. Sue pulled a face at him and shouted,

"This isn't a By-way, it's a Bridleway, that means horses and bicycles not motorbikes!"

The quadbiker looked at her from under his multi-coloured helmet, his breath puffing out like e-cig vapour with the effort of controlling the quad on the hard, slippery ground.

"Fuck you hoity-toity pants, there's no Police for miles so jog on luv!"

"So big and clever! Riding a kids bike when you're a grown man, bet your willy's the size of a peanut, that's why you need so something so big."

Polo began to skitter sideways, sensing the tension in the air and not liking the blipping of the throttle that the biker was doing, simply to annoy the horse.

"You know what, you horsey women don't own the countryside and yeah, this used to be a road years ago, until you posh fuckers started moaning to the council. Get a life and ride some cock not a horse!"

Then he whacked the gas open on the bike and ploughed up a scarred trench of solid earth and ice, where a tractor tyre had dug a wet channel a week before. The sudden racket sent Polo in to a fright and he bolted, with Sue hanging on as best she could. The horse gathered speed very quickly, then Polo made an attempt to jump the hedge to escape the bike's blatting exhaust pipe, but failed, pitching Sue over the thorns and into a heavy, messy heap of bones and bruised flesh on the grass.

The biker tore off, not wanting to see the consequences. He was content to leave her to it and didn't want any dog-walking witnesses to come along and survey the scene.

Polo picked herself up and then limped down the lane for about 50 yards or so, before snorting to a halt and pawing the ground mournfully. Her leg was broken. Sue sat in the field for a minute, getting her breath back and feeling a terrible jolt of pain spread from her scaphoid and radius bones, transmit tiny blades of agony beyond her wrist and into her brain. Tears welled up and ran down her face. She stood up and walked along the field, calling Polo's name out as the dusk gradually fell. She found a gate and clambered over it, driven by adrenaline, fighting the pain in her wrist and arm.

She walked slowly towards her beautiful horse in the copper-sky gloom, seeing the awkward outline, the bowed shape of her, looming up. She knew straight away that Polo's leg had gone. She kissed his nose, nuzzled her neck gently, stoked his mane with her good hand, and then let out the most maternal cry, from the very depths of her soul.

"Polo, No…no. My beautiful friend."

\*\*\*\*

Night had just about fallen. There were still two cars that needed fixing up with tyres, plus an exhaust back box on an old Peugeot, but Kev washed his hands carefully and left Davey boy to sort it all out, cash up and lock the shop. Kev was still in holiday mode, plus had a general sense of well-being after giving it to Sue the night before. All was well.

He drove the van the three miles or so to the Travelodge meeting room that Dooley and the Isle of Man team had chosen. Once there, he clambered out of his overalls and put on his clean shirt than he had hanging up in the back of the van, checked his hair wasn't skew whiff from wearing his baseball cap at work and that there were no grease marks on his nose. He didn't want to look like a dipstick, not on a day when he would become an almost millionaire after flogging off the tyre business. Kev switched off his mobile phone and went inside the hotel lobby.

Dooley greeted him in the bar area, warmly shaking his hand and making chit-chat about the New Year and the lack of willpower he had regarding resolutions.

"Actually, speaking of the hard stuff, can I buy you a drink, even though you're driving?"

"Yeah, why not? It's a big day after all." agreed Kev, although he stopped short at ordering champagne, choosing a steady pint of Boddingtons instead. Dooley bought himself half a lager, then ushered them through to the little meeting room he had booked. To Kev's surprise the meeting room was empty, the Island trio were not here.

Once sat at the end of the table, Dooley opened his laptop bag, took out his tablet computer, powered it up and placed a large folder of paperwork on the desk between them. Kev wanted to touch the red plastic cover on the folder, make sure it was real.

"Kev, I've got some news for you and I want you to hear me out, on all of it mind, before you say anything."

"Right, OK." said Kev, taking a drink of bitter and feeling baffled.

Dooley opened the folder and laid two sets of paper out in front of Kev. The top sheet said something about the purchase of the tyre business, its land, chattels, fixtures and fittings etc. by a company called AMD Holdings Jersey.

"There's no easy way to say this Kevin, but the guys in the Isle of Man have bought the Peppermint club and all the land around it. Marco dropped the price a fair bit after all that swinger stuff made the papers and then there was all the council bribe business - very messy. So, the upshot is, that they are withdrawing their provisional offer to you mate. They're going with the `Mint. I'm so sorry."

Kev was stunned into silence. As Dooley expected, so he followed up rapidly, flicking the contract onto the fourth page where it described the terms of the instalment plan offer that his own company, AMD Holdings, was willing to make for the tyre fitting depot.

"Now they've shit on you mate, but I'm willing to make an offer, which is detailed here. So have a quick look and take a minute to think it over. Let me know what your first impressions are Kevin."

Kev scanned through the offer and felt his heart sink, became aware of the weight of the bridging loan, the deposit on the French house that had left his bank account over a week ago and the crushing sense of bewilderment that overwhelms anyone who has been duped, expertly played for a fool.

"You can't do this, it isn't legal. It just can't be right? I had an offer, in writing." Kev protested, scratching at his head as he tried to make sense of the legalese peppering the pages. It read like a meaningless car warranty to his tired, angry eyes.

"Well yes, but if you read Clause 36 you'll see that the offer is subject to any and all searches on the land, revealing previously undeclared problems, like say flooding, toxic waste to be removed etc." soothed Dooley, sipping his lager.

Kev simmered in quiet fury. He couldn't really decide what to do for the best. But he knew what he felt and how to express it;

"You're all just a bunch of twats basically. You're a con artist."

"Well, OK yes, the guys on the Island are a bunch of twats, that's how they got rich running a chain of bookies shops, plant hire businesses in the 90s and renting out flats. All without paying nob-all tax. But I'm not a millionaire like them Kevin, and it annoys me that they've turned you over like this. It isn't fair. Listen, what I've pulled together is the best Plan B that you can get right now, or you could go bankrupt of course. There's always that option."

Kev looked again at the offer that Dooley had given him. The figures didn't seem right; surely there was a zero missing?

"I'd rather go bust than hand over everything on a plate to you, for…for a bag of beans basically. I mean seventy grand, a lousy seventy grand? Come on man, that's a rip-off. No way is that happening, the land alone is worth at least quarter of a million."

"Is it really Kevin? Even with a history of flooding, you think that another property developer will pay a decent whack and jump through all the planning hoops to build on it do you? Then there's the residue from old engine oil, rotting tyres and maybe some asbestos from days gone by? Who knows until the diggers go in eh?"

Kev said nothing and Dooley warmed to this theme, taking a quick drink and waving his arm expansively as he sketched out a couple of possible futures for Kevin;

"Let me be totally honest with you, straight up and down; you're a great tyre fitter, but you're no developer. I am, and my company can save you from going under in the next couple of weeks when the bank calls in your loan - and your business overdraft."

Dooley gave Kevin a look that said, `I know the score, I know what you're really worth mate and it's peanuts,' then leaned back in his chair. This chess game was rapidly drawing to a satisfying conclusion.

Kev pictured Sue's face when he told her that the French dream was over, there was no money to complete the deal, and worse still, he'd lost the twenty-five grand deposit, plus legal expenses. It would be a kick in the teeth for her - for both of them - and he knew it.

"Let's think about this Kev; you clear all your debts, walk away with about forty grand after everything's paid off. That's enough to rent a workshop, buy some equipment, and get on your feet, so you won't have to sign on with deadbeats at *Job Centre Plus*. You're still the boss, not some fitter monkey getting told what to do by a 30 year old manager. That's a plus point, one of life's little bonuses when you think about it. What d'ye say?"

Kev looked at the solicitor's search paperwork concerning the flood that affected the land some years ago, the notes relating to building on a flood area. The bleak words imprinted themselves upon his brain, wiping away the dreams that he'd engraved there just a day or two before.

He took hold of Dooley's pen and signed, dashing his name in scrawl, as if by making it illegible, it erased the validity of it. Then he finished his drink, went and sat in the van, and began crying like a child.

Everything he had imagined possible, each daydream moment of freedom in France, the carousel of sunny days and warm nights by the barbecue, drained away. How could he break this news to Sue, explain what had happened, and yet keep her happy? After another five minutes or so, he got his head straight again, watched Dooley drive away at speed in his knob-cheese yellow BMW M Sport, then switched his phone back on.

He received two dings to show missed calls, and a voicemail. Sue had been trying to get in touch. He tapped in his password, opened up voice messages and listened;

"Kev it's me. I'm at the stables. Polo's had a fall and the vet's on his way to put him to sleep. I can't do this alone, and I think I've hurt my wrist so I need driving to A&E afterwards, please come and help me. I need you." she said breathlessly. He could hear the wincing pain in her voice.

Kev put the van in first gear and booted it. A mile down the road, he overtook Dooley at about 80mph, forcing the van into a gap between the BMW and a lorry in front. Then Kev was away again, overtaking like a crazy man, determined to help Sue, hold her, and comfort her. Tell her everything would be OK, even when it wasn't.

"Calm down Kev, you'll live longer." Muttered Dooley under his breath, as Kev sped away.

****

# CHAPTER TWENTY-SEVEN: "YOU DON'T HAVE TO BE RICH, TO BE MY GIRL"

It had been a long week. A series of phone calls with Beth, plus a short chat with Olly had started things off on the wrong foot, and I didn't really know how to deal with it. On the Wednesday night, I'd gone to the Peppermint but just had one dance and barely spoke to anyone, as my heart wasn't in it. All the gossip about Bendy Wendy, soap stars, spanking and the like wasn't interesting to me.

I spoke to my brother on the Thursday and his advice was clear and blunt;

"Get a DNA test done bro before you say, or do, anything else. Just to make sure, even though he looks a bit like you did 30 years ago doesn't mean to say that he's yours, do y'know what I'm saying?"

I agreed with him, but was reluctant to do much about it. There was still plenty of suspicion in my mind about Lisa and her husband, so I didn't need more Jeremy Kyle moments right now. I watched a film on Friday night and ate Chinese food alone in my flat, deciding to stay in rather than go along to the Motown night at Stockport. Life had turned pale, colourless, in the dog days of January.

I texted Lisa, asking if she was OK and hoped her weekend was going to be relaxing. She texted back that she had a pile of housework, plus a new presentation at work she had to prepare over the weekend. She sent me kisses, hoped that I was feeling OK, and asked about Olly.

We texted, on and off, for about two hours, but somehow we said nothing worth remembering to each other. I had a hot bath and then settled down in bed with a classic car magazine. There's nothing like a bit of engine porn for middle-aged men to see you through the winter nights. I wished her goodnight and sweet dreams, she sent the same kind words back to me.

Before I went to sleep I texted Beth and asked her if she thought Olly might like to visit a classic car show in a few week's time. She said he was into `drift cars,' whatever they hell they were. I googled them and suggested I book us three tickets for a performance car show at the NEC which sounded a bit more tyre-smoking and `wikkid.'

**Thanks Cal, you're a good `un x**

Beth texted back just after midnight.

I knew that I wasn't, but still, I was doing a good thing for once.

****

## YOU FIND OUT WHO YOUR FRIENDS ARE

Wendy stared at the bedside clock and willed herself to make a move. It was just after ten a.m and even on a Saturday, that was a massive lie-in. She had to face the world and she knew it. She plugged the landline into the socket again and it started to beep and make funny noises as it downloaded various missed calls and a message from a tatty celeb magazine offering her `an exclusive kiss `n' tell deal.'

Wendy trotted downstairs in her dressing gown, not bothering to do her usual Yoga type stretching exercises. What was the point she mused, nobody would be coming round to her house for quite some time, or giving her a good seeing to for that matter. Men were now terrified of her; she had seen it in a fat bloke's eyes at Asda on Thursday afternoon.

A wodge of post was rammed through her letterbox and the noise made her flinch instinctively. The kettle boiled and clicked itself off. Everything was normal, and yet strange, almost other-worldly as things had unravelled before her eyes and the party was most definitely over. She scanned the letters quickly. Junk mail, more junk and one from HMRC.

*Dear Ms Bamford,*

*You are hereby given notice that I have opened a special investigation into your tax and financial affairs, subject to the conditions set out in the attached rules concerning undeclared income, assets and non-payment of tax owed. This investigation is the result of information received by us concerning your occupation and income.*

*Our investigation may include checking on all tax and NI contributions owed dating back approximately ten years.*

*You should seek legal advice and be prepared to submit any receipts, bank statements or other relevant documents for investigation as soon as possible. We would request you attend our office on Tuesday 22nd January for a meeting regarding your tax affairs. If you cannot attend, then please let us know as soon as possible.*

*If you fail to pay tax owed this is a serious matter, which may result in court action, a fine, or possibly imprisonment. Please contact us to resolve this matter.*

"Oh life just gets better and fucking better, doesn't it?" muttered Wendy to herself, as she digested the contents of the letter, realising that someone had dobbed her in. People were just so jealous and bitter.

She made a cup of camomile tea and had a serious think. Then Wendy traipsed back upstairs and opened her bedroom safe, counting out cash, googling the secondhand value of her watches and jewellery. There was about seventy-eight grand in total, maybe more if she auctioned the jewellery at the right place. But still, not much to show for a lifetime's work - and having sex with annoying, drunk, sweaty men was very hard work indeed sometimes. Especially when you were married to them, she mused, remembering her deeply annoying ex-husbands.

Wendy took an old diary from her bedside drawer and began working out some figures, based on her nocturnal activities over the last three or four years, and the money she'd made from parties, plus `gifts' received from various lovers and sugar daddies. It came to a measly one hundred and thirty-ish thousand pounds.

Then she began to weep as she realised that she was likely to lose everything once the Taxman had finished with her. She might even pay back all the money owed, and still get a conviction for fraud or something, that was how vindictive HMRC were with ordinary people. Companies could hide their cash in a hundred different overseas banks and fiddle their books all day long, but little people had to be made an example of, from time to time. She realised that it was her turn; someone was out to get her.

"That fucking councillor, that's who it is. Bastard." she sobbed out loud, but in reality, she had no idea who had grassed her up, it could have been any one of half a dozen ex-lovers who felt cheated out of caravans, cars, new kitchens or cash, after she had finished milking them dry.

Wendy didn't know who to trust, but she had to take a chance. She was in a corner and couldn't simply tickle someone's balls, until there was a happy finish, to get out of this one. She picked up her mobile and called Joe the Builder, she needed a friend today, one true friend.

****

Sue lay on the sofa, tired of this miserable, chilblain Saturday already and wanting to crawl back to bed. Her plaster encased wrist ached and throbbed, at a level than Panadol couldn't cope with. Kev was at the tyre shop; mainly because there was nothing else to be done now, except to get on with things, at least that's what he said. Whether Kev felt that philosophical about things, deep down inside, Sue couldn't say. All she could think of was Polo, poor Polo, lying on his side, whinnying in pain as the vet checked her leg and then lowering her head back down again, a look of confusion and fear in his big, beautiful eyes.

"You should step outside now, or go home. You've said goodbye and the kindest thing to do now is let her go." said the vet, whose words would never leave Sue's heart.

"I can't leave her. I have to stay until the end. Please let me comfort her, please."

Sue replayed the final moments over and over in her head. The chemicals going in and Polo twitching a bit, then settling, softening his great, grey outline somehow as his muscles relaxed and sleep began to claim her. There was just a second where he looked at Sue, as much as to say, `can't you help me, stop me falling away?' and then he was gone. There came a sudden ghostly blankness in the stallion's eyes, as all his strength drained away, his mighty head lolling onto the tarpaulin that they had placed beneath his broken frame. The most wonderful animal, the greatest and most loyal friend, that Sue had ever known, and loved, had faded away and left her completely bereft. Alone.

Kev texted her and it sparked her out of her reverie, back to the painful world.

**Hi babe. Hope you are feeling OK and sending big hugs to you. Ta for understanding about the house and**

**business. I have ruined everything, but so long as I have u then it's all OK. Love you xx**

Sue laughed at the text, at the futility of it. How helpless Kev was without her. It was a shame he didn't have four legs, a big black mane and like carrots. She texted back;

**Ta hun. Don't work too hard and we are having takeaway tonight as I can't face cooking. Hope that's OK. Love n kisses xx**

Sue dried her eyes and flicked the TV on. She scrolled through the channels; cookery, antiques, Saturday sport, reality cop shows. Then up popped *Escape to The Country*. It was all a bit depressing. She picked up her phone and texted Angie instead.

**Angie it's been a terrible week, although I dare say I feel better than you do, even with a broken wrist. Fancy meeting up for a coffee and comparing war wounds hun? X**

The reply took a Nano-second.

**Fan-fucking-tastic. You're the only friend who has given two hoots about me since the funeral. Ta hun and will pick you up as I have to get a taxi everywhere, still on sticks n that x**

Friends. Life is a hard place without them.

\*\*\*\*

Laurence and Trish looked at other and smiled.

"You have a shower first, go on." said Trish, who was quite happy snuggling down under the duvet for half the day. It was bitter cold outside and apart from housework, she nothing else to do, as the shopping had all been done yesterday.

"I thought we were going to have lunch out today at the Trafford Centre, maybe see a film?" said Laurence, stroking her hair as she read her horoscope in one of her several celeb and chat magazines.

"Well, we haven't even had breakfast yet, so that's put the tin hat on that one matey. You and your frisky little willy, it spoils all the best laid plans!"

Laurence laughed and then laid his arm across Trish's ample bosomage, cuddling up to her and absorbing some of her cosy warmth.

"Go on then, read me my daft stars. Amaze me with the predictability of my life." he wittered into her shoulder. Trish pushed her reading glasses back up her nose and focused on the tiny printed box.

"Virgo. You are feeling ready for big changes in your life, as the new moon lifts your mood and your finances too. Now is the time to invest in moving home, a new car or perhaps a holiday. Love: You want more closeness with that special someone, and if you're single now looks a great time to mingle, so join a dance class or try a new social activity."

Trish gave Laurence a big `Ooohh' type of look. He burst out laughing, and then leapt out of bed. Trish looked on astonished, as he opened the wardrobe door and rummaged for his trousers.

"Are you going somewhere dear, have you left the iron on at your place?" enquired Trish, arching her eyebrows.

Laurence came back into bed and drew his hand slowly from behind his back, revealing a small red velvety type box. He flipped it open and revealed an 18 carat white gold ring, set with five beautiful, glittering diamonds. Trish sat upwards with a start and pulled the duvet across her boobs.

"I can't get down on one knee at my age, I might never get back up." began Laurence, his eyes full of smiles at her surprise, "but I would like to ask you Trish Fairbrother, if you would do me the honour of becoming Mrs Lewis instead, as it's shorter and easier to spell?"

"Oh you daft thing."

"I'm not joking, it's a real ring, from a jewellers shop, not Argos."

Trish laughed at his crinkly eyes, then put her arms around him and said `yes, yes of course I will, I love you so much Mr Lewis,' as she kissed him, and then let him push the ring onto her finger. It fitted perfectly. Trish burst into tears, and flushed with joy and shaky emotion.

"I was going to propose over Christmas, but your friend had the crash…and your other friend lost her Mum, there was too much going on somehow." Laurence explained, as he surveyed how the ring looked on her finger.

"Ah how thoughtful. That's why I said yes to you Laurence, because you always think about other people and most men are just selfish buggers. You're a keeper, yes you are and you're also my best friend, which is the best thing of all."

Then she wiped tears from the edges of her eyes, pulled his head towards her and kissed him, moving her mouth in slow circles, letting him touch her breasts, cup them, and then bring them near his lips, play with her. Caress her. Take her.

"I'm all yours, totally yours." she breathed, as he held her so close, so tenderly.

**\*\*\*\***

Saturday morning Trev came round to mine and we headed off to the car show. We could have left it until Sunday, but the weather forecast was snow tomorrow, so we switched plans. He was in his Alfa GTV and once I had clambered inside the cabin, I felt like we were inside a vintage bobsleigh. Everything creaked, the brakes had a tendency to send the vehicle sideways and there was a distinct lack of heater, which meant the blowers had to go full tilt to keep a reasonably sized patch of windscreen clear of condensation.

"If the sun keeps peeking out like this mate, I might take the top down." shouted Trev cheerfully, as he turned up Wish FM on the radio.

"No you won't, because either I will kill you, or you will be eaten by a frigging polar bear. Just go steady here Trev, this roundabout looks like a sheet of ice."

The car twitched left at the front end, then it gripped again and we fell miraculously back into our lane. Trev glanced at me, with a casual mix of fear and bravado.

"You're with an Alfa enthusiast today my friend, watch and learn, watch and learn..."

"Actually Trev, I wanted to ask your advice about something, well it's the Lisa thing really." I countered; deciding that if we talked about woman troubles it might slow his cavalier driving, and take my mind off the strange scuttly-rattly noise that seemed to be coming from the front suspension area. It worked, Trev slowed down, so that the wind noise didn't drown out our conversation.

"Ah yes, I thought you looked down in the dumps on Wednesday at the `Mint, in fact Penny was saying we should all get together soon for a cheer-up type of dinner party, as it's been such a shit Christmas for almost everyone." noted Trev, unzipping his anorak a tad as we slowed down to around 60mph.

"Sounds good, yes. The thing is, I'm not sure that Lisa would come along to it, you see we've had some problems over the last few weeks."

"Oh right."

There was an awkward silence between us, which hung in the air like the tension during an exhaust emissions test on a classic car. Nobody knew what to say next. In the end, it was down to me to confess an edited version of what had been happening between me and Lisa.

Trev listened in silence, nodding and tipping his head onto one side during the news about my mystery son appearing from the past, the change in text message tone, the constant working Lisa did etc. But Trev couldn't stop himself from speaking out when he heard that Lisa was still married and the husband had stayed over at Christmas time.

"Ah, I'm gonna stop you right there mate, because I can tell you one thing about separated women, they are NEVER truly separated until that divorce paperwork is signed. That could be a long road ahead, if what Penny tells me is true."

"Oh really, what's that then?"

Trev pulled a special face, and continued, moving his left arm in the air to emphasise his point;

"Now you're not allowed to say that I told you, because Pen and I made an agreement that we wouldn't interfere, as it's your life, we're all grown-ups etc. But she works with a lady who used to deliver training courses at the hospital where Lisa works. Anyway, long story short, this woman knows Lisa fairly well and was friends with her a few years back."

"OK, go on." I wanted to know more, even if it was a third-hand bit of gossip from an ex-friend, which is never the most reliable of testimony.

"Well Lisa – lovely as she is - has a bit of previous in this regard; she meets a guy, dates him, everything is hunky-dory for a while and then she just stops replying to messages...cancels dates and so on. That's what she does."

I didn't reply as Trev shot me a glance. I was still adding up the evenings cancelled due to `mad busy at work' text messages.

Trev elaborated a bit as he over took a Nissan Micra at a fair lick.

"Maybe it's like this? She likes the idea of seeing someone, but she also likes the idea of not selling her house and living on chips and beans in a small flat, which is what often happens after a bitter divorce. I probably shouldn't say all this, but well, we're mates. That's all there is to it."

We drove on for a bit longer, as I mulled it over.

"You've gone quiet mate," observed Trev, "I hope I haven't offended you, but thought you had a right to know. If you don't believe me, just ask her about dating Doctor Simon in the past, and see what she says."

It was an odd feeling, learning that my friends – one of my best friends – had so much dirt on Lisa and yet hadn't said anything up until now. People always had hidden reasons for saying, or doing, certain things. Maybe it was just gossip, perhaps not, but either way I had to dig deeper one day, I just knew those questions would never lie still inside me forever.

"Thing is Trev, I haven't seen her this week, as I'm not happy that she's still married, on paper at least. Plus I have to meet my son, build some bridges there." I gazed out of the steamy window at the frost-tipped hedgerows whizzing by, "I've really made some massive mistakes in the past, now I'm paying for it I suppose. My life's a mess, a big mess."

Trev turned the radio up a tad, as Maroon 5 came on and shifted gear to make the Alfa rev up nicely.

"You know what, classic cars may break the bank, but they don't break your heart. Let's go look at some nice old Capris, cheer you up." winked Trev, who knew it was time to change the subject. No man likes to talk about woman troubles for too long, as it wastes valuable time when cars, sport, beer, DIY projects or new gadgets could be discussed in great detail.

That day out was exactly what I needed; a breath of old engine oil, faded vinyl roofs and an ocean of memories made metal. Retail therapy for blokes is rarely about clothes, or sensible things like kitchen appliances. No, it's all about finding a mint, unmarked copy of the Autocar Motor Show Special from 1979, with a feature on the new Audi Quattro in there, all for just £1. I mean that, ladies and gentlemen, is what you call a bargain.

****

## CHAPTER TWENTY-EIGHT: "HOW DO YOU SLEEP AT NIGHTS?"

Let's rewind 24 hours. It's important.

That Saturday morning was an iron-clad ship of frost as Kev set foot out of bed at six o'clock and pad-pad-padded, cat-quiet, into the bathroom to get ready for work. He made a brew and shaved downstairs, so that he didn't wake Sue. She was knocked out with a sleeping tablet anyway, due to her knackered wrist, but Kev wanted her to rest, sleep as deeply as she could, for long hibernating hours.

After some corn flakes and toast, which he munched with military precision, he got the van windows defrosted with the magic squirty stuff, and then headed off to the shop. He drove in silence, his overalls creaking and crinkling as he steered around tricky, icy junctions. Once at the depot he unlocked the gates, then opened the doors and ducked underneath the roller cover rapidly to unset the alarm. He flicked all the lights on and took a long look around.

"Fucking shame."

Then he went inside the office and began sifting through paperwork, checking VAT and tax letters were filed away, punching holes in expense receipts and the red `jobs to do' folder. All the usual drab, mechanical gestures of the working day completed, Kev drove a blue Renault Clio onto the ramps and hoisted it up, then air-hammered the nuts loose, swearing occasionally and pausing to sip at a mug of tea.

An hour or so went by and then Davey and Phil turned up. They exchanged a bit of banter with Kev and then got busy on a couple of jobs that Kev had written on the whiteboard in red marker pen. Traffic began to build up on the arterial road nearby, the radio crackled over the speakers with weekend chirpiness. Daybreak eased itself, creaking boned, over the horizon.

Then a yellow BMW pulled into the yard, slicing the air with a crunchiness from its fat tyres, as the driver parked on a frosty puddle. Dooley got out, along with two large, anorak-clad men. Their faces looked pinched, raw with cold, heavyset with whatever job at hand concentrated their minds.

Kev went out to meet them. Dooley opened his coat and produced a sheaf of papers.

"This grants AMD possession of the site Kevin. Now we can do it the hard way, with bailiffs and the Police next week, or we can do what I suggested yesterday, and settle this like businessmen. That's all it is now, a bit of business – you've sold it to me, so come on, time to pack up and move on."

One of the two men produced a large heavy duty chain and padlock, and then began attaching it to the outer gates, dragging them noisily across the concrete of the car park.

Davey and Phil came out and asked Kev what was going on, as they knew nothing about the sale of the shop – Kev had said nothing to them. In a few terse sentences Dooley explained the situation to Davey and Phil, relishing in the knowledge that the two workers didn't know squat about being laid off so soon after Christmas.

"What a shit trick Kev, I've fuckin' worked for you for thirteen year. Twat." spat Davey, pulling off his overalls and grabbing his coat from the office. Phil just stood by Kev, utterly baffled. Phil wasn't the sharpest tool in the workshop.

One minor detail had escaped Dooley however. He didn't know that Kev had been a black belt at Tae Kwan Do about ten years previously. So when he approached Kev with his minder, ready to shove him out of the way and take the keys to the shop by force, things happened at an incredible speed.

It took about three seconds for the minder to take three rapid blows to the guts, neck and nose. Then Kev kicked the big fellow in his shinbone, sending a vicious bolt of pain up through his beefy leg. The jarring, needling blow froze the big guy and it only took one more neat chop of the ledge of Kevin's hand, to his Adam's apple, to put the guy down, choking for air as his throat tried to close up in bruised reaction.

The other guy suddenly came waddling from the gates, chain and lock still in hand, but Kev bundled him sideways as he took a wide, almost slow-motion swing at him with the padlock. He lost his balance and hit the frozen concrete hard. Kev stood on his cock and balls and pressed his boot into weak flesh.

"Stay there, if you get up I will make you lose a testicle, do you understand?"

"OK, yeah, I'm not doing anything."

Dooley backed away as Phil came at him with a mole-wrench in his hand. There would have to be a Plan B on this deal, thought Dooley, swearing at Kev as he got back inside his BMW and waited for the gasping, wheezing minders to drag their sorry fat arses back inside the car.

"Don't get oil and shit on the seats, take your coat off!" said Dooley as they struggled to fold their bruised bodies back inside the safety of the car. As he drove away Dooley pushed the button on the passenger window and shouted at Kev.

"We'll be back with the law next week Kev. You take care now, OK? Think about what I said, it's over mate, all over."

Kev had a chat with Phil and Davey, split the week's cash takings with them both, and then said goodbye. Davey felt bad about what had gone on, so he finished off a Toyota Yaris job, and then drove it to the owner's house, which was just a mile away. Kev gave Davey a man-hug and said `I'm gutted mate' as they parted. Then Kev phoned the owners of the cars left outside the yard, parked on the strip of waste ground near the road, and locked up the shop for the last time. He didn't bother setting the alarm. No point.

It was just past ten in the morning. He didn't know what to do, so he just sat in his van at McDonalds eating a McMuffin and texted Sue, hoping she was OK, telling her that he loved her. Then he threw his rubbish in the bin, started the engine and drove to a place that he knew from when he was a kid. It had a little bridge, and a place where you could park up nearby, unpack fishing gear and have a little dabble in the canal. But if you walked in the other direction, for about half a mile, you found the main West Coast railway line, with a bigger bridge crossing its electric avenue of iron, wires and limitless emptiness.

Kev stared at the railway tracks, the stains of diesel on the sleepers, the sheen on the metal where the wheels bent the rails, with their immense weight. He watched his own living breath steam and dissipate into the winter morning air, as he looked up. The skies of France seemed a million miles away now, although the trees nearby seemed just as threadbare, and stark.

He took his phone out of his pocket and turned it over in his bruised hand a few times, before smashing it to pieces against some slabs of concrete that were stacked near the line. He pictured Sue and then imagined her crying for a few days, but maybe buying another horse, meeting a guy next Christmas at the Peppermint. Life would keep turning without him. The world didn't change, it never changed. It just kept on crapping on you from a great height and there was nothing he could do about it.

Nothing.

All he wanted was for darkness to engulf him, swallow his troubles and take him somewhere else, where debts and loans and bastards with pieces of paper, didn't exist. The next train might take him there, thought Kev.

****

Saturday lunchtime and Angie was getting animated, as the red wine kicked in and began to mess with her medication. She confessed to Sue that she had texted Gary a few nights ago, eventually asking him if she could see him again when things died down. Sue pulled a face, partly in pain as she forgot about her wrist and accidentally leaned on it, but also in dubious shock that Angie could contemplate such a thing.

"Yes but he is so fit Sue," justified Angie, getting a faraway look in her eyes, "and why shouldn't I have some fun in a few months' time when my leg has healed up? I can't be a fucking Nun for the rest of my life can I?"

Sue had to agree that wasn't really an option in Angie's case. But countered;

"Don't you think that things have changed though Angie, I mean changed forever between all of us? Gary isn't going to stay a barman at the `Mint forever is he? There's no future in it."

"Well, I suppose. But I don't want a big future Sue. There's got to be fun, or else I may as well see myself off in Switzerland at that Drug-me-Fast clinic."

Sue pondered on this prospect for a while, but consoled herself that Kev was almost ten years younger than she was, so he would look after her if she was struck down with some awful wasting disease.

"Hey talking of fun, Penny texted me on the way over here. Her and Trev are having people over tonight for a bit of a belated New Year buffet thing. Vera, Cal, Larry and Trish have already said they're going along – what do you reckon?"

Angie raised her glass and took a deep swig, almost draining the contents in one smooth swallow. Then she made an exaggerated `schhlup-aahhh' lip-smacking sound.

"Let's get the party started babe. Bring it on."

\*\*\*\*

Trish saw Penny's text message and replied `yes' immediately. Then she realised that she hadn't even checked with Laurence, but it was OK, he was planning on staying the weekend with Trish anyway, so a night out with company would be great.

"Are we going to tell them our news then?" he asked Trish as they had ham and cheese toasties for lunch. Trish realised that there would be about 150 questions if they did tell the group, but she also knew herself very well.

"I've got to Laurence, I'm rubbish at keeping secrets and even my grandchildren can tell if I'm fibbing – I'm hopeless at it."

"Oh well, bit of pressure. We'd better choose a date I suppose?"

"Oh God yes…and then there's the bridesmaids, the wedding venue and all kinds of things – not to mention the colour theme for the dresses. Oh bloody hell, there's loads to organise."

"It will cheer everyone up though I expect, so we should maybe ask a couple of your friends to be bridesmaids? My brother will be best man." chipped in Laurence thoughtfully.

"Oh yes, we all need cheering up after a Christmas from Hell. But at least none of us died. Ahh, it will be so lovely having another wedding, shall we get somewhere booked for this summer?"

"Well I'm not getting any younger Trish, let's crack on while we can manage the first dance thing eh?"

"Speak for yourself, I'm still in my prime Mr Lewis." she chided, kissing him and wiping away crumbs from the corner of his mouth. Trish then phoned Vera, unable to contain her excitement any longer, plus ask Vera to be her maid of honour.

Vera screamed down the phone so loud that Laurence could hear.

"Yesssss, get in Trish! I'm so pleased for you love, you deserve some happiness and he's such a nice chap too, a real gentleman. Ah congratulations Trish, wonderful news! We can really party tonight eh? Ce-le-brate good times come on!" she sang the line from K C and the Sunshine Band's top tune down the phone line. Laurence shook his head in mild amusement - it was going to be an eventful evening.

****

**RAINCHECK**

I Whatsapped half a dozen photos of classic cars to Lisa as Trev and I left the show, including one of a Mini Clubman 1100, which had been Lisa's first car. There was no answer until I sent a picture of an Aston Martin DB7, with a message that read;

**Would love to take you for a spin in one of these one day, do you like that idea? xx**

And then a curt message came pinging back.

**Not really. Listen my husband is here and we are trying to sort things out, he wants you to leave me alone and stop bothering me. Sorry that's just how it is.**

The message stopped me short for a few seconds and then I realised that her fella had got hold of her phone whilst she was doing something else, as he might well know her passcode. In any case, it was unlikely that she would be coming along to the party tonight, so that little plan had gone up in smoke. But in a way I was relieved, I felt like I was learning about Lisa's true nature and I really didn't have the time for it all anymore. I put my phone anyway and started browsing music stations on Trev's GTV.

Trev's phone suddenly rang. He chatted briefly to Penny, and then nudged me out of my brooding, slightly miserable state.

"Bloody hell, big news! Trish and Larry are getting hitched - wedding of the year on the cards!"

The rest of the drive home was a bit of a strange affair, with me faking happiness for the sake of Trev, Trish and all the gang, who were looking forward to the evening. I pretended that Lisa had thrown a sickie on me last minute as we drove home about tea-time and Trev didn't say anything more than, `Ah well, her loss.'

I got home and dropped off a pile of magazines in my spare room, then made a cuppa. I sent Lisa a short text and plugged the phone in on charge.

**Hiya, hope you're OK. Let me know if you need anything, that's all. Not much else to say really, but thinking of you x**

After a few minutes the phone rang, but it wasn't Lisa, it was Beth. In tears and upset after having a blazing row with Olly, who had packed a bag, pushed her over in the hallway and headed off to 'live with his mates.' Beth begged me to help and speak to him.

"Why would he listen to me Beth? He doesn't know me."

"Just go round to this mate's house and try will you? I can't leave Josie and little Louis here on their own, and I don't want to ask the neighbours to mind them, as 'her next door' probably heard all the shouting and swearing, so she'll have her nose in our business. My Mum says I should let him stew over things for a night or two, but he's angry and upset about things. Please speak to him, you owe me that much at least. Be a Dad Cal, this is what it's all about..."

She was right about that. Lisa gave me the address of Olly's mate's house; I set it in my Sat Nav and headed off into the sleet and rain. It took me about an hour to find the house, a nondescript council property, in the middle of a rough estate. A child's BMX lay in the unkempt garden, there was no gate on the gatepost and as I walked up the path a dog barked an alarm inside. The door opened and a blowsy, short-haired woman, dressed in her jim-jams and smoking a ciggy greeted me.

"Yeah mate?"

"Is Olly here please, I'm his Dad and I just wanted a quick word."

"Oh right, yeah, the famous Dad who *did one* years ago. Well he's out with my Darren, so I'm afraid not, no chance of a word at all." she smirked, before taking a drag and folding her arms.

I spent a few minutes explaining a bit of background to her, even though it was none of her business, because she was the only person who could help me find Olly. Finally, she agreed that I seemed `alright really' and led me through to the back garden, where Olly and Darren were stood in the doorway of a large shed, drinking cans of beer and smoking. Darren unloaded some abuse in my direction, but the bag lady dragged her son back inside the house and left us to it.

"Why are you here? I don't know who the fuck you are. Leave me alone." mumbled Olly, shifting uneasily on the step of the shed, seeking cover from the sleet under the thin eaves.

"I don't deserve a second chance, I know that. But no matter what you've heard from your Mum, I didn't just leave you, in fact I didn't even know that you were born. She never said anything to me."

"Fucking liar!" Olly threw the dregs of his beer at me. I wiped it from my eyes and carried on talking, apologising for being a rubbish Dad anyway and praising Beth as a good woman, who had made a few mistakes like the rest of us.

"Olly people say things out of bitterness, or embarrassment because they feel stupid. I've done it loads of times. We re-write our own history every day, without even knowing that we're doing it."

"What the frig does that shit mean? Darren's my mate, I know where I stand with him, he's straight with me. You just talk shite. Mum talks shite and she's a liar too. I'm staying here."

"Right, OK, Darren's straight is he? No, Darren will teach you how to shoplift, smoke weed and stay in bed all day playing *Assassins Creed*. Look around you Olly, do you see a stable home life here, or the chance of a proper job interview with this address on your CV? I had a mate like Darren when I was your age, and he was a fucking knob-end too."

"He's not a knob-end, he's cool." protested Olly.

"Cool? Fuck's sakes Olly, he's wearing a *Where's Wally* onesie and staying in with his Mum on a Saturday night! Look at him in the kitchen...eating Pringles like it's an Olympic sport. Get a grip mate."

Olly's anger fizzled out and an alcohol-fuelled chuckle fell from his mouth. He told me that I wasn't cool either, that I was, in fact, a `sad old git who wears gay shirts,' and that I deserved a slap for what I'd done to his Mum. This was all true, but I pointed that it was Beth's job to dish out the slaps, if any were due.

After a while, he got his bag from upstairs, gave Daz a man-hug, and then hugged Darren's Mum too. She told Olly to `keep out of trouble and always stick something on the end of it.' Class. We drove back to Beth's place in a state of uneasy truce, but I felt a million times better because I was starting to get to know my lad. I was helping him a little bit and it felt brilliant.

I spent a couple of hours at Beth's that evening, chatting with her younger children, learning a bit more about her life and confessing more stuff from my own chequered past. After a second cup of tea, she told me to stop apologising for everything - that I'd made a new start – and I should leave it at that. As I left the cosy house, I jokingly offered her a man-hug, and she led me out into the porch to say goodbye.

"Cal you're a much nicer person now you're older, thank you for tonight. Listen, I'm sorry I emailed people on Facebook saying you just walked away from Olly all those years ago. I was stupid for saying that stuff."

I forgave her, told her not to worry about it, and how all that mattered was how we thought about each other, not what Facebook trolls thought.

Then she kissed me, passionately, placing an arm around my neck and pulling my head to one side. She stroked my neck and jawline, and then broke away. She looked at me with her dark eyes, gave me that sinful smile, full of promise that women can turn on so well. Her lips didn't open, but she translated years of lost chemistry into a new scent, a fresh longing.

"That was wrong of me, sorry." she said, knowing exactly what she was doing. I hugged her, platonically, and kissed her cheek and said goodnight to her with a smile.

"In a different lifetime Beth. In the next life maybe. Take care of Olly, talk soon."

\*\*\*\*

# CHAPTER TWENTY NINE: SIX MONTHS LATER

Finally, all the wheels had been greased, the boxes ticked and the dust had settled after the evening at Bendy Wendy's. Two council planning officials had taken early retirement, and – handily – signed gagging orders as part of the settlement, so they couldn't talk to the press, ever. Well they could, but then they'd have to repay the sums of £156,000 and £87,000 respectively.

Miss Emma Holland, former freelance journalist, was now working for a recruitment agency, specialising in IT sector staff. Her shaming on Twitter and Facebook was damning in every way, and when the truth came out about the ex-Corrie star actually being abroad on holiday, not at Bendy Wendy's shindig, Emma's career was finished within seconds of Retweets and viral memes.

As Emma's story fell to pieces, any real credence in the accusations of graft in the Peppermint land acquisition also fell by the wayside. The boys in the Isle of Man made an official libel complaint, with the threat of High Court action, to the newspaper which ran the story, but the owners settled quickly, for a basic £50,000, plus £22,500 in legal fees. Both sides wanted closure, so it was a sweet deal all round, except for Emma. Life's like that of course, scapegoats have to be sacrificed so the real hypocrisy can be swept under the carpet.

Come with me now then, like an angel on my shoulder, on this cool June Monday morning, as the thin, high cloud clears away, and shafts of sunlight pierce the boards and shutters over the windows of the graffiti-scarred, abandoned shell of the Pink Peppermint.

Behind the double-doors the reception desk still stands on guard, but the till, the desk drawers, with all their paperwork and the phone console have all vanished. In the back office, there's a deep wound in the floor, where Marco's ancient 1970s steel safe was ripped out using chains and a mini-digger. The safe's bolts had rusted solid to the concrete.

The back lounge has just one brown leather sofa left on show, with its seat cover torn and gaffa-taped up. Unloved, unwanted, and so unlike the many couples who spent countless hours pressing their bodies ever closer upon its welcoming folds. The curtains hang forlorn against the French windows, caked in dust from the months of darkness and gloom, since the padlocks went on and the security fencing went up in February, straight after the Valentine's Day farewell dance. The windows at the far end still have Sadie's hand prints on the outside, where she braced herself as Brian the fisherman banged her senseless from behind.

In the main room, there is a yawning space in the centre, over a foot deep and stretching for some twenty-five feet in either direction, where the illuminated `Night Fever' disco floor tiles were carefully lifted out and sold on as salvage to another club owner. The DJ's console is bereft of decks and wiring, all stripped out and sold for scrap, as was most of the lighting from the four ceiling rails and the stage area. The stage curtains, complete with sequins and stars, still hang, shroud-like at the back of the room, waiting for the final act.

Delve inside the ladies loos, and you will find all the porcelain pans and sinks have been removed, leaving skewed pipes, some capped off, others simply taped up, spiking up and down at crazy angles. Inside trap three, there's a pair of purple knickers, found stuffed behind a cistern, left like crime scene evidence on the floor.

The gents' toilets have also been gutted of anything useful, as the builders, prepping the club for destruction, methodically stripped the place bare. Likewise the kitchen lacks its cooker range, the steel sinks, and the serving hatch heating lamps. All that remains are waste bins, broken utensils, a burnt saucepan and stained serving trays, grimy with the burnt ochre residue of a thousand hot-pots.

Marco didn't turn up to watch demolition commence, but Steve the bouncer did, wanting some kind of souvenir, a fragment of his past glory days. As the safety team dismantled the fencing, and the demolition guys checked the site before firing up the huge bucket JCB, they let Steve inside for a final look around. Steve spotted something glinting in morning light, wedged in the tiny gap between the carpet and the skirting board in the back lounge. Steve bent down to pick it up and discovered it was an earring.

"Might be gold eh?"

"Well spotted mate. Could be a tenner's worth there." said one of the hard hat fellas. But Steve would never sell it, instead he imagined it belonged to a nice woman, one of the ladies who came to dance each week and never copped off with blokes. Just had a fun night out on twenty pounds and a taxi ride home.

Then Steve and everyone else had to leave. The fencing was pulled wide open, boards removed from the windows and rear fire exits. The digger crunched its gears as it lurched forwards on its tracks, the bucket began to swing, left and right, like an `80s New Romantic dancer in slo-mo, waving their arms in a steady rhythm to an electronic beat.

A ton of steel Glasgow-kissed the side wall, and caved in the spot where supermarket Jenny first set eyes on Gary the lorry driver, starting the affair that ended her marriage. Another four strikes of the digger and a section of roof came cascading down, scattering lumps of plaster on the place where Karen and Heather always sat, smiling at men they liked and grabbing their phones from their handbags, pretending they had a missed call, when they were chatted up by ugly geezers with beer breath.

By lunchtime, half the roof had been stoved in and a good thirty feet of wall turned into rubble. The wooden floor blocks, still carrying slight traces of blood from a five man punch-up back in the summer of 2003, were covered in debris. The fire exit door where Maureen, a chip shop assistant from a slum town called Parr gave oral relief to a member of a rock band called Badger Bell, lay dented, battered like a stretcher during the Blitz, amidst a pile of debris.

All the ghosts of discos past, the fights, the kiss-and-make-ups, the beginnings of wonderful friendships and the sad embraces of mourners at funeral teas, began to smoulder and rise from the broken brickwork.

The Pink Peppermint became dust, a half-remembered tune.

\*\*\*\*

"Now that looks fantastic my love, really nice." encouraged Trev, as he saw Penny adding the finishing touches to the dinner party table. The two tables they had joined together to make room for everyone didn't quite match in terms of height, but once both were covered in a mix of red and white paper cloths, wicker place mats, glasses, party papers and little gift bags, it did look the part.

Trev was already dressed in his costume, for the `Evening of Murder and Mystery,' which was a kind of mash-up of Cluedo and `Allo 'Allo. He wore a black shirt and trousers, with a vicar's dog collar on, plus a long, red velvet lined coat. Penny meanwhile had dressed up as a character called Bon Bon, a French maid who was a strong suspect in Trev's very own scripted comedy-drama.

Both of them had made a huge effort for this summer party night and wanted to heal some wounds in the group. It was also a chance to note that the Pink Peppermint Lounge was no more, and to toast absent friends. On the upside, there was the imminent wedding between Laurence and Trish to celebrate, so it would be an emotional evening. The weather played ball and there was a long, slow sunset in the warm sky as guests arrived. Vera and Joe the Builder were the first, getting giddy straight away on the Prosecco and comparing their fancy dress character outfits. Vera was a kind of vampish Edith Piaf, playing a femme fatale called Roxy la Roux, a cabaret singer. Joe meanwhile was playing Toulouse Lautrec with admirable method acting by wearing old shoes tied to his knees, so it looked pure comedy when he knelt down for photos.

Penny's daughter Joanne, who was heading out to stay with friends overnight, looked in astonishment as middle-aged people parked up in the street, wearing oddball fashions and carrying booze and food.

"No wonder half the street thinks we're all swingers." Jo muttered under her breath, as she drove away.

In an hour or so, everyone had arrived and Penny had corralled them to the table, stressing that the food would be ruined if they didn't start eating soon. Laurence and Trish played Count Del Monte Cristo and his wife Lady Lucia. Trish's tiara kept slipping over her left eye when she moved her head; otherwise she kept her dignity very well. Angie arrived with her new boyfriend, a tubby guy called Mick. Angie sat down with careful precision, using a silver topped cane for support, as her hip still flaring with pain if she moved too quickly. She was playing a strict governess called Madame Bovary, wearing a long black evening dress, with matching silk gloves, and used her walking stick to good effect, whacking

Mick on the behind as he leaned over the table to accept a pint of beer and a Tia Maria from Trev.

Cal sat at the head of the table, not just because he was still single, and it was a bit awkward placing him with couples, but he was playing the part of Inspector Clouseau and had to interrogate various suspects as the meal progressed. Cal's trilby hat and moustache looked the part, but his charity shop suit was more *Big Issue* seller, than Peter Sellers. Nick the Greek had brought along his date for the night, Sadie, who was playing Maria the Farmer's Daughter and wearing a milkmaid's outfit. Nick was dressed in tweeds and a deerstalker, loving every minute of being Mellors the Gamekeeper. As the guests arrived Trev tried to hand a script to each person, and emphasise the part they were meant to play, but mostly, the group simply took the piss out of each other and laughed at schoolyard level banter. It was too hot to sit inside, so Nick led a rebel splinter group outside into the garden, whilst Angie and Mick stayed inside. Penny fussed over them all, offering nibbles from plates and practising her dodgy French accent.

"Mick seems a happy soul Angie, where did you meet?" Penny asked, as Mick went outside for a crafty ciggy.

"Well I can't dance now, so I joined a dating site." confessed Angie, then elaborating, "He messaged me for a few weeks, and then we met up for a drink or two. He's only 52, but took early retirement from the council – think it was in the planning department. Anyway, he's absolutely fucking wadded; got a caravan in Barmouth, drives a Jag and collects vintage wines. He's actually got a cellar in his house, quite creepy really. But there's just wine down there, not his dead Mum or anything."

"Oh right-ho, well that's good news." smiled Penny, emptying another bag of root vegetable crisps into a trio of small bowls, "That's a bit of a change for you from your usual type of guy, but I'm glad you've found someone. Is it going well so far between you then?"

Angie took a swig of Tia Maria, glanced sideways to make sure nobody else was listening, then explained,

"He does seem slightly too keen on spanking Penny. Don't get me wrong, I like a bit of a slapped arse now and then but he is always asking if I'll dress up in some outfit or other and lay into him like it's a re-run of Prisoner Cell Block H. Erm, by the way, do you know what butt beads are Pen?"

Penny almost dropped a bottle of Valpolicelli as Angie made the enquiry. Then admitted she didn't know exactly, but she imagined it wasn't a treatment for piles.

****

The last couple to arrive, Sue and Kev, took their places, with Kev dressed as Colonel Mustardo, a retired Latin-American army type, wearing a yellow suit, with a penchant for poisoning people's fruit cocktails. Sue was super glam, in a sparkling silver evening dress, playing Miss Coco Canal, the wealthy and ruthless boss of a perfume company.

As the food was served and the drinks flowed, the party of twelve relaxed and got into their respective murder mystery roles. Trev's script was funny enough, but the drink-fuelled ad libs and references to people at the Peppermint really brought the night alive. Angie sat next to Cal, looked him in the eye, and asked him straight out;

"Come on Cal, are you giving Beth and Miss Frosty Knickers one at the same time?"

"No, I'm not. I haven't had any action for so long my nuts are the size of sprouts."

"Well, so long as they're not the same colour, that's all that counts," noted Angie, winking at Vera, "but if you'll take my advice Cal, watch *This Morning* on catch-up and knock one out over Holly Willoughbooby, because you have to keep your prostate in full working order."

Mick almost choked on a chicken wing at this witty aside, but stopped himself from sharing other tips for prostate checking methods.

"Cal's at a dangerous age, it's true. I've had experience." added Vera, as the table fell silent in anticipation, "Many years ago I got friendly with this fella called Ronnie from my church and he hadn't had sex for over four years – I mean can you imagine it? Anyway, we got intimate one night and I could feel his balls were huge, I mean the size of lemons, but when we got down to business I noticed they were slightly blue!"

"Blue balls?" gasped a shocked Nick, "are you sure he didn't have a blue moon as well?"

"No they definitely had a hint of RAF blue about them, a tinge, if you know what I mean."

Trev placed his glasses onto Penny's nose and interjected;

"Cal, we need Doctor Bon Bon here to check the colour of your nuts, just for health and safety reasons you understand."

"I can weigh them first if you like Cal?" offered Sadie, cupping her hands suggestively. Laurence and Trish just looked at each other and Trish shook her head slightly.

"Look, can we get back to the plot and stop all this smut and innuendo?" protested Cal, taking a sip of water and flushing red in the face, "now someone was seen leaving ze library, with a massive tool, did anyone see a big tool earlier in ze day?"

The noise of the good company's laughter and smutty jokes was carried outside, the haze of summer lifting it over the fences of suburbia, irritating neighbours who sat in stony silence in their conservatories, watching TV and not speaking to each except to ask if the other party required tea.

The evening progressed naturally, to a full-blown shambles, with Colonel Mustardo found guilty by Inspector Clouseau, a large portion of chocolate cake dropped down

Angie's impressive cleavage and Penny forgetting about the Banoffee pie, which was pleasantly burnt in the oven. Half of it was consumed by the cat, which got stuck in the pedal bin foraging for caramelised cream residue.

When the meal was over, the group split up and chatted, with Trish and Laurence sitting next to Vera and Joe. Trish told Vera how much it meant to get married again and to have her old friend Vera as her Maid of Honour.

"Tell me when you and Joe got together, when did this happen?" she asked Vera.

"Well Joe got binned off by that awful Wendy woman; apparently she's running a gay bar in Tenerife or Lanzagrotty. Anyway, Joe came round to fix my wonky washing machine a few weeks ago and we got talking didn't we Joe?"

"Yeah, you did." observed Joe, smiling at Laurence.

"Well, he told me some shocking stuff about that Wendy's sex parties – oh what a brazen old slag - but the top and bottom of it was that lots of his friends didn't want to know him after all that stuff in the papers. But I'm not like that, y'know judgemental-"

Laurence almost spat out his mouthful of Theakstons beer at this remark, and then Trish nudged him back to normality.

"So I said to Joe, let's just go out as friends and see how it goes. Do you know what, he's a real gent and not some filthy swinger like everyone says." continued Vera at breakneck pace.

"Thanks," said Joe, smiling weakly and rolling his weary eyes heavenwards, "If I ever need a reference for my CV I'll let you know love."

****

Sue and Kev were sitting in the summer house, with Angie holding forth on the topic of Rahim once again, and how she missed Gary. Mick was chatting to Cal, instructing him on the finer points of keeping a prostate in full working order, so Angie felt free to talk.

"I texted Gary the other night, but he's got a girlfriend now and they're moving to London. I will miss him, bless. Cheers Gorgeous Gary, we miss you mate!" toasted Angie, knocking back half a glass of Isla Negra in one fell swoop.

"Probably for the best though eh, he's so young isn't he, poor lad?" offered Sue, in a motherly way.

"I suppose, but Gary wasn't just some young guy I bonked y'know, he cared about me. He came to see me in hospital and everything. He's got a heart of gold, and a large package. His girlfriend's a lucky cow." sulked Angie.

"Well, it's all in the past now," said Sue, "just like the Peppermint. We drove past it the other morning, as I was taking Kev to work, just a pile of sticks and stones left. Sad to see it gone like that, makes you think."

Kev said nothing and looked at the floor.

Angie sensed the mood needed lifting a touch, and wanted to cheer up Kev, who was still having counselling after his breakdown near the railway line.

"Kev how's the new shop going love, is it better?"

Kev brightened up immediately, like a puppy dog that has just been stroked.

"Yeah, it's so great having the *Timpsons* thing, `cos it's just me on my own, no VAT bills, and no payroll to work out, just a lad on Saturdays who helps me out. Brilliant."

"Oh well, that's a good thing love. You don't need all the headaches of running a business, it can get too much, all that paperwork, massive bills and so on."

Sue shot Angie a look, and reminded her, via psychic powers, that it was best not to dwell on Kev's failed business, big bills and paperwork – of any type. Things were too raw, and the day that Kev had been gently lifted by two Police officers from the side of the railway line, as he wept uncontrollably, was still too close for comfort in Sue's mind. Secretly, Kev was closing up early some days and spending hours drinking alone in his local pub, there was still a deep well of bitterness within him. He googled Dooley once a week on average, to see what he was up to, and check on the housing development on the old tyre fitting place.

Sue moved the conversation onto the topic of her new horse, Minty, to take the burden off Kev's shoulders.

\*\*\*\*

Later on, around midnight Nick the Greek cornered Cal by Trev's Alfa Romeo and stood chatting about cars for a few moments. Then, in his usual way, Nick steered the conversation towards women.

"Hey Cal, good to see you my friend - you've lost weight by the way, good for you! Hope you've been burning calories by banging lots of ladies, you can tell me, I'm a man of the world."

"Just keeping out of trouble Nick, not going out much to be honest."

Then both the guys watched as Sadie, Sue and Penny began dancing to a bit of Barry White. Sadie wiggled her behind and shook her boobs in perfect rhythm, almost as if she was using an invisible hula-hoop. The milk maid's dress was struggling to contain her pumping assets, as Nick raised a glass in her direction, then he explained his position to Cal;

"Just look at Sadie, now that's the kind of woman you need my friend. Likes dancing, swallows on the second date and takes it up the ass on the third! Amazing hip action. She's one hot mama. Actually, she's a grandma, but who cares with tits like that eh?"

"She seems a lot of fun." agreed Cal diplomatically, taking a sip of peach tea with ice.

Nick placed a friendly arm around Cal's shoulder and lowered his voice to a whisper,

"Tell me something Cal, are you still seeing that married woman...Alicia is it?"

"Lisa."

"Yeah Lisa, the miserable blonde one. Well, are you still meeting her now and then for a bit of fun? I hope so, because let me tell you something; no man lies on his deathbed and says, `I really regret making love to so many women, it was a big mistake.' No, don't miss a chance my friend, sort her out yes, give her what she wants, what *all* married women want – a bit of no-strings, sex on the side now and then. That's the way of the world Cal, never forget it."

Cal shifted on his feet and shook his head.

"Mainly, I'm trying to stay out of marriages, good or bad, and look after my son Oliver. It's a strange thing to suddenly be a Dad to a teenager, but it's the best thing that's happened to me for years. Years."

Nick smiled broadly, raised his glass, and slapped Cal on the back.

"Fantastic! My sons live in Greece, so you must bring Olly over and stay with my family sometime. Good for you and I'm happy that you're a new Dad too! You're right you know, in the end family and friends are what matters, not these crazy women always messing with your head...or your dick. Ha ha! Come on, let's all have a drink."

"I don't drink Nick."

But Nick led Cal back into the kitchen grabbed a bottle of Prosecco, and then popped the cork in the garden, signalling for silence. Trev switched off the music and the group all gathered under the summer stars. Nick made a short speech congratulating Laurence and Trish on their wedding, wishing them good luck and thanking everyone for being his friend, and finally thanking Sadie for showing him that sometimes, ` a woman does belong on top!'

"To the best of times, and to the very best of friends – let's wish Larry and Trish love and happiness, always! Yamas!" finished Nick triumphantly, with a flourish of his glass.

"Yamas!" shouted the group and then Trish corralled them into a posed selfie photo session, as she wanted to remember the night forever. It had been such a great laugh. The party continued long into the night, with dancing in the dining room, a few smashed plates, plus a few more smashed people. The music thumped out, past the patio and into neighbouring gardens. There were shouts of complaints around two in the morning and reluctantly, the guests began to leave.

"You know what," slurred Trev to Penny, as the last couple, Sue and Kev left in their taxi, "we have to find another club where we can have a disco. I really need a disco, badly."

\*\*\*\*

**TWO WEEKS LATER**

I was in Morrisons, looking for ready meals, fruity muesli and biscuits, when I saw her, reaching up to get a packet of doggy treats. She dropped them in her trolley and then looked straight at me. Lisa, and all her mixed emotions, came flooding back into me.

I smiled and greeted her, awkwardly pecking her on the cheek, as I didn't know what else to do. A handshake would felt like a work seminar, but doing nothing would have betrayed coldness, a touch of bitterness. She took the kiss on her cheek in surprise and smiled nervously at me.

"Cal, it is so nice to see you – how are you?"

"I'm very well. How are you, are you OK?"

She looked tired, worn out in fact, with dark rings under her eyes and folds of skin hanging from her arms, which poked from her summer dress. She had lost weight, but didn't look better for it. She could have been ill, but I didn't want to press the issue.

"Oh I'm still whizzing about here, there and everywhere, chasing after Sarah, even though she's moved out with her boyfriend. It's all go, never stops."

She was just making conversation, killing time until she could think of an excuse to leave my company. I could sense it, so I took a deep breath, and said what I'd rehearsed, and turned over a dozen times in my mind, months before.

"Lisa, it was wonderful being loved by you last year, but I can't get beyond the fact that you're married and you kept it secret. Plus, you never really had any time for me; it always felt like I was on call-out or something. In the end, I suppose I'm worth a bit more than that, and I need to find it one day. But I wish you happiness too, you're a lovely woman and you deserve better than that husband of yours."

She stood in silence and a trace of a teardrop welled up in her eye. It was hard to gauge whether my words had really struck a chord, or maybe I'd become a sharp reminder of how dead her marriage was, what a charade it all was.

"I wish we could still be friends Cal, I need a friend like you."

For a tiny moment, I wanted to put my arms around her, tell her that everything would be alright, and she would never be alone in this world, so long as there was breath inside me. But I didn't. Something stopped me.

"I can't, I have to look after my son, get on with things. Anyway, it's all in the past now.

She agreed and smiled at me, touched my arm with her hand and wished me good luck with Olly. Then she posed a tricky question;

"Do you see much of Beth now that things are OK with you and Olly?"

I was aware that Beth had `unfriended' Lisa about three months ago, after an exchange of messages about my past and enquiries as to `how things were going?' I didn't want any bad feeling, couldn't stand to hurt anyone again, so instead I pulled the shutters down again between Lisa and myself. I blandly explained that mother, father and child were doing fine, and had all sat down for a few meals. It was nobody else's business really, and I wanted to leave it at that. Lisa didn't like being shut out of the loop, and she instantly became that bossy, hospital manager lady once more, her voice changed in tone, became more business-like.

"Well that's wonderful Cal, I'm happy for you and *you take care*." she emphasised, making it clear what she thought about Beth now. Then we parted, for the final time;

"Ah, bye-bye Cal. I shall always think about you, and smile. We made some good memories, didn't we?"

"We did, you look after yourself too, and Jess, give her a pat from me." I said goodbye and began to walk away.

"You're an interesting man Cal, and a decent guy too - I shall miss you." she admitted, staring into my eyes. I shrugged, went back and kissed her goodbye properly on both cheeks.

"I'm not that good really,' I countered, as I took a last look at her, standing in her white summer frock in the pet food aisle, "I just did the decent thing for once in my life. `Bye.'

**THE END**

.

15795344R00210

Printed in Great Britain
by Amazon